FOLKTALES of JOHA

Jewish Trickster

The publication of this book was assisted
through a generous grant from the
Maurice Amado Foundation, whose mission
is to perpetuate Sephardic heritage and culture.

FOLKTALES of JOHA
Jewish Trickster

Collected and edited by
Matilda Koén-Sarano

Translated from the Judeo-Spanish (Ladino) by David Herman

Illustrations by Ezra Masch

2003 • 5763
The Jewish Publication Society
Philadelphia

Design and composition by Sandy Freeman

Library of Congress Cataloging-in-Publication Data

Folktales of Joha, Jewish trickster / collected by Matilda Koen-Sarano; translated from the Judeo-Spanish (Ladino) by David Herman ; illustrations by Ezra Masch.—1st ed.
p. cm.
ISBN 0-8276-0722-9
1. Nasreddin Hoca (Legendary character)—Folklore.
I. Koen-Sarano, Matilda, 1939-
PN6231.N27 F65 2003
398.2'089'924—dc21
2002153401

To my dear grandchildren,
so that they won't lose the habit of laughter.

Contents

Preface

Until recent times, folktales were told in the course of everyday life, from father to son, from mother to daughter, among neighbors and friends, around the fireside, during long winter evenings, and on a thousand other occasions. These stories, with all their delightful spontaneity and innocence, have nearly disappeared from contemporary society, as other means of communication have taken their place. And so, those of us who cherish the genre feel more than ever a great need to preserve and transmit the tales we know and love.

A principal function of folktales has always been to educate by means of example. A no less important aim is to evoke laughter. In making people laugh, the tales free them, if only temporarily, from personal and social concerns. Other aims, often undeclared, are to give refuge in a regal and magical world far removed from the grayness of reality, or to sound a note of heroism amid failure and persecution. Oral folktales also reflect a bygone past rich in history, culture, and tradition. Their world contains much that speaks to younger generations and says it in a figurative and pleasingly picturesque manner, arousing the imagination and leaving vivid traces of sermons and moral teachings.

A researcher faces several challenges in the effort to rediscover popular folktales and rescue them from oblivion, thereby making known their historical, literary, and sentimental value. One such challenge is to find ways to transmit them in a manner as faithful as possible to the tales' very essence. It is practically impossible to preserve oral folktales in writing. They are formed in the very act of narration, passing from one person to another, from country to country, from generation to generation. Each narrator adapts and alters the elements of a tale around a more or less fixed nucleus, frequently by means of mimicry and according to his or her memory, mood of the moment, character of the audience, and circumstances in which the tale is told. And so every time a tale is told, it emerges differently. With each telling, it is unique and unrepeatable. The real fascination of the folktale resides in this oral quality, which unfortunately is non-transferable. Once set down in writing, a tale loses the theatricality that the narrator's tone of voice and gestures give it.

A researcher must therefore decide what written style is most appropriate for a tale. That choice ultimately turns out to be straightforward though not easy, because the author is "writing"an oral text. This may seem a paradox, but it is the only way to preserve the freshness. Then the researcher has to search for narrators among the elderly, encourage them to tell their stories, and free them from the prejudice that makes them think such tales have no value in modern society. Once this initial resistance is overcome, the narrators demonstrate in telling their tales that this art form is indeed a vital one, and they are usually willing to become informants* for the researcher. One obtains the best results by having a regular circle of narrators, men and women, meet periodically to tell once more the tales they call to memory.

After a tale has been recorded, the researcher transcribes it word for word, preserving the tone of the original narration.

* A narrator simply tells a story as he or she has heard it. An informant, on the other hand, tells a story or speaks about a story to a folklore researcher who is writing it down. A narrator can be informant as well. In my books the narrators are all also informers because they gave to me, the scholar, the information.

Finally, it undergoes the indispensable editing process, to render it "readable"and give it a literary shape. Only in this way can folktales be presented to the public with their truest characteristics preserved and be read without difficulty. Each tale requires editing that is specific to it, because each informant has an individual manner of narrating.

Tales of Joha delighted us in our youth, we children of Jews who emigrated from the region of the former Ottoman Empire and from North Africa to Italy, France, Israel, and the Americas. So it is that these tales link us with our parents. We received them in the most direct manner possible: face to face. Along with these tales we also received two fundamental things. Our fathers and mothers, and frequently our grandparents, instilled in us the virtues of good manners and good works. They set an example that would remain ingrained in us for a lifetime. They also taught us to laugh, something of prime importance in life. And so this comic Mediterranean antihero, with roots not only in the ancient Arab world but also in Christian Sicily and in the Jewish Mediterranean world, is so vivid and entertaining that he continues to this day to make us laugh and our children laugh as well.

Our Joha is a little boy but he is also an adult. He can be intelligent and stupid, honest and dishonest, sad and joyful, poor and rich, believer and nonbeliever. No possible situation exists, whether realistic, fantastic, or absurd, for which he does not propose his personal solution. The results can be quite laughable—sometimes even ludicrous.

This book of Joha tales is appearing in English for the first time. It includes stories about the traditional character and also those about the "modern"Joha, who is the traditional hero now in contemporary situations. I chose both types of tales for this volume because his figure is still alive among the people. His characteristics are well known, and new tales are to this day created around him, adapted to his personality. The tales here were narrated to me in Judeo-Spanish, sometimes called Ladino, which is the language of the *koiné*, the community of Jews expelled from Spain in 1492. For 500 years, in the various countries of the Sephardic Diaspora, these stories were preserved and enriched.

Between 1979 and 2000, I recorded the greater part of the present collection in Israel, Turkey, and Italy. Some I recorded in France, the United States, Canada, and South America. The tales attributed to me are a part of my narrative repertoire. For the other tales, my editorial method was to preserve the linguistic register of individual narrators, so as not to deprive the stories of their particular characteristics and flavor. By taking this approach, I aimed to show that these tales still live in the mouths of our parents, as the fruits of collective popular fantasy. I also sought to present varied styles of narration, rather than one single style or my own personal tone, because the tales' polymorphism is their primary characteristic and it is what makes them so vivid and immediate.

To my narrators, who devoted themselves to their task with the enthusiasm and pleasure the tales of Joha inevitably arouse, I convey my heartfelt thanks. I also wish to express gratitude to my parents, Alfredo and Diana Sarano of blessed memory, who transmitted to me the Judeo-Spanish language, their culture, and their love of folktales.

I am grateful to my husband, Aharon Cohen, and to my family, who enabled me to complete this research. Their interest and encouragement inspired my untiring labor. I wish especially to thank the translator, David Herman, for his marvelous English rendering. The Jewish Publication Society and Dr. Ellen Frankel, CEO and Editor-in-Chief, had the initiative to publish this book and thus bring to English-speaking readers this rich part of the Judeo-Spanish cultural heritage.

MATILDA KOEN-SARANO
JERUSALEM, OCTOBER 3, 2002

Introduction

Joha is a well-known character in oriental folktales and especially in Sephardic folktales. Stories about him are told in Sephardic communities all over the world.[1] The origin of his name is unclear, but we do know that he is first mentioned in Arabic stories dating from the ninth century. A similar character, Nasr-a-din Hodja, appears in medieval Turkish stories. According to the Turkish literary tradition, such a man really existed and is buried in the town of Akshehir. Eventually, the two characters' names merged, to become Nas al-din Hodja (or, in modern Turkish, Nasreddin). During the seventeenth century, Turkish migrants brought this literary tradition to North Africa, where it became intermingled with similar local traditions. On the eastern coast of Africa and in Iraq, parallel stories refer to Abû Nuwâs. Parallel stories also exist beyond the Islamic world, for example, in Sicily, where the popular fool is named Giufà. The unique shapes this character assumes in each culture reflect the particular context and circumstances in which the tales are created.

Joha has Janus's double face: On the one hand, he is innocent and stupid; on the other, a trickster. He is a cheater and is cheated. He sets traps for others and himself falls into traps; he is simpleton and liar, victimizer and victim. But as a literary figure, he never dies. He continues to live on in jokes told by the very young as well as the old. In traditional stories he is the king's or the sultan's fool, yet he also moves through time and meets real people, such as Baron Rothschild and even Hitler. He is very familiar with Jewish religious practices *(halakhah),* and some stories about him can only be understood in a Jewish context.

The Book and Its Tales

This translated English compilation of traditional and contemporary tales is Matilda Koén-Sarano's second book about Joha. The first was published in Judeo-Spanish (Ladino) and Hebrew.[2] The close to 300 new or renewed stories in this volume are a representative sample of Sephardic oral literature and ethnic culture, organized by chapter according to life cycle. The stories range from Joha's childhood (chapter 1), to his relationships with his mother and his teachers at school (chapter 2), through marriage and his relationship with his wife (chapters 5 and 6), to fatherhood (chapter 7), the elderly years and death (chapter 15). Other chapters are dedicated to his prominent traits, such as "Joha the Glutton" (chapter 13), or different life situations, as in "Joha in the Hospital" (chapter 14) and "Joha and the Law" (chapter 12), or his roles in society, as in "Joha and Work" (chapter 3) and "Joha and the King" (chapter 8). Each chapter opens with a Judeo-Spanish proverb concerning him.

The stories were told to Matilda Koén-Sarano in their original ethnic language, Judeo-Spanish (Ladino), and documented over a period of 21 years. Thirty-one of the narrators are male and 51 are female, spread among 17 countries, representing the traditional geographic distribution of the Sephardic communities. These countries include Turkey, Egypt, the island of Rhodes, Morocco, Italy, Bulgaria, Greece, Yugoslavia, Israel, Italy, and France. Relatively new places of settlement like Argentina and the United States are represented as well. Most of the narrators are from Turkey (28) and Israel (25). Lebanon, Morocco, Tunisia, and Spain are represented by one narrator. The age span of the narrators ranges from Koén-Sarano's grandchildren, born in 1992 and 1993, to narrators born in 1898, 1902, and 1904.

The relationships between the narrators and the collector also vary. Members of Koén-Sarano's family, her husband, grandchildren, and sisters, contributed several tales. She has worked for many years with some of the narrators, who meet regularly to tell stories. Others she met only once or sent her stories by mail. The 40 stories contributed by Koén-Sarano come from her cultural heritage or are re-creations of tales she has heard performed on various stages. The second prominent narrator (after Koén-Sarano herself) is Beki Bardavid, with 27 stories, who is from Turkey and is herself a collector. Eliezer Papo, from Sarajevo, provided 19 stories. The 16 stories from Greece were narrated by Sara Yohay. Nine stories originated with Esther Levy, in Jerusalem.

The Sephardim and Their Folkales

Readers from other backgrounds might ask why so many stories are told about Joha, even today. One entrée into the world of tales about him and their special brand of humor is to know something about the Sephardim and what makes a folktale Sephardic.

The Sephardim are Jews who were exiled from Spain (in Hebrew, Sepharad) in 1492 and consider that country their historic place of origin.[3] More than 15 generations have passed since these Jewish communities were dispersed to various lands: Turkey, Greece, Yugoslavia, Morocco, and especially the Balkan countries. Distinct groups of Sephardim emerged as each country left its unique cultural mark. One group has lived in Israel for several generations, making them veteran settlers in a society of immigrants.

A common feature uniting Sephardim is the Judeo-Spanish language. As with all Jewish languages, Judeo-Spanish is also a fusion language composed from major and minor determinants. The two major components are medieval Spanish (grammar and most of the vocabulary) and the Hebrew Aramaic lexicon, which contributes the language's unique traits and its high prestige, as taken from the holy language and texts. Minor determinants are interwoven from the environmental languages, such as Turkish, Greek, and Arabic.[4]

But western Judeo-Spanish, or Hakitia, which is spoken in northern Morocco, is very different from the eastern Judeo-Spanish, or Ladino, of the Balkans. Individual cities have their own dialects, too. The Salonika dialect, for example, is distinct from that of Monastir, Izmir, and Jerusalem.

Despite their differences, the Sephardim consider themselves one group with a common origin, language, literary tradition, style of prayer, music, norms of behavior, customs, material culture, and foods. These same differences and similarities infuse the particular qualities of Sephardic narrative folktales.

In terms of plots and motifs, folktales are a universal and general literary form. Many cultures have their own version of the Cinderella story,[5] as does each Jewish ethnic group, whether Yemenite, Moroccan, Polish, or Judeo-Spanish.[6] Folk motifs are rarely unique or exclusive to a certain culture, but they are organized in a special way that echoes a people's physical environment and way of life.[7] For Sephardic Jews, as for any other ethnic group, folk literature has been a narrative means to express ethnic identity.[8] What makes a folktale specifically Sephardic is its texture, context, and content.[9]

Literary texture is the language and style of the narration. With audiences that have little Judeo-Spanish, a storyteller might incorporate Ladino expressions and adages into the Hebrew or English narration to preserve some of the Judeo-

Spanish style. Often, the narrator's aim is to preserve and foster a communal Jewish heritage and to emphasize ethnic values and perceptions. The audience, too, influences how a folk narrative becomes an expression of Jewish identity. Audience members may identify a story as "our story." They remember versions from their home tradition and enjoy the individual variations the narrator presents. In Jewish culture, ethnic identity has traditionally been expressed mainly through the synagogue, the family circle, and among peers, and this is where folktale narration has taken place. Sometimes a story can reflect even a specific tradition of a certain family.[10] Contemporary Sephardic stories are often performed in public places like the theater, where the audience may consist of different Jewish ethnic groups and the narrator might select stories from collections published in languages other than Ladino.[11]

The Sephardic context of folktales is reflected in place names and settings. A legend about a blood libel, for example, might take place in the Yohanan Ben-Zakkai Sephardic Synagogue in Jerusalem, with a rabbi who lives in the Sephardic neighborhood of Ohel Moshe.[12] Or a story may be set in cities with sizeable Sephardic communities, like Salonika, Istanbul, Monastir, or Saragossa. In the Sephardic tradition, the town of fools is Makeda, rather than the Ashkenazic Chelm or the Libyan Kuzbat.

The character of the fool and the trickster who makes fun of others fulfills different social and emotional functions in each society. And so we find versions of the Joha stories (or stories of parallel characters such as Hersheli) among all Jewish ethnic groups. The tales in this compilation are uniquely Sephardic, however, from narrators defining themselves as Sephardic Jews who reshaped plot and characters recognized as universally Jewish. Their audiences were composed of Sephardim, who received them in a Sephardic context—at home or in the courtyard, among friends and neighbors—as "our stories." They are Sephardic stories because they express a "group self"and an ethnic identity, along with a particular physical and geographical environment, worldview, and way of life. The Sephardim conceived of themselves as an elite group living according to concepts of tolerance, moderation, dignity, and honor. They preferred in-group marriages to maintain their group borders.

In Joha stories we can see expressions of Sephardic mores. And we can also see many of the taboos, for Joha does and says things that are inappropriate and often culturally forbidden. In such instances Joha serves as an outlet for human desires and emotions.

Simpleton and Trickster

Joha the simpleton is full of good will. With all good intentions, he performs tasks given to him but without any ability or flexibility to adapt to circumstance. And so he fails. He understands instructions in a literal way and evokes laughter. He sees problems where others do not, arrives at what he thinks are logical conclusions where a normal person would perceive them as absurd, and lacks basic knowledge of the laws of nature and reality. In one story, for instance, his mother sends him to the market to buy nuts. To save time, Joha empties the bag into the street and asks the nuts to roll home (p. 28). Joha's judgment is based on only one aspect, the rapidity of the rolling. Of course, his faulty logic ignores the essential problem: Nuts cannot return home by themselves. His absurd judgment is what creates the comic effect.

Joha also interprets metaphorical idioms literally. When his mother advises him to "cast an eye"on his bride, he buys a cow's eyes and throws them at her (p. 89). In the same way, when his mother sends him to the butcher to see if he has "cow's feet,"Joha checks the butcher's feet (p. 27). He fails to fulfill instructions, so he tries again and again. He finally manages to carry them out correctly but in the wrong context. When his mother tells him he should not carry margarine on his head but should wrap it up and carry it in his hands, he tries to do this with a puppy and nearly chokes it to death (p. 25). He does exactly as he is told and means well but doesn't underst and the reality of his actions. He lights all the matches in a box to see if they work properly (p. 23). Or he doesn't understand why he's missing one of his donkeys, even though he counts them again and again—he fails to include the one on which he is riding (p. 71).

Nor does Joha differentiate among humans, plants, animals, and objects. He thinks a human being can be transformed into a donkey and vice versa (p. 74). He thinks that the reflection in the mirror is his actual self (p. 118) and that camels can grow from the earth (p. 224). Usually such stories are told about Joha as a child and reveal his strong connection with his mother, who accepts and understands him.

His father expects more of him and sends him to America to study English. When Joha writes that he has no money and soon will be thrown into the street, his father answers: "Then be careful a bus doesn't run you over"(p. 132). In these stories, Joha's parents fulfill traditional, stereotypical roles. Their relationship changes from story to story, however. In some of the less well-known tales, father and mother cheat on each other and have children outside of marriage (p. 31). With his absurd logic, Joha can sometimes find comfort for his travails, as in the story in which a cat steals his fish but he manages to keep the recipe for cooking it (p. 70).

Joha has become a stereotype, not only for the listeners of the stories but also for the fictional characters who appear in the stories. Thus, when he enters a hardware store and asks for a tuna fish, the storekeeper identifies him immediately, exclaiming "You must be Joha"(p. 53). Joha the innocent is hurt by almost everything—people around him, animals, objects, and situations, not only in childhood but in adulthood as well. If he is married, his wife is ugly (p. 108), tries to harm him as much as she can (p. 110), or is depicted as a snake (p. 110). She spends her time with her lovers (p. 116) and chases him out of the house (p. 110), but she won't divorce him (p. 109). The misogynistic stories featuring Joha's wife belittle women and warn men against them. The function of such stories may have been to allow men to feel sympathy for Joha's suffering at his wife's hands. But because he is downtrodden, tellers and listeners have the satisfaction of feeling that such misadventures could not happen to them; they're not as foolish. Those stories do not necessarily reflect reality; being jokes, they serve as an outlet to what is forbidden in society. According to the declared norms, women should be treated with respect.

Many of the stories concern the erotic or even pornographic aspects of life, subjects that were not supposed to be discussed openly. The jokes enabled people to get around this taboo. The humor arises from Joha's portrayal as an innocent, and his innocence, as well as the subject of the story, evokes laughter. On his wedding night, for example, Joha has no idea what to do (p. 102).

The other side of his ridiculous innocence is his sacred innocence. Here the roles are reversed, for the tales reveal that a man considered inferior by people may be highly regarded by God. Because Joha suffers so much in our world, he has a promised place in the world to come (p. 110). In one very unusual story, Joha tries to pray but cannot pronounce the word describing God as "The One"(*Echad,* in Hebrew). He inadvertently changes the word to *"Acher"* (the other), which makes the prayer blasphemous. But God understands his good heart and values his good intentions (p. 202). This story belongs to the international tale-type "the simpleton's prayer,"[13] told in Jewish as well as in Christian and Islamic cultures.[14] It is hard to see this story as humorous, and it is usually defined as a saint legend. That Joha figures in this story shows how his character has been transferred to different genres and cultures.

In other tales, Joha answers the king's questions and saves the Jewish community (p. 151). This legend is well known in Jewish tradition and is usually attributed to cultural heroes like Maimonides or Rabbi Abraham ibn Ezra. In one variation on the well-known fairy tale about a brave tailor, Joha boasts that he has killed "seven with one blow."[15] Then the king orders him to kill a giant. Another tale, in which Joha gives King Midas the golden touch (p. 150), incorporates elements from Greek mythology. These examples show how the character of Joha exceeds genre boundaries and is found in legends, fairy tales, and myths. He also figures in modern jokes, such as one famous among students—tie yourself to a pillar on campus for three years and you'll receive a degree (p. 42).

In the trickster stories, Joha uses deception or practical jokes to achieve his ends, even to the extent of hurting others. He cheats his aunt while selling her cloth (p. 60) and sells fake flea medicine (p. 52). He forges money (p. 66) and sells his house except for one nail, on which he hangs a dead cat that makes his buyers leave the house and run away (p. 61). He has no feelings of repentance or a bad conscience. He treats his wife terribly, hits her (p. 109), wishes that she be hanged like a mezuzah (p. 106), and sends her to the Angel of Death (p. 104). When she dies, he does not mourn her but mourns the cow he has lost instead (p. 122). He is not afraid of God and tries to do business with Him (p. 194). He breaks all taboos, takes the dead from their graves in order to sell their shrouds (p. 57), and even mocks the king (p. 148). Sometimes he uses a trick for moral reasons, as when he feeds his sleeves because people respect the cloth more than the human being (p. 177).

Most of the jokes are based on universal humor, like those about human defects or gender relationships. But some stories are unique to Jewish culture; they are based on Jewish laws or rituals. In one such story Joha offers to build sukkot (the special booths Jews stay in during the holiday of Sukkot, the Feast of Tabernacles) for the whole community if he is invited to eat with the families (p. 253). This story requires some knowledge of Jewish customs to appreciate it fully.

The choice to use one or another face of Joha depends on the character of the storyteller and the circumstances of the story's telling. The naive and childish Joha enables listeners to see things from the point of view of a game, to laugh at him from a position of superiority but at the same time to feel empathy and compassion.

The cunning Joha lets listeners see things from another point of view. He expresses forbidden wishes and acts as many would like to do but dare not. For a moment, he enables listeners to feel what is not considered normative, like enjoyment in the face of another's calamity. Joha's attitudes to sacred subjects and taboos, like death, fatal illness, and God, also help listeners overcome deep fears and tensions.

Laughter as a social device has two faces, like Joha himself. It helps preserve social norms, and it permits the individual to not submit tamely to society. Society can use laughter as a vehicle of sanction; individuals can use it as a defense against social pressure. Little wonder, then, that Joha has two faces: Joha the trickster acts for his own good against social norms and institutions. But the innocent simpleton is unable to adapt to the laws of society and nature, and this makes him pathetic or ridiculous.

Although Jewish humor has often been ascribed to the experience of Eastern European Jewry, every group that participates in Jewish culture and society has its own special humor that reflects its time and place.[16] Every Jewish group in foreign lands and in regions with oppressive regimes used humor as a protest, as strategy and tactic, to survive and prosper in spite of the difficult reality. And for the Sephardim, it is Joha who embodies this humor.

TAMAR ALEXANDER
ESTELLE FRANKFURTER CHAIR FOR SEPHARDIC CULTURE,
CHAIRPERSON, FOLKLORE PROGRAM,
HEBREW LITERATURE DEPARTMENT,
BEN-GURION UNIVERSITY OF THE NEGEV, BEER-SHEVA ISRAEL

NOTES

1. Alexander-Frizer, T. *The Beloved Friend-and-a-Half: Studies in Sephardic Folk Literature* (Jerusalem: The Hebrew University, Magnes Press; Beer-Sheva: Ben-Gurion University of the Negev Press, 1999) (in Hebrew), forthcoming in English from Wayne State University Press, pp. 354–87.

2. Koén-Sarano, M. *Djohá Ke Dize? Kuentos Populares Djudeo-Espanyoles* (Jerusalem: Kana, 1991); M. Koén-Sarano, *Kuentos del folklor de la famiya djudeo-espanyola* (Jerusalem: Kana, 1986).

3. Díaz-Mas, P. *Los Sefarardíes: Historia, Lengua y Cultura* (Barcelona: Riopiedras Ediciones, 1986); P. Morag-Talmon, "The Integration of an Old Community within an Immigrant Society: The Sepharadi Community in Israel"(Ph.D. thesis, in Hebrew, The Hebrew University of Jerusalem, 1980).

4. Bunis, D. M., *A Lexicon of the Hebrew and Aramaic Elements in Modern Judesmo* (Jerusalem: Magnes Press, 1993); Y. Bentolila, "Le Composant hebraique dans le judéo-espagnol marocain,"in I. Benabu and J. Sermoneta, eds., *Judeo-Romance Languages* (Jerusalem: Misgav Yerushalayim, 1985).

5. Dundes, A., ed. *Cinderella: A Casebook* (New York: Wildman Press, 1983).

6. Bar-Yitzhak, H. "Smeda-Rmeda': Multi-Dimensional Study of the Cinderella Story As Told by Moroccan Jews,"*Jerusalem Studies in Jewish Folklore* 13–14 (1991–92): 323–49 (in Hebrew). For Sephardic versions of Cinderella, see note 1 above, pp. 280–311.

7. Honko, L. "Four Forms of Adaptations of Tradition,"*Studia Fennica* 26 (1981): 19–33; C. W. von Sydow, "Folktale Studies and Philology: Some Points of View," in A. Dundes, ed., *The Study of Folklore* (Englewood Cliffs, N.J.: Prentice Hall, 1965), 219–43.

8. Alexander, T. "The Judeo-Spanish Community in Israel: Its Folklore and Ethnic Identity," *Cahiers de Littérature Orale* 20 (1986):131–52.

9. Dundes, A. "Text, Texture, and Context,"*Southern Folklore Quarterly* 28 (1964): 251–65.

10. Alexander, T. "Literary Tradition, Family Self-Image, and Ethnic Identity,"*Jewish Folklore and Ethnographic Review* 15, no. 2 (1993): 39–49. The paper deals with the literary tradition of the Meyuas family.

11. Alexander, T., and M. Govrin. "Story-Telling As a Performing Art,"*Assaph Studies in the Theater* 5 (1990): 1–35.

12. Alexander, T. "A Sephardic Version of a Blood-Libel Story in Jerusalem,"*International Folklore Review* 6 (July 1986): 131–52.

13. Aarne, A., and S. Thompson. *The Types of the Folktale: Classification and Bibliography* (1961; rpr. F.F.C. 184, Suomalainen Tiedeakatemia Academia Scientiarum Fennica, Helsinki, 1973). Tale type no. 827.

14. Heller, B. "Gott wünscht das Herz: Legenden über einfältige Andact und über Gefährten im Paradies," *Hebrew Union College Annual* 4 (1927): 365–404.

15. Aarne A., and S. Thompson. Tale type no. 1640.

16. Ziv, A., ed., *Jewish Humor* (Tel-Aviv: Papyrus Publishing, 1986) (in Hebrew).

The Myth of Laughter

One thousand years ago there was a great *hoja,* a Muslim cleric, who had twelve pupils. One was Joha. The pupils remained with the *hoja* for the entire day. He taught them and also fed them.

This great *hoja* had a sheep. Every day at exactly the same time the *hoja* would take the sheep, slaughter it, and cook it. All thirteen would sit down and eat. Afterward, the *hoja* would take the bones of the sheep and murmur a few words to re-create the lamb, because there was much hunger at that time and nothing to eat.

One day a woman fell very, very ill. For whom did they go looking? The *hoja*!

"*Hoja! Hoja! Hoja!* This woman is going to die!"

The great *hoja* called his pupils to him and said: "Look, I am going to go to visit this sick woman. For God's sake, do not slaughter the lamb! Even if it is one or two o'clock do not slaughter the lamb, because only I know what to say when it is slaughtered. You know how to read, you know all, but you do not know what I know. Therefore, do not do it!"

The man went off to see the sick woman. . . . An hour passed.

At 12 o'clock he would usually slaughter the lamb. . . . One o'clock passed . . . two o'clock passed. . . . The great *hoja* still had not returned. The pupils waited for him.

They ate only once a day. They were hungry.

One of them said: "Come, let us slaughter it."

"No! The *hoja* said to us: 'No!'"

Another one said: "Come on, let's slaughter it."

The third one said: "I am not afraid! I already know what the *hoja* said. I am going to do it, and he will come and find the lamb whole nevertheless."

One said: "What are you going to do?"

"I am going to take the knife. . . ." And he took the knife.

"And what are you going to do?"

"I am going to slaughter it. . . ." And he slaughtered it.

"And you?"

"I am going to skin it. . . ." And he skinned it.

"And you?"

Each of the pupils did something. Only one did nothing. He was standing in front of the others and laughing. It was Joha.

It was past two o'clock when the great *hoja* arrived. He went black in the face because he immediately understood that they had eaten the meal and were not able to re-create the lamb. Only bones remained in its place.

He said to them: "What? Didn't I tell you to wait!"

"But, *hoja*, we were hungry."

"Didn't I tell you? . . . Now, all of you stand in a row. . . . You, what did you do?"

"I took hold of it."

"You took hold of it? Thus they will take hold of you, they will squeeze you, you will die. . . . And you?"

"I slaughtered it."

"Thus will they slaughter you! And you?"

"I skinned it."

"You, if they do not remove your skin, your soul will not go out from your body! And you?"

"I cooked it."

"You they will throw in boiling water and you will die!"

And so he cursed each of the eleven in turn. At length he came to the end of the row, to Joha.

"Joha,"he said, "what did you do?"

"I," said Joha, "didn't do anything. I stood in front of them and laughed at each one and at what they were doing."

"As for you," said the great *hoja,* "they will relate your whole life forever, as long as the world exists and until it ends, and at you, people will laugh!"

NARRATED BY HANA CORDOVA – 1994

CHAPTER 1

JOHA and his family

*"Joha laughed,
the whole family laughed."*

One at a Time

At that time, before departing, the train would whistle one whistle . . . toot . . . toot . . . toot. . . .

Joha's mother, together with her little son, was running to catch the train before they blew the whistle.

"Climb aboard, my soul! Climb aboard, my soul!" his mother said to him.

The man from the train, who was waiting to blow the whistle, said: "First, you climb aboard. After that, let your soul climb aboard!"

NARRATED BY POLA GREGO – 1990

Like This!

Joha's mother said to him: "Go and buy me two liters of milk."

So Joha went to buy her two liters of milk.

He arrived home and knocked at the door, with one liter of milk.

His mother said to him: "I asked you for two liters. Where is the second one?"

Her son said to her: "It broke, Mother!"

"How?" his mother said to him.

Joha took the other liter and . . . pulled it . . . and broke the second one. "Like this!"

NARRATED BY SARA BEHAR – 1998

Which Half Hour?

Joha asked his mother: "Mama, can I go out to play with my friends?"

"Yes, but come back in half an hour."

"How will I know when half an hour has gone by?"

"Ouff!" his mother said to him. "Ask someone in the street."

A good listener needs few words.

Joha went out and played, and played. After some time had passed, he approached a man and asked, "Sir, sir, can you tell me—has half an hour gone by?"

NARRATED BY ELIEZER PAPO – 1999

All Good

Joha's mother sent him to buy matches from the grocer's. She said to him: "Look, Joha, make sure that the matches are all good!"

Joha went to the grocer's and bought a box of matches.

On the way home he said to himself, "I will look to see that the matches are good, so that my mother won't shout at me afterward."

Joha opened the box, lit a match . . . it was good. He put the matchstick back into the box.

He took another one and lit it . . . saw that it was good. He extinguished the matchstick and put it back inside the box . . . and so on and so on. He tried them all and saw that they were all good.

When he arrived home, he gave the box to his mother.

She opened the box and saw that all the matches were used.

She said to him: "Joha, what is this? The grocer cheated you! All the matches are used!"

"No!" Joha said to her. "What happened is that on the way home, I tried them to see if they were good, as you told me. They were all good!"

NARRATED BY KOHAVA PIVIS – 1999

He Is Different

There were three youths. One of the three was Joha. They strolled about, looking in shop windows.

They passed a shop window filled with dolls and toys.

One of the youths said: "You know, my parents shopped for me in here!"

"Come on! What are you talking about? Your parents are rich!"

They walked farther and came to a much more fashionable shop, filled with all kinds of games and toy animals.

The second youth said: "You know what? My parents shopped for me in here!"

"Goodness!" the other two said. "Your parents must be very, very rich!"

Joha said: "Me they didn't buy. They didn't have any money, so they made me!"

NARRATED BY ESTER LEVY – 2000

Mother's Advice

Once Joha's mother said to him: "Go, sweetheart, and visit your grandmother."

Joha said: "Fine!" And he went to visit his grandmother and stayed with her for a few hours.

When he was about to leave, his grandmother said to him: "Look, I have some margarine and I am not using it. Take it. Bring it to your mother, so she can make you cakes."

She wrapped it in paper and gave it to Joha.

Joha took the margarine and said: "Ouff! Do I have to carry this home?"

On the way he took off his hat, put the margarine under the hat, and played with a ball.

Meanwhile, the margarine was dripping . . . and dripping. . . .

When he got home, his mother said: "What is this? This is how one carries margarine? By putting it on the head? Margarine is wrapped in paper, and one carries it in the hand. . . ."

"Fine," said Joha. "The next time!"

Some time passed, and his mother said: "*Yalla.** Go visit your grandmother! It's been a long time since you went to visit her. . . . "

Joha went to his grandmother, who had a little puppy. Joha said to her: "Grandma, give me the puppy! I want the puppy. . . . "

His grandmother said to him: "All right. *Yalla,* take it!"

Joha took the puppy and went off. Along the way, he said to himself: "Mother told me to wrap it in paper. . . . "

Joha searched and searched until he found a paper. He wrapped the puppy up and held it tightly in his hand. The dog was choking and began to scratch him because it wanted to get out of the paper. So Joha held it in his other hand and the dog tore that hand, too. What was he going to do? By the time he

* Go on

got home, he was all covered in blood.

His mother said to him: " How did you get like this?"

Joha said to her: "Look, I held the dog— "

"Is that how you hold a dog? . . . You must tie him at the throat with a loose string and pull him along like this. . . . "

"Fine," said Joha. "The next time!"

A little time passed. His mother said to him: "*Yalla!* Go visit your grandmother!"

Joha went to see his grandmother.

She had bought some good meat and said to him: "I will give you a piece of good meat for your mother, so she will make you meatballs."

Joha said: "Fine!"

His grandmother wrapped a good piece of meat in paper and gave it to him.

Joha said: "Grandma, have you got a string?"

"Yes! What do you need it for?"

"I want a string."

His grandmother looked for a string and gave it to him. Joha went out, tied the meat to the string, and pulled it along like this. . . . By the time he reached home, the meat was all dirty with earth and mud.

"What is this?" his mother said to him.

Joha said: "Look! Grandmother gave me meat for you to cook—to make meatballs."

"Good God!" said his mother. "Stupid you were born and stupid you will die! You will not go to your grandmother's anymore!"

NARRATED BY SOL MAYMARAN – 1990

Special Eggplant

Once Joha's mother said to him: "As you live, Joha, go out and buy me an eggplant!"

"What is eggplant?" Joha said to her.

Said the mother: "A thing that is green on top, and underneath the green is a dark color—a dark red."

Joha went into the street, looked and looked, but didn't see anything like it.

Finally, he found a sheikh who had a green turban and a coat in an eggplant color, and he brought him to his mother.

He said: "Here, Mother, I have brought it to you!"

"What did you bring me?" his mother said to him.

"Here, this is eggplant!" Joha said to her. "Didn't you tell me that on top it is green and underneath red? Take it!"

NARRATED BY SIMHA MEYUHAS – 1988

The Cow's Feet

Joha's mother said to him, "Joha, go to the butcher and see if he has cow's feet," because she wanted to have everything ready for the Sabbath *hamin** dish.

Joha went to the butcher and lifted up the butcher's trouser leg, to see if he had cow's feet.

He returned home and said to his mama: "No, Mama, the butcher hasn't got cow's feet."

The following day his mother said to him once more: "Go, Joha, and see if the butcher has cow's feet."

Joha went to the butcher and again lifted his trouser leg.

* stew

The butcher didn't understand what this creature wanted. He gave him a kick. Joha got up from the floor and left.

When he got home, his mother said: "Joha, does the butcher have cow's feet?"

"No, Mama!" replied Joha. "He hasn't! I already told you that he hasn't!"

On Thursday morning, Joha's mother said: "There's nothing else I can do but go to the butcher myself and see if he has cow's feet!"

She entered the shop and saw lots of cow's feet hanging there.

She said to the butcher: "All week I sent my son to you, to see if you had cow's feet. So why did you tell him that you hadn't any?"

The butcher looked at Joha's mother and said to her: "Ah! Was it your son? Every day he came and lifted my trouser leg. . . . Now I understand. He wanted to see if *I* had cow's feet!"

"Oh!" Joha's mother said. "Forgive me! It's my fault! Because I told him to go and see if you had cow's feet! Don't you know—he takes everything literally!"

NARRATED BY MATILDA KOEN-SARANO – 1996

Independent Nuts

Joha's mother told him to go to the market to buy a kilo of nuts.

Joha went and bought a small bag of nuts. Returning home, a nut fell out of the bag and began to roll along the street.

Joha emptied the bag into the street and said to the nuts: "Roll home!"

When he arrived home, he asked his mother: "Have the nuts arrived yet? I saw that they knew how to roll, so I sent them home by themselves!"

NARRATED BY NELLA ADDADI – 1991

What a Family!

The mayor of the village where Joha lived wanted to give charity to the poor. He said: "I'm going to give a loaf of bread to each member of the family."

Joha, who lived alone with his mother, came and said: "Two loaves of bread are too few!"

He went before the mayor, who said to him: "You . . . how many are you?"

Says Joha: "Wait a moment while I count, because I cannot remember well. . . . Now, let's see . . . Joha, the glutton, the lazy one . . . my mother, she who bore me, and me. . . . We are six!"

NARRATED BY MARIA BAHBOUT – 1988

The Bear's Tail

One day, Joha's father had people at home, and they were all telling tales.

Joha jumped up and said, "The bear we caught today had a tail two meters long!"

Said his father: "No! What are you talking about? Two meters? . . . Much less!"

Said Joha: "No, not two meters! But it was one meter long!"

"No, no, no, no! Much less!" said the father. "Go down, go down!"

Said Joha: "Half a meter!"

"Lower! Lower!" said his father.

"Hey," Joha said to him, "you will leave the bear without a tail!"

NARRATED BY VALENTINA TSOREF – 1987

The Rich Uncle

Joha had a multimillionaire uncle in Argentina, and Joha was living in Turkey.

The uncle wrote to Joha that he wished to come to Turkey to meet the family. And he had no children. He had no one to leave his inheritance to.

Joha's mother was very excited. She said to Joha: "Look, everything that your uncle asks, you must do! You must! You have to receive this inheritance for us. If we become rich, it is you who will get us out of this mess!"

"Fine, Mama, fine," Joha said to her.

The uncle came, and they received him with great joy. He stayed with them for a month, two months. . . .

And then one day it rained in Ankara. The uncle came home completely soaked . . . drenched . . . pickled . . . and fainting with hunger.

Joha was alone in the house. He saw his uncle and said: "Uncle, what happened to you? How did you get soaked? It isn't good. You will become ill!"

"Joha," said his uncle, "I promise to give you my inheritance if you give me one thing. But if you don't give it to me . . . I won't give it to you!"

"Well, uncle, what do you want me to give you?" Joha said to him.

"I want you to give me an egg with a good beating," said the uncle.

Then, an hour later, Joha's mother arrived. She looked: Outside was an ambulance, taking away the uncle, who was injured all over. She did not understand what was happening.

She said to Joha: "Joha, what happened to your uncle? What is going on?"

Joha said: "He asked me for an egg with a good beating. So I gave him an egg and a good beating, so that he wouldn't forget me and would give me the inheritance."

NARRATED BY DOLLY BURDA – 1999

To Everything There Is a Solution

Joha came home one day and said to his father: "Look, Papa, I have fallen in love with the daughter of the butcher, and I want to marry her."

"No, my son!" his father said to him. "You cannot marry the butcher's daughter!"

"Why, Papa?" Joha asked him.

"Because she is your half sister!" his father said.

"Very well, Papa." Joha said.

A few weeks passed. Joha came home and said to his father: "Papa, you were right. I met a much better girl, the milkman's daughter, and I want to marry her as soon as possible!"

"No, my son!" his father said to him. "You cannot marry the milkman's daughter!"

"But why, Papa?" Joha asked.

"Because she is your half sister!" his father said.

A month passed, and Joha came and said to his father: "Papa, now I met the best—the daughter of the baker! I am going to marry her!"

"No, Joha," his father said. "You cannot marry the baker's daughter either!"

"But why, Papa?" Joha asked.

"Because she is your half sister!" his father said.

"She too?!" said Joha, and he began to cry.

His mother arrived and asked: "Joha, why are you crying?"

"Look, Mama," Joha said to her, "I wanted to marry the butcher's daughter, and Papa told me that she is my half sister. I wanted to marry the milkman's daughter, and he told me that she is my half sister. Now I wish to marry the baker's daughter, and Papa told me that she, too, is my half sister! Well, what will be the end? Who am I going to marry?"

His mother said to him: "My dear boy, don't take it to heart! You can marry anyone you wish, because Papa is not your father!"

NARRATED BY MATILDA KOEN-SARANO – 1994

The Paper Shoes

Joha's mother had a lover. Joha saw him come every night and was very upset by this.

The festival of Rosh Hashana arrived, and Joha's mother said to him: "Listen, Joha, for the festival of Rosh Hashana buy me a pair of shoes."

"All right, Mama!" Joha said to her, and on the night of Rosh Hashana he brought her a pair of paper shoes.

His mother said to him: "Joha, why did you bring me this pair of paper shoes?"

"Mama," Joha said, "if you put them on only on Rosh Hashana night to meet your boyfriend, they will last a very long time!"

NARRATED BY MARIA BAHBOUT – 1988

The Joys of Joha

Joha was staying with his sister. One week passed, two, three, four. . . .

And they waited for him to go.

Joha understood this and made as if to go.

They said to him: "Go with God, and return when there are feasts and rejoicings."

Joha went off and returned two hours later.

They asked him: "Why have you returned?"

He said: "I returned because you are rejoicing that I left!"

NARRATED BY ALEX KORFIATIS – 1998

CHAPTER 2

JOHA at school

"Learning makes you sweat blood."

To the Letter

When he was a child, Joha came home one day, took a button, and put it in his ear.

His mother arrived and said: "Dear God! What are you doing?"

Joha said to her: "Today the teacher told me: 'You don't understand what I am teaching. It goes in one ear and out the other!' So I am trying to see if it is true!"

NARRATED BY SOL MAYMARAN – 1987

Knowing How to Ask

Joha was in class, and the teacher wanted to teach the children about the animals.

He said to them: "How does a dog go?"

They all went: "Bowwow!"

"And how does the cat go?"

They all went: "Meow! Meow!"

The master said to them: "Good. Who knows how the wolf goes?"

Joha raised his hand and said: "My grandfather knows!"

The teacher said to him: "Bring your grandfather here."

Joha brought his grandfather to the class, and the teacher asked him: "How does the wolf go?"

The grandfather went: "Eh . . . . "

The teacher repeated, "How does the wolf go?"

The grandfather went: "Eh . . . ."

Said Joha: "Not like that, teacher. . . . Grandfather, how was it when you were a young man with the beautiful young girls?"

The grandfather went: "Oooo . . . !"

Narrated by ALEX KORFIATIS – 1993

Mother's Dear

Joha always got up very late in the morning to go to school, when his father and mother had already left the house to go to work.

When Joha got up, he couldn't find his shirt, his trousers, his shoes. . . . He couldn't find any of his things and began to look for them like a madman: "Where can they be? Where can they be?"

Actually, at night, before going to bed, he had undressed and thrown his clothes here and there: The jacket and the shirt he left in the living room, the trousers in the bathroom, the socks under the chair . . . one shoe under the bed, another behind the door.

And the books and school notebooks—who knew where he had left them?

And so, by the time he got dressed, found the books and notebooks, and arrived at school, the *hacham** had already arrived and the lesson had begun.

When Joha arrived in class, the *hacham* began to make fun of him: "*Pasha de la madre,* mother's dear, how quickly you came! Where were you until now, mother's dear?"

"Excuse me, Señor Hacham!" Joha said to him. "I didn't know where my things had gone to. . . . I had to look for them. . . . Someone hid them from me, while I was asleep."

"Yes, mother's dear," the *hacham* said to him. "Go to the

* rabbi

corner right away!"

The other boys began to say slowly: "*Pasha de la madre,* mother's dear!" They looked one another in the face and began to laugh like madmen. And so they stuck Joha with the name "*Pasha de la madre.*"

A week later, the *hacham* took Joha aside and said: "Look, Joha, I am going to teach you what you are to do each night, before you go to bed. You will take a piece of paper and write down where you have thrown your clothes and your things, before going to bed. And when you get up in the morning, study well what you wrote, and you will find everything in its place."

Joha did what the *hacham* told him. He took a pencil and wrote: "The shirt is on the chair, the trousers on the small stick, the shoes under the bed, the socks under the chair, the books above the table in the parlor" . . . but when he went to bed he added: "Joha is in bed."

When he woke in the morning he found everything in its place: the shirt, the trousers, the socks, the shoes . . . the books—everything. But where was Joha? He was not in bed!

Joha began to look for him, lifted the blanket . . . he wasn't there! He removed the headboard! He wasn't there! Dear God! He was going crazy . . . Where was Joha?

Joha was late again for school and arrived during the middle of the lesson.

When he entered, the *hacham* put him in the corner once more, with his face to the wall. The other pupils began to call out slowly: "*Pasha de la madre,* Mother's dear!"

When the *hacham* finished the lesson, he called Joha aside and said: "Tell me, Joha, what happened today. How did you come late once again?"

And Joha told him how he looked for himself in the bed and couldn't find him.

The *hacham* said: "Look, Joha, the first thing that a person has to do is to find himself. If one doesn't find oneself, one can do nothing in life!"

"What does it mean 'to find oneself,' Señor Hacham?" Joha asked.

"Think well, and you will understand it!" the *hacham* replied.

Joha thought and thought and didn't find himself. He went to his mother and said to her: "Mama, where can I find myself?"

His mother, who was busy, said to him: "Look at yourself in the mirror!"

Joha looked in the mirror and said: "There you are, Joha!"

He took the mirror and placed it above his bed. When he went to look for himself in bed, this time he found him and so did not look anymore. And from that day on, Joha was never again late for school.

The *hacham* asked him: "Mother's dear, did you find yourself?"

"Yes, Señor Hacham," Joha said to him. "I found myself in bed. I left him there and came quickly to school!"

NARRATED BY MATILDA KOEN-SARANO – 1999

Born Merchant

The teacher asked Joha in class:

"Five eggs at twenty cents each one, how much is that?"

"Sixty cents."

"No!"

"Seventy . . . "

"No!"

"I won't go higher than ninety!" said Joha.

NARRATED BY BEKI BARDAVID – 1996

The Patient Teacher

When he was small, Joha went to school. He always insisted on making bets with his friends. And he always won the bets.

One day, coming out of school, a boy said: "What a good teacher we have. He never gets angry. He is always patient."

Another said: "He never gets angry."

Joha said: "I am going to make him angry! Do you want to see? But," he said, "how much will you give me if I make him angry?"

His friends said: "We will give you one hundred liras, each one of us, if you make the teacher angry. *Aval,*"* they said to him, "you always beat us, and we want to win against you for once. How much will you give us if you don't succeed?"

"I will only give you one hundred, but I want one hundred from each of you!" said Joha.

Joha went home, thought and thought, and said: "Now I know what to do!"

He got up at midnight, went and knocked on the teacher's door.

The teacher got up, went downstairs, looked. What did he see? Joha was there.

"What do you want, dear?" he said, without getting angry. "What do you want at midnight?"

Joha said: "I wanted to ask you why they all have long legs in France. . . . Why do the French have long legs?"

The teacher said: "There, they are all tall; that is why they have long legs. You did well to ask me," he said to Joha. "This is something you must know. Have you anything else to ask me?"

"No!" Joha said to him.

"Well then," the teacher said, "go now, dear, go home. Go in peace." The man did not get angry. He went back indoors.

* but

"What am I going to do?" said Joha, "I didn't make him angry. . . . " He turned around and knocked on the door once more.

The teacher got dressed again, and again he went downstairs. He opened the door and said: "You have come again? What do you want?"

Joha said: "I came to ask you why in Japan they all have broad feet."

The teacher said: "That is how they are there. It is because there are many sands. They walk barefoot, and so their feet are broad. You did well," he said, "to ask. . . . Now then, my dear, go home."

When he said this, Joha began to cry.

The teacher said to him: "Why are you crying? You came to learn, didn't you? So why are you crying?"

Joha said: "Because of you, I will lose one hundred liras!"

NARRATED BY ESTER VENTURA – 1992

A Dangerous Language

Joha very much wanted to study.

He said to his father: "I want to teach myself French."

"And I will send you to France, that you should learn the language!" his father said and sent him to France.

After a month, his father wrote a letter to Joha, saying: "Joha, how is the language you are studying?"

Joha wrote: "Papa, I'm not picking up this language, and I am forgetting the language we speak at home."

His father wrote back: "Hurry, Joha, come home immediately, before you become mute!"

NARRATED BY ESTER BEN-YOSEF – 1992

Still Waiting*

Joha went and tied himself with string to a pillar next to one of the classroom buildings at the university.

A student passed by and asked: "What are you doing here, Joha?"

"What? Don't you know?" said Joha. "Someone told me that even a donkey tied to the university by a string still leaves with a degree and a certificate in the end! That is why I put myself here and am waiting."

NARRATED BY SMADAR AZULAY – 1999

Don't Know Which

Joha, at the age of forty-five, was already learning to read and write.

"Oh, is it true, Joha? Now you know everything. You know how to write; you know how to read. There is no word you cannot write, and you even know how to write the numbers from one to a trillion."

"Yes, I know everything. I am being held up in only one place."

"Go on, Joha, tell me! I will teach it to you immediately."

"Three hundred and thirty-three . . . "

"Huh?"

"I cannot manage to write three hundred and thirty-three."

"What is there not to know? You put down three threes, one next to the other!"

* This joke was originally told by Yeshayahu Leibowitz.

"I know, but which one do I put first? . . . That's what I don't know!"

NARRATED BY BEKI BARDAVID – 1999

If Not Now, When?

Joha's father came to an agreement with his son. He said to him, before Yom Kippur: "Look, Joha, now we are going to the tailor. I will have him make you a completely white suit for Yom Kippur. . . . " Knowing that Joha always did the opposite of what he told him to do, he said: "Look, you will be well dressed . . . so that you will bring me honor. You should do everything that I tell you!"

Joha said: "Fine!"

Yom Kippur came, and they ate the last meal before the fast. Joha put on his white suit and went with his father to synagogue.

On the way there, they saw a pool of water. His father said, so that he should do just the opposite, "Look, Joha, you are dressed so well—go into the pool of water!"

Joha went into the water and got his white suit all dirty.

His father said: "What have you done?"

Joha said: "I did exactly what you told me to do! I went into the pool!"

"But you always do the opposite of what I tell you to do. How is it that you did exactly what I told you to do this time?"

Joha said: "If on the eve of Yom Kippur, I don't do what my father tells me, when will I do it?"

NARRATED BY SARA SAADON – 1999

CHAPTER 3

JOHA and work

"Joha wanted to die in order to get enough sleep."

Lazy Joha

Joha's mother said to him: "Look, do me a favor: go to the marketplace and bring me a kilo of meat, a kilo of fish, and a kilo of flour. But come back quickly!"

Joha went off and very soon returned home and said: "Mama, I forgot what you asked me to buy!"

The same thing happened again. Finally, his mother said to him: "Write the three things I told you on the palm of your hand."

Joha wrote them and went off. Along the way he came across a pool of water. He played in the water, and what he had written on his hand got washed off.

He returned home and said to his mother: "I'll try just this once more, but not again!"

His mother told him again and he walked the whole of the way, repeating: "Meat, fish, flour . . . meat, fish, flour . . . meat, fish, flour."

When he had bought everything, he stood there saying, "I don't know what to do! These things are very heavy!"

A dog passed by. Joha said to it: "Carry this meat home for me."

The dog cried: "Bowwow!"

Joha gave him the meat. The dog went off.

A cat passed by. Joha told it to carry the fish home.

As for the flour, he said: "This is heavy, too!"

He said to the air: "Carry this flour home for me!"

He came home and asked his mother: "Has everything I bought arrived?"

His mother said: "No!"

Joha told her that he had sent the meat with the dog, the fish with the cat, and the flour with the air.

And his mother said: “Get out! Until you bring everything back to me, you won’t sleep at home!”

Narrated by ESTER COHEN – 1994

Pedantry

Many years ago, they didn’t sell ready-made bottles of oil in the grocer shops. Everyone brought a bottle, and it was filled for them.

One day, when there was no oil in the house, Joha’s mother put a bottle in his hand and said: “Go, buy me two liters of oil.”

Joha went to the grocer’s and said to him: “My mother told me that you should give me two liters of oil.”

The grocer measured out the oil and poured it into the bottle. The bottle was smaller than his mother had thought, so a bit of oil remained.

The grocer said: “Joha, there is still a little oil left. Where shall I put it for you?”

Joha turned the bottle upside down and said: “Put it here. There is a hollow in the bottom of the bottle.”

In this way all the oil that was already in the bottle spilled out, and Joha went home with only the little bit in the hollow.

His mother said: “Joha, where is the oil?”

“Here!” He turned the bottle upside down again, and the rest of the oil was emptied as well.

Narrated by ISSAHAR AVZARADEL – 1991

Tasty Work

Joha wanted to have some income. He didn't know what work to do, what employment to take, or what to trade. He went to the marketplace and saw many there selling grapes.

Said Joha: "It seems that this is a prime trade! Selling grapes!"

"But," he thought, "If I go and sell grapes where all these vendors are, I won't be able to sell anything."

He asked himself, "Where should I sell?" and decided to go to the entrance of the cemetery.

He took two baskets of grapes, sat down at the entrance of the Mount of Olives, and waited: No cock crowed, no dog howled. And he stood there, shouting: "Come, buy grapes of Muscat and grapes of Hebron!"

But there was no sound or reply. Finally, as he waited for some client to appear, he began to taste the grapes. He filled his throat, grape by grape, and finished all the bunches. Then he returned home with the empty baskets.

His mother saw him with empty baskets, was very happy, and said : "How was the sale?"

And Joha said to her: "You can't imagine what a time I had. Next to me were all the dead people, silent, and grape by grape I ate all the grapes!"

Narrated by PINHAS TOKATLY – 1989

Business Is Business

Joha had six hens and a rooster, and he went to the market to sell them.

A man came and said to him: "Look, I only want to buy the hens."

Joha said: "No! I won't sell only the hens. If you want to buy, you must buy the seven together."

The man came back and said: "You know what? I want you to give me the hens. I will go to my wife and ask her. If she tells me that the hens are good, I will buy the rooster as well."

Joha said to him: "What, do you think I am stupid? I'm not going to give you the hens. Go and don't come back again!"

The man replied: "Look, you know what? We will make a contract. I will take the hens; I will show them to my wife. And I will leave you the rooster as guarantee."

"That's fine!" said Joha.

The man took the hens and brought them to his wife.

His wife said to him: "The hens are very good. Leave them here, and let Joha stay there with the rooster!"

And the good Joha is still waiting there for the man to come and buy the rooster as well!

Narrated by LEVANA SASSON – 2000

According to Circumstances

Joha was working as a chef for a very wealthy man.

One day the man came to him and said: "Look, I want you to prepare a very fine meal for me: Take a sheep. Take out the best parts of its insides, cook them, and bring me the meal."

Joha went and took the heart and tongue of the sheep and cooked them.

He came to the patron and said: "Please, look what a fine meal I have cooked for you!"

The man ate and said: "Truly, it is very good! I will give you a lot of money, because I enjoyed this meal you made for me very much."

Several weeks passed. The rich man came back, called Joha to him, and said: "I want you to make me a sheep meal again. But this time give me the worst parts inside it."

Joha went and took the sheep, took out the heart and tongue, and cooked them.

The man sat down to eat. He saw at once that the meal was the same as the one he had had previously.

He said to him: "What is this, Joha? A few weeks ago I asked for the best inner parts of the sheep, and you gave me the heart and the tongue. Now I wanted the worst parts, so why have you given me the heart and tongue again?"

Joha said to him: "Look, for the one who has a good heart and tongue, the meal is good. For the one who has a bad heart and tongue, the meal is bad!"

NARRATED BY LEVANA SASSON – 2000

The Nudnik

Joha owned a restaurant.

One day he had a bowl of yogurt in front of him.

A nudnik customer came up to him and said: "What is there to eat?"

Joha said to him: "There is dolmas, stuffed squash."

"What else is there?"

"There is *kubbe*."*

"And what else?"

"There are *borekas*."†

"And what more is there?"

"There is *mejadara*."‡

The customer was standing in front of him, and Joha's nerves were becoming very strained.

"And what else is there to eat?"

In the end Joha became so unnerved that he took the bowl of yogurt and threw it at the customer: "There is Joha with yogurt! Eat!"

NARRATED BY ALEX KORFIATIS – 2000

There Is an Answer for Everything

Joha was the owner of a restaurant, and it had everything in it.

One night a nudnik came and said to him: "Can you give me a kilo of nothing?"

"Yes!" Joha said. He opened the door of a dark room and asked, "What can you see there?"

The man said, "Nothing!"

"Take a kilo of it!" Joha told him.

NARRATED BY ALEX KORFIATIS – 2000

* Iraqi rice pastries with minced meat filling
† salty pastries with cheese or spinach filling
‡ rice with lentils

What Is the Best Method?

There was a poor man who was constantly being eaten by fleas and didn't know what to do.

One day he walked through the market and saw Joha, who was selling some packets, which he said contained an anti-flea medicine.

The man asked, "What is this?"

Joha said, "This powder works miracles! You kill fleas with it."

The man didn't think twice, paid, took a bag, and went home.

He sprinkled the powder on the floor and went to bed. The fleas bit him just the same as before.

The next day, angry, he went to the market, to the man who had sold him the medicine, and said: "Now, see here, you cheated me. Now, see here, the fleas still ate me up! See here, your medicine is good for nothing!"

"I cheated you? How did I cheat you?" Joha said to him. "It works! But what I want to know is if you knew how to use it correctly."

The man said: "Of course! I threw it under my bed."

"Ah," said Joha, "the medicine is useless that way. You must take the flea with both fingers, open its mouth, and with the other hand put a bit of powder in its throat."

The man thought and said: "But you are stupid! If I take the flea with my hands, I go like this . . . and I flatten it under my fingers, then I don't need your medicine."

And Joha, seeing that the other man was not such a fool, replied: "Well, you can do it either this way or that way."

NARRATED BY SARA YOHAY – 1994

It's Obvious!

Joha went into a shop.
"I want a kilo of tuna fish, but it must be fresh!"
"It seems you must be Joha?"
"Yes!!! How did you know?"
"Here we sell only ironware!"

NARRATED BY BEKI BARDAVID – 1996

Once Too Often

For Joha's wedding his mother bought him a beautiful jacket.

Joha wore it for years because he wasn't able to buy another one; he always had more important things to buy: shoes, clothes for his child, things for the home.

When the jacket had gotten very old, he went to a tailor and asked: "How much will a new jacket, the same as this one, cost me?"

The tailor said: "Fifty liras!"

"I'm sorry," Joha said to him, "but I haven't got that much money. Can't you give me a discount?"

"Look," said the tailor, "I can't give you a discount, but if you wish, I can do something else. Give me your jacket, and I will reverse it for you. It will cost you ten liras, and you will have a jacket that is like new."

"Fine!" said Joha. He took off the jacket and left it with the tailor.

A week later he came and took a marvelous new jacket, which the tailor had made for him by turning the old one inside out.

Very pleased, Joha put on the jacket, paid, and went off.

Years passed. Joha continued to wear the jacket, until it became very worn once more.

One day he said: "I will take it to the tailor. He will reverse it for me and make it like new."

He went to the tailor and asked: "Can you reverse this jacket for me?"

"With pleasure!" the tailor said, setting to work.

But what did poor Joha see when he came to collect the jacket soon after? A jacket just as old as the one he had given him!

"What is this?" he asked the tailor.

The tailor said: "Señor, in the past did you have this jacket reversed?"

"Ah, yes!" Joha said to him. "Once."

"Ah, well," the tailor said, "you should know that one cannot reverse a jacket more than once!"

NARRATED BY MATILDA KOEN-SARANO – 1999

Only to Think of It!

Two friends were complaining about the heat. One of them was Joha.

Joha said to his friend: "Do you know what it's like to carry bricks to the eighth floor of a building under construction?"

The other one asked: "How long have you been working?"

Joha said to him, "I'm starting tomorrow!"

NARRATED BY HAYIM REFAEL – 1992

"Joha Wanted to Die in Order to Get Enough Sleep"

Joha was lazy. Whatever work they put him to, he never could adapt. He preferred to go without eating rather than work.

Finally, a friend said to him: "Go to the cemetery and collect the leaves. Go and trim the grass!" And he took Joha there.

As Joha was trimming the grass, he suddenly saw on a gravestone the words "Avraam Esfornes—May his soul rest in peace in the Garden of Eden," and also, "Señor Cuencas—May his soul rest in peace."

Then . . . he saw that five or six souls were resting.

Joha said: "They are all resting and only I am working. And I want to rest as well!"

NARRATED BY HAYIM REFAEL - 1992

"A Woman May Not Have Much Sense, but Whoever Does Not Use It Is Dense"

As usual, Joha was without work.

Each day, his wife would say to him: "Now then, Joha, go and find yourself some work. We have to feed the children!"

And he would say to her: "Where will I find work? There is no work today. What can I do?"

One day she got angry and said: "Go play music at the cemetery!" (to keep herself from saying "Go to the devil!").

Joha, who always took everything literally, picked up a drum and went to play at the cemetery. While he was playing, a bear stepped out from among the graves and began to dance.

Joha played and the bear danced. . . . When he stopped dancing, the bear gave Joha a sack of gold ducats.

Full of joy, Joha went home and gave the money to his wife.

"Where does this come from?" his wife asked. "Did you steal it?"

"No!!" Joha said. "I did as you told me. I went to the cemetery and played music."

"Ah, that's good!" said his wife. Happy and content, she went to buy them food to eat and clothes for the children.

A month passed. Joha took the drum once more and went to play at the cemetery.

Again the bear came out. Joha played and the bear danced.When it stopped dancing, the bear gave Joha another sack of ducats.

Joha went home and gave the money to his wife.

They bought everything good. And they bought a house. They were extremely rich.

Another month passed. Joha took the drum and was about to leave the house to play at the cemetery.

"No, Joha!" his wife said. "Don't go anymore! We have enough money for the rest of our lives."

"On the contrary. I want to go!" Joha said to her, and he went to the cemetery.

Barely had he begun to play when the bear came out and began to dance. When it stopped dancing, the bear motioned with its finger to Joha: "Come here, my dear!"

"Yes," said Joha. "What is it?"

"Look," the bear said, "the first time you came here you were flesh and bone. You were not to my taste. The second time you also were not fat enough for me. But now," he said, "you are fat enough. Now I am going to eat you!"

"No!" Joha said to him. "Don't eat me! Do me a favor!"

"Fine," the bear said."I am going to do you a favor. Tell me where you would like me to start eating you."

"Start with my ear, because I didn't listen to my wife!" Joha said to him.

Narrated by MATILDA KOEN-SARANO – 1994

How Many Eggs?

Joha was selling eggs under the bridge.

Just then Monsieur Pilosof passed by. "How much is one egg?"

"A hundred cents."

"Very expensive!"

"For you, Monsieur Pilosof? You are rich!"

"How many eggs have you got there, Joha?"

"I don't know. I must count them."

"You don't know how many eggs you have. . . . How, then, do you know how much money I have?"

Narrated by BEKI BARDAVID – 1992

What a Way to Make a Living!

Joha didn't have any work.

His wife said to him: "What will happen to us? We have children! You must find work!"

Joha said to her: "I looked. I looked for work but didn't find any!"

One morning he got up and said to his wife: "I have an idea. Every day they bury the dead. At night I will go and remove their shrouds. They have no use for them anymore. Then I will sell them, and then we will have enough money to live."

He went during the day and saw that they were burying dead people. Then he went there at night, removed the earth, took away the dead people's shrouds, went and sold them, and brought bread home.

To make it short, Joha was making a living.

One day, he went to the cemetery to conduct his business. While he was removing the shroud from a dead body, the dead man gripped his hand.

"For heaven's sake!!" said Joha. "Why are you holding me?"

"Why are you taking my shroud off? I have only one shroud, and you want to take it from me!" said the dead man.

From that time on Joha, the poor soul, gave up his new way of making a living.

NARRATED BY ESTER VENTURA – 1999

Neither Buying nor Selling

Joha was walking around the bazaar, looking at the vegetables and the oranges. A young man whom Joha did not know, a prankster, came up to him and wanted to joke at his expense.

Finally, the unknown man made Joha angry when he said: "Tell me, Joha, what day is it today?"

And Joha said: "How should I know, son, what day is today? I am a stranger here."

And the other replied: "Really, you don't know what day is today? You don't know that?"

Joha raised his eyebrows, as if in wonderment, and said: "Ah, my dear young man! As you see, I am walking around the market, but I am not buying or selling days!"

NARRATED BY SARA YOHAY – 1992

The Mathematician

Joha began to work as a waiter in a restaurant.

One day a man came in and asked him for a cup of tea.

Five minutes later, he called Joha over again and asked: "How much does the tea cost?"

"Seven dinars," Joha answered.

"Well, bring me another one."

Joha brought him another cup of tea.

The man drank it and wanted to pay.

"Eleven!" Joha said to him.

"It is not my job," the man said, "but it seems to me that seven and seven make fourteen."

"Don't you teach me!" Joha said. "I was married, I had four children with my first wife, and my second wife was also married and had four children with her first husband. Now we have three children together. Thus, she has seven and I have seven, and altogether it makes eleven!"

NARRATED BY ELIEZER PAPO - 1999

Each to His Business

Joha was selling chestnuts in front of the Rothschild bank.

"Chestnuts! Hot chestnuts! Chestnuts that burn your hands! Tasty chestnuts!"

At that moment Rothschild passed to enter his bank, and the warmth of the chestnuts in the fire appealed to his spirit.

"Joha, give me a hundred grams."

"Certainly, Señor Rothschild!" And he weighed him a hundred grams of chestnuts, so hot and tasty.

Then Rothschild saw that he hadn't any small change.

"Joha, I will send you the money shortly. I haven't any small change."

"Nooo, Señor Rothschild! Give me back the chestnuts. Everyone should know his business. Today you make me your banker, and tomorrow you might begin to sell chestnuts and take my work from me. Come on now, let each of us return to his own work. . . . Chestnuts! Hot chestnuts! Who wants chestnuts . . . ?"

NARRATED BY BEKI BARDAVID – 1996

His Way of Counting

Joha opened a clothing store.

Aunt Sinhulachi came in: "How are things, Joha? Going well? Good business?"

"Thank you, Aunt Sinhaluchi. What do you want?"

"I want to buy some cotton material for my granddaughter. We are going to sew sheets for her."

"With the greatest pleasure! How many meters?"

"We shall need about sixty meters."

"Please tell me . . . one, two, three, four . . . how old is the new granddaughter?"

"She is already eleven months."

"Yes?. . . twelve, thirteen, fourteen . . . and the eldest one, how old is she?"

"God be praised, she is already sixteen years old."

"You don't say! . . . seventeen, eighteen, nineteen, twenty. . . . And how long to the wedding?"

"About twenty-five days."

" . . . twenty-six, twenty-seven, twenty-eight, twenty-nine, thirty . . ."

NARRATED BY BEKI BARDAVID – 1992

Joha's Nail

Joha wanted to sell his house and began to tell people, "I have a house for sale at a very cheap price." But they already knew about Joha's craziness and didn't want to do business with him.

Eventually, Joha came across a family who was new to the city and didn't know about him. They came and asked him to sell them the house.

Joha said to them: "Look what a beautiful house, and what a price! I have only one condition: that a nail in the wall of the living room remain mine, because it is a souvenir of my father."

"Fine! What does it matter to us?" they said, and signed a paper that said the nail was his.

Joha went away. The family began to live there, and all was well.

Suddenly one day, while the family was eating, Joha entered like a whirlwind, without knocking on the door or anything.

"Why Joha, what has happened?" they asked.

"Nothing!" said Joha. "It was very hot in the street. I came to hang my coat on my nail."

"Fine," they said, and he went off.

At night, Joha entered again without knocking: "I came to take my coat. Now it is cold!"

"What can we do?" they said.

Two days passed. They were all in bed and were about to go to sleep when suddenly Joha entered, without knocking.

"What's the matter, Joha?" they asked.

"I came to visit my nail." said Joha. "I longed for my father, and I came to see the nail. It is the only thing that I have left from him."

"But goodness, why at this hour?" they asked.

"Eh, what do you want?" Joha said. "Didn't you sign a paper saying that this is my nail? I can come to see it whenever I wish!"

Two weeks passed, and one day Joha entered the house with a dead cat in his hand. He went straight to the nail and hung the cat on it.

"What is this?!" the family asked him.

"Eh, we are going through very difficult times. I don't earn enough. I am working with stuffed cats. I am going to leave this cat here, and next week I'll come and take it!"

"How can you leave it here?!" the family members began to shout.

"I already told you that this nail is mine, and I can do whatever I wish with it. Here is the paper you signed."

Seeing this, the poor people said: "We can't stand this any longer! Let's go away from here, quickly!"

And so Joha took back his house with his nail . . . and kept the money.

NARRATED BY MATILDA KOEN-SARANO – 1994

Profitable Ignorance

They asked Joha: "Pray, Joha, how did you become so rich? You don't know numbers or how to keep accounts!"

"It's very easy!" Joha said to them. "I buy for one hundred and sell for two hundred. Thus I earn my ten percent!"

NARRATED BY BEKI BARDAVID – 1996

Foreign Work

Joha went to Germany to look for work. He rented a house with a Chinese man and a black man.

The first day, the black man went to look for work and they told him: "We don't want black people here!"

The next day, the Chinese man went. They told him: "We don't want yellow people here!"

Joha said: "Don't you worry! I am white. Me, they will take!"

The Chinese man, who didn't want them to take Joha, painted him with crude oil during the night. And in the morning he woke him very quickly, saying: "Run! Run! You will be late!"

Our poor Joha didn't have time even to wash. Straight from the bed he went to work.

The boss said to him: "We don't want black people here!"

Joha said: "I know. That's why I came."

The boss said: "You're also black!"

Joha said: "Do you think so?"

The man gave him a mirror and Joha, looking pensive, concluded: "That Chinese man is a fool. He woke the black man again, instead of me!"

NARRATED BY ELIEZER PAPO – 1999

How to Sell the Bible

There was a publisher who was looking for salesmen to sell the Bible. He put an advertisement in the newspaper: "We are looking for salesmen to sell Bibles to private people."

Joha presented himself.

"What is your name?"

"My . . . my name is Joha."

The man explained the conditions to him and gave him three Bibles, but he noticed that Joha was a stammerer.

Joha went off with the Bibles. Two hours later, he returned without them.

The owner, marveling, gave him five more Bibles, and Joha went off. Two hours later, he returned without the Bibles.

The owner said: "Bravo, Joha, bravo! The best salesman that I have is you! How do you do it? Tell me your secret."

And Joha told him: "Well . . . we . . . ll, I . . . I . . . ring the . . . the doorbell. A lady opens for me . . . me. She says: 'Wha . . . wha . . . what . . . do you want?' I . . . I . . . tell her: 'Ma . . . madam . . . I . . . I . . . came . . . here . . . to . . . sell . . . Bi . . . Bibles. The . . . the . . . Bible costs this much money. What . . . what . . . would the lady prefer: that I . . . sell it to her or that . . . that . . . I . . . I . . . I read it to her?'"

NARRATED BY ALBERTO MODIANO – 1999

The Mortgage

Joha went to the bank to ask for a mortgage.

They sent him to the bank manager.

The bank manager said: "My dear Joha, are you working anywhere? Have you got money? Do you have a wage?"

"No!" Joha said.

"Look," said the bank manager, "you are not solvent. I can't give you a mortgage!"

Joha went home sadly.

A few days passed. Then Joha learned that the manager had died. Joha right away called the bank and asked to speak to the manager.

They said to him: "What for?"

He told them: "For a mortgage."

They told him: "The señor manager has died!"

He said to them: "Ah, yes?" and put down the phone.

Half an hour passed. Joha called again.

They said to him: "Señor . . . you can't get any information because the manager has died."

Half an hour later, Joha called again. They told him: "Señor, we already explained to you that you cannot receive information about the mortgage, seeing that the manager has died!"

Joha answered: "I already know about the mortgage, but, you see, I get pleasure from hearing that the bastard is dead!"

Narrated by ELIEZER PAPO – 1999

What a Relief!

Joha started a business with a partner.

The two managed to sell some merchandise and to make a wonderful profit.

Then a client said to them: "If at the end of a week you do not receive a letter from me, it is because the merchandise has been sold, and I will surely very soon come to pay you."

The two partners began to wait impatiently for the postman. No one arrived.

The more days that passed, the happier the two partners became.

Who was that coming now? The postman, bringing them a letter.

Joha started to panic: "Do you see? Do you see," he said to his partner, "what bad luck we have? Look, he is already going to send us back the merchandise!"

With a black face, Joha opened the letter and read. Suddenly, he let out a cry of relief and joy: "You know what!? Your mother died!"

NARRATED BY BEKI BARDAVID – 1999

Nonexistent Banknotes

The days of the Turks were over. New days came, and with them new money, but this time made of paper.

Joha noticed how people were buying with these new banknotes.

He asked one person: "What is this?"

They told him: "Money!"

He said to them: "Anyone can make it!" No sooner said than done. He sat down and began to make paper money.

His wife came and said to him: "What are you doing? Madman! There is no banknote with a value of five thousand dollars!"

Joha said to her: "Why not?"

His wife said to him: "Go to the market and try to exchange it, and we will see who is right."

Joha went out and returned after half an hour, crying:

"Look! You see, I did change it!" And he showed his wife two counterfeit banknotes of 2,500 dollars each.

NARRATED BY ELIEZER PAPO – 1999

The Real Reason

Joha read an ad in the newspaper advertising for a television announcer. At once, Joha set out. He looked for the building mentioned in the ad but didn't find it.

It happened that Joha had a speech problem: "S . . . s . . . eñor pol . . . iceman, c . . . c . . . can you tell me where the TV studio is?"

"Look, the building that you see, that's where it is."

"Tha . . . a . . . nks."

The policeman could not resist asking: "Why are you asking?

"There is a . . . a . . . a . . . te . . . est for an a . . . nn . . . noun . . . cer . . . ."

The policeman didn't move away from the door of the TV studio, and he waited for Joha.

Very soon, Joha came out, after barely five minutes.

"Well, Joha, did they accept you?"

"S . . . c . . . ound . . . rels! A . . . a . . . all anti-Semites!"

NARRATED BY BEKI BARDAVID – 1999

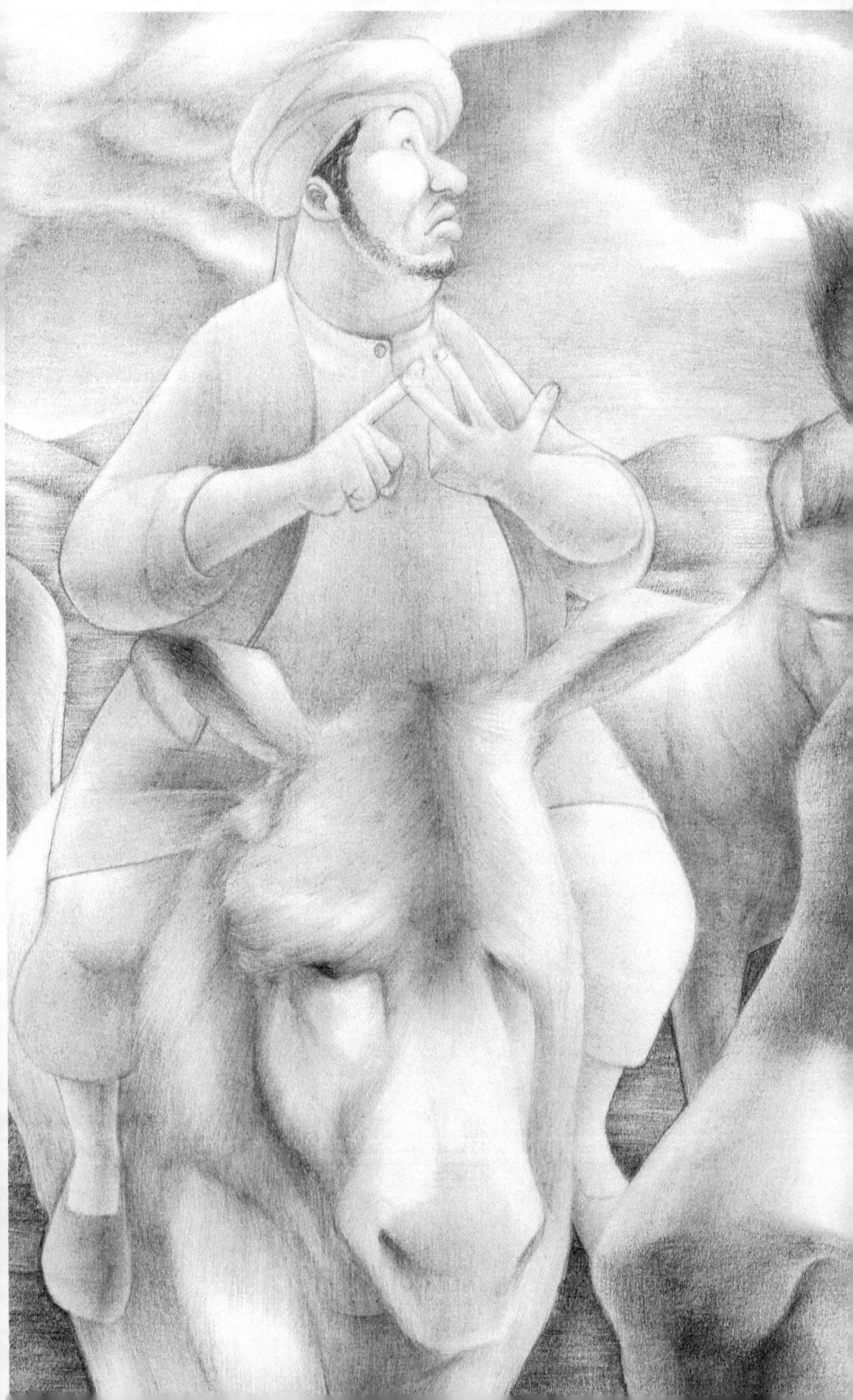

CHAPTER 4

JOHA and the animals

"Don't die, donkey,
until the new grass grows."

A Fish Recipe

Once Joha's mother sent him to buy fish. Joha went to the grocer with a little basket and said to the man working there: "Look, my mother sent me to buy her fish. But my mother doesn't know how to cook it. She said that you would tell me."

The man put the fish into a newspaper and handed it to Joha. Then he said to him: "Look, first of all you must clean it . . . you have to put lemon . . . and salt . . . and you have to cook it."

Joha went dizzy in the head with all this.

The man said: "Look, perhaps you should write it down."

"But where should I write it ?"

"Write it on your fingernail," the man said.

Joha stretched out his finger, and the man wrote a few notes on the nail: Lemon, salt, do this, do that. Joha left very happy. But he left the basket he had brought from home at the grocer's and went out with the fish in his hand, wrapped in a newspaper.

Joha walked along happily, thinking: "Now I will go home and give the fish to my mother. We will eat it on Friday night, like kings."

He walked along, and behind him was a dog—God forbid!—a big dog. Joha began to run and the dog followed behind him. He ran, and the dog ran after him. In a moment the dog had opened its mouth, grrr . . . and swallowed all the fish.

Joha stood there, empty-handed. Only the newspaper remained in his hand. He said: "Son of a *mamzer*!* Now look at my finger. . . ." He put his finger in his mouth and with his tongue rubbed out all that was written on the fingernail, saying to the dog: "Look, I won't tell you how to cook it!"

NARRATED BY HAYIM TSUR – 1992

* bastard

If You Wash a Cat

Early one morning, Joha took his cat to the riverside and began to wash it.

A neighbor passed and said to him: "Joha, what are you doing!? You don't wash a cat! It washes itself by itself. You are harming it!"

But Joha continued washing it.

A little later, another neighbor passed by and said to him: "Joha, look here, you don't wash a cat! Don't you know that if you wash it, the cat will die?"

But all Joha did was let out a snort.

A little later another neighbor passed by and said to him: "You silly thing, Joha. Are you crazy? You mustn't wash the cat; it will die!"

Joha didn't answer him.

In the afternoon, three neighbors passed by the riverside and saw Joha, sitting and crying. They asked: "Joha,why are you crying? What happened to you?"

Joha said to them: "My cat has died!"

"You see!" the three neighbors said. "Didn't we tell you this morning that if you washed your cat, it would die?"

"Ah, no!" Joha said to them. "When I washed it, nothing happened to it. But when I squeezed it out to dry, it died!"

NARRATED BY VITTORIA (VITTO) ESKENAZI – 1992

The Six Donkeys

Joha was going to the market on foot to sell six donkeys. On the way he grew tired and climbed onto one of them.

As they went along he began to count the donkeys: "One,

two, three, four , five. . . . Why only five?" But he wasn't counting the donkey on which he was sitting.

Joha got down from the donkey and went to look for the sixth one. He walked and walked and didn't find it.

He went back, counted the donkeys: Now there were six of them!

"Ah, so you came back?" Joha said to him, and very content, he got up on the donkey and continued on his way.

A little time passed, and Joha once again began to count the donkeys: "One, two, three, four, five. . . . Son of a *mamzer,* the donkey has run off again!" Joha got off the donkey and went to look for it, cursing. But he didn't find it.

He went back and saw the donkey. "Ah, you *mamzer,* why are you going off, and where to?" Joha said and got on it.

I'll make this brief. . . . Joha once again counted the donkeys, and once again the same thing happened.

Joha stopped by the side of the road, filled with confusion.

A friend passed by and asked: "Joha, what are you doing here? Aren't you going to the market to sell six donkeys?"

"Yes," Joha said to him. "But I don't know what's happening: From six, the donkeys are becoming five, and from five, six! I don't know what to think anymore."

"Look, Joha," the friend said to him, "it's simply a matter of counting. I am going to count them," he said, "and you will see that they are seven."

"How seven?!" Joha said to him, in great amazement.

"Yes, Joha. Now then, look," his friend said to him, counting the donkeys. "One, two, three, four, five are the empty donkeys, six, the donkey on which you are seated, and seven, the donkey who is seated on the sixth one!"

NARRATED BY MATILDA KOEN-SARANO – 1994

A Bad Name

Joha met a friend walking in the street with a horse by his side.

He asked: "What is this horse?"

His friend said: "Don't you know! This horse is a marvel! It does everything for me at home. It washes the floors, makes my bed and does the laundry, brings me coffee in bed in the morning. . . ."

Joha, hearing all this, was dying to buy the horse.

After many discussions, the friend sold it to him for a hefty price.

A week passed, and the friend met Joha, who was in the street with the horse.

Joha's face was black with anger. He said to the friend: "This horse that you sold me is worthless! It is lazy! All day long it eats, drinks, and makes dirt! It does nothing at all!"

The friend said to him: "Shh! Take care that the others don't hear you talking this way about the horse. Afterward you won't be able to sell it!"

NARRATED BY YOSEF (MORDO) COHEN – 1999

A Tested System

Joha had a little donkey, and he always walked around the village with it.

One day he decided to go down to the city with the little donkey. He came to the curb, and the donkey refused to budge.

What was Joha going to do? He wanted to get to the city.

But cars were passing by; the donkey was frightened. It was not accustomed to seeing cars in the village.

Joha waited for an hour, two. . . . The little donkey didn't move.

Finally, Joha gave it two big blows, and the donkey began to bray. All the cars stopped, and the donkey crossed over.

From that time on, whenever people saw Joha on the little donkey, they stopped their cars immediately and let Joha and his donkey pass.

NARRATED BY ESTER VENTURA – 1992

The Transformations of the Donkey

Joha had a little donkey and always went out walking with it. One day he put it in the stable and went off alone.

Thieves came, took the donkey, and brought it to the market to sell. They tied up a young man in its place in Joha's stable.

Joha came to take the donkey and in its place saw the young man.

This young man said to him: "My father cursed me and made me into a donkey. The time of the curse has passed, and I have become a human being again."

Said Joha: "If that is the case, I will free you!" And he untied the young man. As soon as Joha gave him his liberty, the man left the stable and went about his business.

But Joha needed the donkey. So he went to the market to buy another one.

Walking through the market, he saw his donkey, which was

for sale there, and he said to it: "Once again you disobeyed your father and turned into a donkey? But I will not take you again, because you might turn into a human being once more!" And he went to buy another donkey.

NARRATED BY ROZA SALINAS – 1984

Donkey on a Diet

Joha had a donkey for sale. He found a Napoleon coin, stuck it on the donkey's rear end, and walked around the market with it.

People passed them and said: "Joha, what is this?"

Said Joha: "This donkey goes to sleep at night, and in the morning the whole stable is full of Napoleons."

They said to him: "How much do you want for it?"

"I want," he said, "five Napoleons."

"And what do we give it to eat?" they said.

"You give it," said Joha, "a big bucket of barley to eat and a big bucket of water to drink. It doesn't need anything more. In the morning," he said, "the whole stable will be full of Napoleons."

They bought the donkey from him and took it home. They gave it a big bucket of barley to eat and a big bucket of water to drink, and the donkey went to sleep.

The next morning, the young boy went to open the door and see if the stable was full of Napoleons. He saw the donkey's foot and thought he saw something shining there. "Aiee!" he said. "The stable is full of Napoleons!"

"What!!?" said his father.

"I saw them!" said the young boy.

"But I could not open the door!"

What did they do? They broke down the door, and what did they see? The donkey stretched on the floor and dead!

They called Joha right away and said to him: "What is this, Joha!"

"It is nothing!" said Joha. "The thing is that you did not feed the donkey properly!"

"How so, we didn't feed it properly? We gave it a big bucket of barley and a big bucket of water!"

"Ah," said Joha, "surely there were a few grains of barley and a few drops of water too many. That is what did the damage and caused its death!"

NARRATED BY VALENTINA TSOREF – 1988

Difficult Counting

They asked Joha: "How many donkeys have you got?"

Joha said: "Wait, I will count them."

He went off and returned ten minutes later. He said: "Look, there were nine donkeys standing in a row. I counted them without problems. But there was one donkey that kept moving from one place to another and wouldn't stand still. Him I couldn't count!"

NARRATED BY YOEL PEREZ – 1999

The Counting of the Omer

In order to count the days of the Omer,* Joha made a knot every day in the the donkey's rope. Thus he knew which day of the Omer it was.

One night, while he was on a journey, he arrived at an inn. He tied the donkey at the entrance of the inn and entered, forgetting to feed the donkey.

He got up in the morning and went to leave. And what did he find? That the donkey had eaten the whole rope! So Joha did not know any longer which day of the Omer it was.

NARRATED BY YEHUDA ASSERAF – 1991

The Villager's Cow

Once Joha went on a journey. In order to not be molested, he decided to dress as a dervish. On the way, a Turkish villager approached him, thinking that he really was a dervish.

This villager had a very precious and valuable cow, and his main income was from the milk of this cow. And so it was that when this cow became sick, this villager decided to do everything possible to make the cow well. And when he saw this dervish, he felt a great joy and asked him to accompany him to his village, so that he should say some prayer or, at the least, write him an amulet.

Our good Joha, who had not the slightest wish to accompany the villager to his village, took out a small piece of paper

* In ancient times Omer were grain offerings made at the Temple in Jerusalem; the Omer was counted on the 49 days between the holidays of Passover and Shavuot in a tradition known as Counting the Omer.

and wrote some words on it, giving it to the villager, who began to jump about with joy.

That villager's cow regained its health, and the story would have ended there were it not for a Jewish neighbor of the Turkish villager.

Two, three months after the incident, the cow of this Jew fell ill. Not knowing what to do, he began to complain to his Turkish neighbor.

The latter said to him: "Look, where cows are concerned, there are no religions, and if this amulet helped my cow, it can help yours as well."

The Jew, who had nothing to lose, and knowing that the amulets of the Muslims are not idolatry, agreed to try using this amulet.

When the neighbor brought him the amulet, the Jew, unable to wait, opened it and was full of wonderment when he saw in it these Spanish words, written in Rashi script:

"Turkish cow, live say I.
If you won't, you will die."

NARRATED BY ELIEZER PAPO – 1999

Change of Identity

Joha had a donkey he loved very much, because he had nobody, neither wife nor children, except this donkey.

Joha worked, and the donkey worked with him. The whole day long they were together.

One day they went into the street. Suddenly, the donkey fell down and died.

Joha was very sad. He said: "Now what am I going to do? I

loved it so much. I am not going to leave it like this," he said. "I will make a grave for it and bury it."

He went and buried it and put a stick and a piece of colored cloth next to it, as a sign that his donkey was buried there. And he sat there crying, next to the donkey that had died.

People passed by and said to him. "Say, Joha, what is this? Why are you crying so hard? Who is buried here?"

Said Joha: "Here is buried a very great and very holy sheik, and he came to me in a dream in the night and told me that no one was visiting his grave. He said to me: 'I want them to come, that they should cry at my grave.'"

And the people . . . one told another, who told another, who told another . . . until the place was full of people.

Each one took out money and put it on top of the grave.

Joha came, saw that they had all gone home, collected all the money. He saw that he had already collected a lot of money, took it all, went home, and said: "I can already buy a new donkey in place of the one that died!"

He bought the donkey and began to work with it. He took it here and there so that it should do all the work. After some time, he passed by the grave of the donkey that had died.

As he watched, they built a big chamber there . . . and it was full of people. And they all were coming and crying and putting money, putting money.

Joha said to them: "What is this? Who has done these things here?"

They said to him: "This is the grave of this great sheik who died, and we come and always put money here and weep."

Joha said: "What are you talking about? This is not the grave of a sheik! This is the grave of my donkey. It died here and here I buried it."

They said: "This one is crazy!"

"No!" said Joha. "I buried it here with my own hands!"

They said to him: "Come, we will go to the *kadi*,* that he should judge you."

They took him to the *kadi*.

The *kadi* came and said to him: "What are you saying? Aren't you ashamed to say that in the grave of this great sheik there is a donkey?"

Said Joha: "But my donkey died and I buried it there!"

The *kadi* said to him: "No! We don't wish to hear such nonsense!" he said. "Take Joha, give him a few blows, and throw him out of here!"

Joha suffered the blows and went home, and from that day on he always said: "Ah, how good was my first donkey! After it died, they made it a sheik!"

NARRATED BY LEVANA SASSON – 1999

It's a Secret

Once Joha was riding to the city on his horse. On one side of the horse was tied a sack of barley. Joha dismounted the horse for a minute, to rest.

A friend passed and asked him: "Joha, what have you got in that sack?"

Joha said to him in a low voice: "Bar . . . le . . . y."

His friend asked him: "So there is barley there? Why are you telling it to me in a low voice?"

Joha replied: "I don't want my horse to hear. . . . "

NARRATED BY MAOR ARZI – 1999

* Muslim religious judge

The Little Donkey That Learned Not to Eat

One day Joha wanted to buy a little donkey. He went to where they sell little donkeys and bought one. He said to the one who sold it to him: "How much does this little donkey eat?"

The other one said: "Three kilos a day. Two in the morning, one in the evening."

Joha took the little donkey, and the first day gave it as much to eat as the man who sold it to him had told him to.

He did not have much money, so the second day he gave it two kilos to eat.

During the day the donkey worked.

"Ah!" said Joha. "Why should I give it three kilos? Two is already enough!"

Several days passed, and Joha found himself without money. He gave it a single kilo.

The little donkey worked.

A few more days passed. Joha forgot to buy it food. During the day he took it out to work.

The little donkey worked.

Joha said: "It's good! Why should I buy it food to eat?"

Three, four days passed, and the little donkey died.

Joha came and said to his wife: "You know what, wife?"

"What?"

"Look at that bastard of a donkey!" said Joha. "After I taught it to live without eating, it died on me!"

NARRATED BY SHMUEL BARKI – 1992

Giraffe Love

In a zoo there was a giraffe, and when the time came for mating they didn't know what to do. Finally, they asked Joha if he would be prepared to make love to the giraffe for a thousand dollars.

Joha said to them: "Yes, with three conditions: first, that no one should see it. Second, that my wife should not know. Third, could you wait for the thousand dollars? The reason is that I don't have that much money at the moment."

NARRATED BY ELIEZER PAPO – 1999

Thank the Lord!

Joha went to the market to buy a horse. He bought the horse, got on it, and shouted "Dio!" to make it move.

The horse did not budge.

Joha said to the person who sold him the horse: "What is this? The horse is not moving!"

The dealer said to him: "This is not a horse like the others.When you tell it 'Thank the Lord!' it goes off, and when you tell it 'The Lord is One,' it stands still."

"Aha! Very good!" said Joha. "Now I understand!" and he said, "Thank the Lord!"

The horse moved off.

The horse was trotting along with Joha on its back, and suddenly Joha saw that they were on the edge of a precipice. He shouted to the horse, "The Lord is One!"

The horse stood still.

"Thank the Lord!" said Joha.

The horse ran and fell down the precipice, with Joha on it!

NARRATED BY MAOR ARZI - 1999

Whom to Believe?

One day the neighbors came to Joha to ask him for the urgent loan of a donkey, to go to a village. And the *hoja* did not want to give it to them.

They came to him and asked: "*Hoja effendi,** could you lend us your donkey?"

Joha said to them: "Ah, don't ask, don't ask. Yesterday as I was going to a village, my donkey died—died!"

At that moment the donkey began to bray "Hia, hi-a, hi-a!" in the stable.

The neighbors said: "But *hoja,* didn't you say that it died!"

"Well, do you believe the donkey or me!"

NARRATED BY ITZHAK HALEVA - 1999

* Sir

CHAPTER 5

JOHA and the bride

"Don't look at the bride or the cloth by candlelight."

The Wishes

Joha was left an orphan, without father or mother, and he grew up with a grandmother.

One day his grandmother said: "Look, I am going to die. This is the way of the whole world. And this child . . . who will look after it? Who will protect it?"

Then she said: "We will get him betrothed. . . . We will marry him off, so that he should have a family," because Joha was an innocent one.

No sooner said than done. They found a young girl, and they made a match.

Everything was fine. Two, three months passed, and his grandmother said: "Joha, did you cast an eye* on your bride-to-be?"

And he said, "No!"

The grandmother said: "You didn't cast an eye on her? You must cast an eye! What kind of thing is this?"

Well, Joha went off to do as his grandmother had said, and what did he do? He slaughtered a cow, took its eyes, came to the house of his bride-to-be, threw the eyes in her face, and returned home running, saying to his grandmother: "Look, grandmother, you told me to throw her one eye. I threw her two!"

The grandmother said: "What did you do?"

He said to her: "I slaughtered a cow, I took both its eyes, I threw them at the bride-to-be. But," he said, "they all looked at me so peculiarly."

Said the grandmother: "And the bride-to-be?"

Said he: "She began to cry. . . ."

Said the grandmother: "Uhhh . . . ! Now this is what you must do: Wait a few weeks, until her rage should pass, and then

*In Judeo-Spanish, *echar un ojo* (literally, "throw an eye") means "to glance at," "take a look at."

go there again. And you must make her laugh, that she should be happy."

Well, two, three weeks passed. Joha went again and told her jokes, but the bride-to-be . . . not a sound from her, not a word.

Then he returned to his grandmother, crying.

The grandmother said: "What happened?"

Said he: "Look, I did what you told me to do. I told her jokes, that she should be happy, but she did not look at me or answer me or greet me, nothing. . . . "

Said the grandmother: "And the others? What did the others do?"

He said: "All the others were crying."

"Crying?"

"Yes!"

"Why?"

"How why?" said he. "Because the grandfather died!"

"Look, son," said his grandmother, "if the grandfather died, you shouldn't have gone telling jokes. You should go and say to her: 'May he attain the World to Come; may God forgive him; may his soul rest in the Garden of Eden. May you have a long life. . . .'"

Two, three weeks passed. Joha went there, knocked on the door, said to the bride-to-be: "May God forgive him! May his soul rest in the Garden of Eden! May you have a long life!"

But no one greeted him, no one wanted to see him.

Once again Joha went running away from there and came to his grandmother, crying.

Said the grandmother: "What happened?"

Joha said: "Look, I did exactly as you told me, and nobody, nobody, nobody greeted me."

Said the grandmother: "And the others, what did they do?"

Said Joha: "They were singing, dancing."

Said the grandmother: "For what?"

"How for what?" said Joha. "They were celebrating a *brit mila!*"*

Said the grandmother: "Look, if they were celebrating a *brit mila,* you should not have said to them 'May you have the world to come,' and all the rest. You should have said: 'He was born in a good time! May he grow big and strong! May he become great!'"

Well, two, three weeks passed—as Joha wanted the bride-to-be to calm down and her anger to pass—and then Joha went there. And the father of the bride-to-be was standing in the garden with a big wart on his chin.

Approaching him, Joha said, just as his grandmother had told him: "May he grow big for you! May he grow big and flourish."

Once again, neither the father nor the bride-to-be greeted him, nothing.

And Joha went out of there running, crying, came to his grandmother and said: "Grandmother, do you know what happened to me?" and he told her everything.

His grandmother said to him: "Look, if he had a wart, you should have told him: 'May it dry up for you; may it shrivel for you. May you not see it anymore!'"

Well, two, three weeks passed. The father of the bride-to-be was in the garden, watering the flowers.

Came Joha and said to him: "May it dry up for you! May it shrivel for you! May you see it no more with your eyes!"

Once again, the father of the bride-to-be looked at him, said nothing, was very enraged.

Joha went out of there and once more returned home.

"Poor little one!" said his grandmother to him. "What happened?"

And Joha told her everything.

His grandmother said: "Look, if he was in the garden with

* circumcision ceremony

all those flowers, with all those fruits, and he invested so much labor in them, you should have said to him: 'May a great quantity come forth and give you endless pleasure!'"

Well, Joha waited again for two, three weeks, so that the future in-laws should calm down. He came there, and by misfortune, the father of the bride-to-be was in the toilet.

Joha entered, and just as his grandmother had told him to do, he said: "May a great quantity come forth and give you endless pleasure!"

Then, the bride-to-be fled, and Joha certainly did not get married to that bride, as long as her father lived!

NARRATED BY ELIEZER PAPO – 1994

Joha's Wedding

Joha's mother said to him: "You know, Joha? I have found you a beautiful bride. Soon you will get married. We have to prepare fine food . . . cakes. Take this sack of wheat. Take it to the miller to grind it for you and bring the flour. We will make cakes . . . cookies. . . ."

"Fine. How should I do it?"

"Look, take the donkey and go!" His mother put the wheat in two sacks, one on each side of the donkey; one half here, one half there.

The donkey was brown. Joha sat between the sacks and took the wheat to the mill. He arrived at the mill . . . knock, knock, knock: "Hey, miller!"

The miller came out: "What do you want?"

Joha said to him: "I want you to grind this wheat for me. Soon I am going to be married. My mother wants the flour. She said that you should grind it well."

"Fine!" said the miller. "Come. Come on up!"

Joha tethered the donkey below, so that it shouldn't run away, and climbed up. "How much do you want?"

"Two *mijities*!"*

"Fine!"

They began to grind. All the flour fell into a tub.

The miller said to Joha: "You put it where you want. Put it into a sack."

Joha put it into the sack. He tried to lift the sack but couldn't.

"Have you got a sieve?" he asked the miller.

"Certainly!"

Joha took the sieve and began to strain the flour through the window, saying: "Wind, take this flour. Flour, go to my village! Flour go to my village!"

All the flour fell on top of the donkey. The brown donkey became white.

"Great!" he said. "I have already sent all the flour to my house. Now my mother will make cakes."

Afterward he went down and looked for his donkey. He couldn't find it. He said: "Miller, come here! You have stolen my donkey! You have exhanged it. This is not my donkey! It is yours!!"

"I haven't got a donkey!" the miller said to him. "What do you want from me? Didn't you bring the donkey? This donkey here is your donkey!"

"How can that be? It was brown. How did it become white? This isn't it!"

The miller brought a brush and . . . trak, trak . . . brushed the entire donkey.

"Now, can't you see?" he said to Joha. "Didn't you empty the flour on top of him?"

"Ah! I did this?"

* Turkish coin named after a sultan

"Yes, you did it!"

"Ay! Now what am I going to do?"

"Go back where you came from."

Joha paid him the money and went home with his tail between his legs.

His mother said to him: "Joha, where is the flour?"

"Ah, I sent the flour with a sieve through the window. I told the wind to bring it to you."

"My God! Why didn't you bring it with you?"

"Because the sack was very heavy, and I couldn't lift it!"

His mother gave him two slaps: "Fool! Stupid! All the flour has been wasted! You should have sent it with a porter! Now I have to buy flour that is ready-made. Another time when you buy something, don't get tired. Send it with a porter. "All right," she said to him, "now don't talk with anybody. Go to the market and bring two packets of pins. I want to mend the lace of the sofas for your wedding."

Joha was silent. He went to the market: "Have you got pins to sell me?"

"Yes!" They gave him two packets of pins.

Joha said: "Mother told me that when I buy something, I should send it home with a porter."

He found a porter and said to him: "Look, take these pins and bring them one by one to such and such a house. Tell my mother: 'Here, your son is sending this pin to you.'"

The porter went to Joha's mother, brought her one pin, and said to her: "Now, your son gave me this pin and told me to bring it to you."

"Dear . . . dear God!!" Joha's mother said to Joha. "Couldn't you bring them yourself?"

"Didn't you tell me not to get tired? That I should take a porter?"

"Did I tell you for pins? For full sacks!" his mother said. "A plague on you!" His mother struck him. "Be a man! Don't do such stupid things! Tomorrow the bride will come! But see here," she said, "you mustn't look at her too much. Every five minutes cast an eye at her."

"Ah!" said Joha. "Cast an eye?"

"Yes!"

What did Joha do? He went to the slaughterhouse where they slaughter cows and sheep and said: "Have you got cow's eyes for sale here?"

He bought cow's eyes, put them in a sack, and carried them home.

The next day they brought the bride-to-be: a good and beautiful bride . . . the daughter of a neighbor. They were already celebrating because the bride found a husband and was going to meet him.

Joha heard cries in the street. They were clapping hands. He asked: "What's this all about?"

"The bride is coming!" his mother said to him. "Now pay attention. I already told you what to do: Every five minutes, cast an eye at her."

"Ah!" said Joha. "Fine!"

The bride came and sat down, and Joha sat down in front of her. He was wearing the fine clothes of a bridegroom, and the bride was wearing a white dress.

Five minutes passed. Joha threw an eye at her . . . chak! Her dress was spattered with blood. She thought that it had fallen on her from above. "Oy!" she said to her mother, who was sitting next to her. "Mama, mama, look what has happened to my dress!"

"It's nothing," said her mother. "Perhaps it fell from above, from the tree."

Everyone was quiet. Joha's mother was serving sweetmeats. She didn't know what her son was doing. Another five minutes passed. Joha took another eye and threw it on the other side.

The bride said: "I don't like this at all! Take me back home!"

Said her mother: "No! Why? Look at him: he's a fine-looking bridegroom!"

The bride was silent again. Barely had another five minutes passed when . . . chak! He threw another eye at her waist. Everything got dirty.

"Aaah!" said the bride. "I don't want to be here any longer! Take me home at once! I don't want this bridegroom!"

They called the bridegroom's mother and said to her: "What is this? Why did he dirty her wedding dress? What kind of a bridegroom is he?"

She said: "Why? What did he do?"

"He's throwing cow's eyes at the bride."

"Hey!" said Joha to his mother. "Didn't you tell me that every five minutes I should cast an eye at the bride? And I am casting eyes at her!"

The bride ran away, and so there the story ends.

NARRATED BY MATILDA MAZALTO BARZILAY – 1990

Married Life

Everyone knows that Joha never wanted to get married. His family always made arrangements for him to meet people without him knowing why they invited them, but from time to time he told them, "As long as I have any sense, I will not get married!"

Once, when his uncle again decided to put it into his head to get married, Joha answered him thus: "Look, I will tell you a fable, and you tell me, as a married man, if in truth the life of married people is not like this:

'An eagle circled around a forest to see if he could find something to eat. Suddenly, he saw a fox down below. He swooped down and caught it in his talons, but the fox would not give in and began to fight with the eagle. And so they fought in the air until, in the end, the fox fell to earth with the beak and talons of the eagle in its mouth.'"

"A good fable," his uncle said to him. "But what has it got to do with marriage?"

"Ah," said Joha, "it is the same with marriage. The man, an unfortunate, thinks that it is he who has carried something off, but in the end nothing remains of him except his boots and skullcap, and the rest the wife swallows up!"

NARRATED BY ELIEZER PAPO – 1999

Big Things

It happened that one day Joha had grown up, and he had not married. His uncle began to search for brides and to recommend him to them. He held interviews with them. The interviews all passed off well until Joha opened his mouth and ruined everything. The prospective bride ran off. Once, twice, thrice . . .

Finally, his uncle said to him: "Come here, Joha. This will be the last time I arrange an interview for you. There is a lady whom we are going to meet, with her family, and you will come and not open your mouth until I give you a signal. And when I give you the signal, start to speak. And don't start talking some nonsense. . . . Speak about big things. Only important things! I will give you the signal . . . and remember, big things."

And so they came . . . and they sat down. The bride's family came, his family came . . . and Joha was there. . . . He didn't open his mouth, just as he had promised.

Finally, his uncle gave him a nudge with his elbow, like this, as a signal. And Joha woke up, began to talk, and said: "Liners, trains, airplanes, skyscrapers . . ."

NARRATED BY VITALI FERRERA – 1998

After the Wedding

Finally, they managed to find a family willing to give their daughter to Joha for a wife. But the daughter didn't see him until it was time for the wedding.

When the wedding ceremony was over, after the festive meal and the Sheva Brachot,* and all the guests had left, Joha and his bride entered the bedroom and he closed the door.

The bride, who saw whom she had married, said to herself: "How am I going to escape from this idiot?" To Joha she said: "Look, Joha, there is a jar of apricot jam up there on the shelf. Climb up, eat, and then bring some down for me."

Joha climbed up to the shelf, began to eat the jam, and lost himself there. The bride opened the door and fled for her life.

Meanwhile, the bride's mother arrived and stood in front of the door, hoping to see how her daughter had passed the night.

At five in the morning Joha's mother-in-law knocked—tap, tap—on the door, saying: "Joha, open the door for me."

Joha said to her: "I cannot, madam. I am up."

"You have been up until now?!" his mother-in-law said. "I will wait a little longer."

An hour passed. The bride's mother knocked on the door again, saying: "Joha, please open the door for me!"

* the blessings that are recited under the huppah during the wedding ceremony

"I cannot, madam, I am still up!" Joha said to her.

"What?! Still!?" his mother-in-law said.

"Yes, madam!" Joha said.

"Get down!!"

"I can't get down!"

His mother-in-law waited a little longer, then said: " I haven't any more patience!" She opened the door and entered the room. And what sight met her eyes?

The bride wasn't there, and Joha was up on the shelf, eating the apricot jam.

And that was how he had spent the entire night.

NARRATED BY MATILDA KOEN-SARANO – 1997

Auto-Matchmaker

Joha got up early, had a bath, shaved, put on his best suit, and was ready to go out to the square.

His mother says to him: "Joha, where are you going, then, well dressed, well groomed? I haven't seen you like this for years."

"Ah, Mama," says Joha, "I am going out to do business!"

"With whom? With what money, Joha? You know well that we haven't got a cent. We cannot afford to eat either bread or cheese, even though we wish to."

Says Joha: "Mother, today I am going to earn five thousand gold ducats!"

"Dear God, Lord of the Universe! Joha, have you gone mad? Five thousand gold ducats! Do you know what five thousand ducats are?"

"Yes, I know, indeed I do, Mother. Don't be afraid. I am going to earn five thousand ducats!" said Joha and went off.

His mother watches him as he goes on his way. "Lord of the Universe," she says, "Lord of all the heavens, when will some sense enter into this Jew. Everyone makes fun of him; they all play games with him. Look and have mercy on him!"

Joha walked, walked, walked . . . until he suddenly found himself standing in front of a palace. What was this palace? No king, no sultan has such a palace, all of marble, with wondrous gardens, flowers, scents, trees.

Joha knocked at the door.

A manservant, strong and tall, emerged. He says to him: "What do you want?"

"I came to speak with the owner."

"Ah!" says the manservant, "have you fixed an appointment or arranged a time with him?"

"No," says Joha, "I don't have anything, no appointment or arranged time." He says, "I came because I want to talk business."

"Ah!" says the manservant. "If you have no appointment or fixed hour you cannot enter here," and he began to close the door.

Joha put his foot in the door, to keep it from closing. He said to the manservant: "Look, tell your master that I came to bring him a very big and excellent business. With this business your master will earn five thousand ducats!"

The manservant, who heard 5,000 ducats, thought: If I let him enter without permission, the master will throw me out. And if I do not let him enter, knowing that he can earn 5,000 ducats, he will cut off my head. . . .

"My good man," he says, "wait here a minute. I am going to speak with the master."

The master was in the salon, busy with his books, with his accounts. He says, "What is it?"

"There is a certain Joha outside," the manservant tells him, "who wishes to bring business."

"Ah! And what business is it?"

"A business in which my master will earn five thousand ducats."

The master, although he was very rich . . . 5,000 ducats are 5,000 ducats . . . says: "Have him enter, and quickly prepare a coffee with baklavas and pastries . . . and other tasty things."

Very shortly, Joha enters.

The master stood up. They shook hands. He gave Joha a seat to sit on. He says to him: "Sit down, sit down, Señor Joha. Speak!"

"No, no!" says Joha. "Wait! We have time now. Let us drink a cup of coffee, and let us eat," he says, "a *baklavayka.** Afterward we shall talk." Inside his heart is pounding. He wants to know if he will succeed in earning those 5,000 ducats.

Well, they finished drinking the coffee and ate everything. And the master says to him: "Well, Señor Joha, here I am, listening. How we are going to earn the five thousand ducats?"

"Look, Señor," Joha says to him, "there are rumors in the city that you have an only daughter, very beautiful."

"Yes," says the master, "it is true. I do have a very beautiful only daughter. What of it?"

Joha says to him: "These rumors also say that you have proposed ten thousand gold ducats as a dowry for your daughter.

"Yes, it is true. . . ." says the master. "First, I wish to give ten thousand gold ducats and, after that, a house in the city, a villa by the sea . . . and other things."

"Fine," Joha says to him. "I have come precisely for that proposition. You are offering ten thousand gold ducats and other things. Give me your daughter. I shall be satisfied with only five thousand ducats. Do you see, Señor, how you are earning five thousand ducats?"

The master stood up in a great rage, called his manservant,

* mini-baklava

and says to him: "Throw this dog into the street and never let him in here again!"

And so Joha returned home sad and dejected, without the 5,000 gold ducats, saying: "But why didn't he accept, Mama? It was a good deal for both of us! He would save 5,000 ducats and I would earn five thousand ducats!"

His mother kissed and embraced him, and said to him, weeping: "Come down from the clouds, Joha! Don't you know the saying: Money goes after money. If you had come to him with five thousand ducats, he would have given you his daughter!"

"Fine!" said Joha. "I am going then!"

But that is another tale!

NARRATED BY ISSAHAR AVZARADEL – 1992

CHAPTER 6

JOHA and his wife

"Joha remembered to kiss his wife only on the day his mother died."

He Didn't Know

The wedding was over. The bride and groom went to sleep, each in their own bed.

The bride was waiting.

A short time passed. Joha hadn't come to her bed.

"Oh!" said the bride. "I am getting cold! I am getting cold!"

Joha came to her, the poor guy, and covered her well.

She said: "I am freezing!"

He took his own blanket and covered her again.

She said: "Ah, when I was freezing at home, my mother would come and warm me."

Said Joha: "But now, at half past one in the morning, should I wake your mother from her sleep?"

NARRATED BY ALIZA TSARUM – 1996

His Wife's Face

Joha married a woman without having seen her face beforehand, because that is how it was done at that time.

When she removed her veil, after the wedding, Joha saw how ugly his wife was.

She came to him and said: "Joha, my husband, tell me before whom you wish me to go with my face covered, and before whom you wish me to go with my face uncovered."

Joha said to her: "With me, always have your face covered, and uncover it before whomsoever you wish!"

NARRATED BY MATILDA KOEN-SARANO – 1997

It Is Useless

One day they told Joha that he should get married.

And they did it so insistently that finally he did get married.

The people he worked with all came and said to him: "Joha, *Mazal tov*! Congratulations! What is your wife's name?"

Joha said: "I don't know."

"How come you don't know?" they said to him. "Didn't you ask her?"

"No!" said Joha.

"Why don't you ask her?" they said. "Ask her!"

"No!" said Joha. "In any case, I have no intention of keeping her!"

Narrated by SHMUEL BARKI – 1992

A Simple Calculation

Joha got married. After three months, his wife gave birth. Joha called his friends . . . a *brit*!

After the *brit* was over, one of his friends said: "Joha, how is it? You got married three months ago! How has your wife already given birth?"

"Aaah!" Joha said to him. "Can't you count? What are you talking about? Tell me," he said, "how long have I been married to my wife? Three months! All right, and she, how long has she been married to me? Three months! How much is that? Six! And how long has she had the little one in her womb? Three months! And how many months does that make? Nine months! What more do you want?!"

Narrated by RASHEL PERERA – 1987

Whose Soul?

Joha loved his wife very much. He called her "Neshama," or Soul.

"How are you, Soul? Where are you going, Soul?" And the entire day he would say: "Neshama! Soul!"

One night the Angel of Death came and said to him: "I came to take your soul!"

"For God's sake, Neshama," Joha said to his wife. "Get up! Get up! He wants you!"

NARRATED BY ESTER LEVY – 1999

What Heat!

Once, Joha was in bed with his wife, and it was hot. His wife said to him: "Ouff! Go farther away!"

Joha got up, got dressed, and began to walk. He walked two, three kilometers. He met someone and said to him: "Do me a favor, and please go and ask my wife: Is this far enough? Or should I go farther?"

NARRATED BY ITZHAK SIMHA – 1987

Not Their Problem

Joha once went for a trip on a steamship with his wife.

In the middle of the ocean a big storm arose, and the ship tossed this way and that.

Joha's wife came and shouted: "Joha, Joha, the ship is going to sink!"

Joha said to her: "Why should you care? It's not ours!"

NARRATED BY KOHAVA PIVIS – 2000

His Wife's Wish

Joha took his donkeys, with his wheat and his wife, and they all went to the mill to turn the wheat into flour. They had to cross a river. When they were ready to return, they put the sacks of flour on the donkeys and then set out on their way home.

They reached the river. His wife crossed. She looked back: Joha was crossing with the sacks of flour. But the sack he had on one side was too heavy for him to carry over the water.

His wife began to shout: "Joha, Joha! Pull the sack on the left side." Then she remembered that Joha always does the opposite of what she tells him, so she said, "on the right side."

And Joha said: "I never do what my wife says! Come, for once I will do as my wife wishes, and I will pull on the right side!" And as he pulled, the sacks fell into the water!

His wife said to him: "Joha, you always do the opposite . . . !"

"But, my dear wife!" Joha said to her. "For once, I wished to do you as you wished, and I did what you said! I never do as you wish, and for once I wished to!"

NARRATED BY RASHEL PERERA – 1987

Beaten Wife

Joha's wife went to complain to the rabbi that her husband didn't love her anymore.

The rabbi asked her: "How do you know that he doesn't love you?"

Then the wife said to him: "Because he hasn't beaten me for a long time!"

NARRATED BY ISSAHAR AVZARADEL – 1990

A Purely Coincidental Connection

In the morning, when Joha went off to work, he would kiss the mezuza.

His wife said to him: "When will you kiss me before the mezuza?"

"When I see you hung there!" Joha said to her.

Before he went out the door, his wife said: "Before you go out to work, say some warm words to me!"

"May I see you fry and toast in Hell!" Joha said to her.

NARRATED BY NAFTALY (NAFI) HALEVA – 1990

Joha's Half

Joha and his wife wanted to go to Paris on a pleasure trip.

Their friends said: "See that whatever price they ask of you there, you say to them, '*La moitié!*' And you will pay half price for everything."

And so it was. They arrived at a hotel. There they told them a price.

Joha said to them, "*La moitié*!" He paid half price.

They entered a restaurant and ate. The bill was brought to them.

They said: "*La moitié!*" And paid half price.

They wanted to buy clothes. They said, "*La moitié*!" They gave them for half the price.

In short, they received everything at "*la moitié*."

One day they entered a cafe. Joha's wife sat down at a table, and he went to the counter and ordered a drink.

They gave him what he asked for and told him the price.

He said: "*La moitié!*" And he paid "*la moitié.*"

At that moment Joha noticed a very beautiful woman there, one of those who sell themselves.

Joha asked: "How much?"

She told him a very high price.

Joha said to her: "*La moitié!*"

She said: "No!"

Said Joha: "No? All right, so don't do it!" and went and sat with his wife.

The two of them were drinking when the beautiful woman passed in front of them, pointed to Joha's wife, and said: "That is your '*moitié*'!"

Narrated by MATILDA KOEN-SARANO – 1999

A Costly Trip

Joha went on a trip to Paris and went to visit the Rue Saint Denis. There he saw beautiful women from all places and races.

Suddenly, he went "Pu!" and spat on the ground.

At that moment a policeman was passing by. The policeman saw him spit, came over, and took him by the collar. He said: "What are you doing? Here one doesn't spit in the street! Pay three hundred francs!"

Poor Joha had to pay.

A week later, Joha flew home. He came out of the plane and met his wife, who was waiting for him.

His wife said: "'Hey, Joha, did you have a good time? Did you like Paris?"

"Yes, very much," said Joha.

"And did you think about me?" his wife asked.

"Oh, yes . . . ," said Joha, "and it cost me three hundred francs!"

NARRATED BY MATILDA KOEN-SARANO – 1992

The Ugly Wife

Joha's wife was very, very ugly.

He said to her: "Look, I want you to leave. You are very ugly. I cannot stand you any longer!"

She said to him: "I am ugly? But you do not understand the meaning of beauty. I will go walking in the street, and you will see. They will all lift their faces to see me!"

The two of them went walking in the street.

The wife walked in front of her husband and made faces at all the men who were passing by.

All the men looked at her, making such funny faces. Joha said: "Goodness me, it seems that I do not understand what real beauty is." And he didn't tell her that she was ugly anymore.

NARRATED BY SOL MAYMARAN – 1997

A Good Answer!

Joha was married and then got divorced. After a short time passed, he met a widow and married her.

A few years went by, and he wanted to divorce her.

He said to her: "Look, I want to divorce. I am tired of being married to you."

His wife said to him: "Oh, no! Widow you took me, widow you shall leave me!"

NARRATED BY ESTER LEVY – 1995

The Neighbors' Seder

The night of Passover arrived, and Joha did not know how to make the Seder.

He said to his wife: "Go to the neighbors, see how they do it, and come and tell me. Then we will do the same."

"All right," said his wife, and she went to the neighbors.

At that moment the neighbor was beating his wife. Joha's wife returned home at once, all afraid.

Joha asked her: "Did you see what the neighbor was doing? Tell me, because I want to do the same!"

His wife remained silent.

Joha repeated the question, and, seeing that his wife didn't answer, he began to get angry. But his wife didn't want to tell him what she had seen at the neighbors'.

Finally, Joha lost patience and began to beat her.

Then his wife said to him, weeping: "If you already knew, why did you send me to them?"

NARRATED BY MATILDA-KOEN SARANO – 1991

What a Woman!

Joha's wife was so bad that she always took revenge on her husband and did everything possible to do him harm.

One day Joha noticed that his wife had changed her ways and became good.

Joha could not resist asking her: "My precious, what happened? Why did you wait so many years to be so good to me? Why weren't you like this from the time we got married?"

His wife replied: "It's only in recent days that they told me that those who suffer in this world go to Paradise."

NARRATED BY LINA ALBUKREK – 1992

The Snake Woman

Joha was married to a very capricious woman. Everything he did she disapproved of. If he just came back home from the market, she would say: "What a housebound husband I have! Nothing will come of him!"

If he stayed at the market, she would say: "What distress you caused me! I am waiting for you, and you? You don't come or send word. May the Lord help me, and one day you won't come back at all. I will be sorry once and for all!"

When he came home with baskets filled with vegetables, she said to him: "Am I a cow? Am I mad? And the meat, where is it?"

If he brought her meat, she would say: "Stupid one, wastrel! What did you think? That it is the Sabbath today?"

Our good Joha understood that whatever he did she would scream, so he stopped listening to her and taking it to heart.

When she, the snake, realized that he was no longer taking notice of her complaints and maledictions, she began to treat him badly in other ways. Sometimes she told him to wash the toilet, and when he had finished she would make it dirty again and say to him: "Hurry up, Joha, we haven't got all day! Come on then, wash the toilet!"

And Joha tolerated it and tolerated it. But one day, when his wife told him to go down on all fours because the stool for the laundry tub had broken, and she wanted to put the tub on his shoulders, Joha's patience snapped and he left the house.

Walking in the desert, he met two friends who were also walking there. He asked if he could join them.

They said to him: "We have nothing in the world, apart from a prayer that we know, and each day one of us says this prayer, and food falls on us from the sky. If you know this prayer, you can walk with us."

"Fine," Joha said. "I already know it."

The first day they said to Joha: "Come on then, my dear, recite the prayer, because we want to eat."

Joha replied: "Today, let one of you recite it. Tomorrow I will recite it."

One of the friends began to recite the prayer, and in two or three minutes a platterful of food and fruits came down from the sky.

Joha stood with open mouth. They ate, said Grace, and went on their way.

The next day they said: "Come on now, my dear, it is your turn to recite the prayer."

Joha said to them: "Let the second friend recite it today, and I will recite it tomorrow."

"Let it be so!" they said to him.

The second friend began to recite the prayer, and Joha watched him closely, to see if he could learn the words of the prayer from the movement of his lips. But with a few words this one finished, and once again a platterful of everything descended from the skies.

On the third day, there being no alternative, our good Joha began to recite the prayer. But since he did not know the secret text of this special prayer, he began thus: "Lord of the world, this prayer that these two are reciting, I neither know it or knew it. But since You are our all-merciful Father, look upon this my prayer as if they were reciting it. Take my intention as if it were theirs, and be gracious unto us, so that neither I nor these people shall lose."

At that moment there descended from the skies three platters: one with cooked foods, one with fruits, and a third with every kind of delicacy. And not only that, but there also fell down a jar of water, so that they could wash their hands and feet, and a towel for them to dry themselves. And, finally, there fell for them a coffeepot with coffee and three *narghila* pipes.*

The two friends were very amazed but even more so was Joha.

The following day, he asked his friends what was the prayer that they were saying. He said to them: "You have seen that I know it too, and it is only that I wish to see if there is any difference between what I say and what you are saying."

They said to him: "We recite as follows:

Lord of the world,
By the merit of that Joha
Who suffers so at the hands
Of the snake, his wife,
Give us wine and food
And grant us a long life."

Realizing that the path to the Garden of Eden lay under the feet of his wife, Joha returned home, went on all fours, and said to the mistress of the house: "Come on then, good woman, bring the laundry tub and don't deprive me of my reward-to-come!"

NARRATED BY ELIEZER PAPO – 1999

* Turkish smoking pipes

When the Compliment Is Worse than the Insult

One day Joha's wife said to him: "Tell me, Joha, is it possible for a compliment to be worse than an insult?"

"No!" said Joha. "That can never happen!"

"And I tell you that it can!" his wife said to him.

"If you say so . . . " said Joha.

A few days passed, and on Sabbath morning, while Joha's wife was going around the house in a rather old housecoat, Joha suddenly raised his eyes from the book he was reading, fixed them on his wife, and said to her: "Well now, Grasia, what a beautiful housecoat you are wearing! Is it new?"

"What?!" said the indignant wife. "New!? Are you kidding?! I made this housecoat for myself three years ago, and I put it on every morning!"

"But I have never seen it before," said Joha.

"Oh, sure!" said Joha's wife very angrily. "It's because when I walk past, you don't notice me. That's why you never saw it!"

"But I wanted to give you a compliment . . . ," poor Joha said to her, "and look what good it did me."

"Quite so!" his wife said to him. "But one must know how to give it. Didn't I tell you that it can happen that the compliment may be worse than the insult? Here you have the proof!"

NARRATED BY MATILDA KOEN-SARANO – 1994

The Last Gift

Joha loved his wife very much. Every year, when it was her birthday, he bought her something big.

One year he bought her a long fur coat, another year he

bought her a big automobile, and another year he bought her a house. The fourth year he bought her a plot of land for the grave.

She became very sad. She said: "Who knows what he will bring me next year?"

She waited and waited . . . came the fifth year that they were married, and he didn't bring her anything.

She said to him: "Look, you love me so much. . . . Every year you bring me big things. Why didn't you bring me anything this year?"

Joha said: "The first year I bought you a fur coat, you wore it. The second year I bought you an automobile, you drove it around. The third year I bought you a house, which you lived in. The thing that I bought you last time you did not use. . . . So what should I bring you now?"

NARRATED BY LEVANA SASSON – 1992

A Legitimate Request

Joha went into the field. He felt the need to relieve himself. So he began to do so.

A wasp came and stung him on his "*brit*."*

Dying with pain, he came home and said to his wife: "Bring cold water, bring ice!"

Nothing helped.

Joha said to his wife:"Tomorrow is the Sabbath. Go to the synagogue, and pray to the Lord that he will rid me of this misfortune."

His wife went to the synagogue.

* *Brit* here means the male sex organ after circumcision.

When they opened the Holy Ark, his wife said: "Almighty God, make it so that my husband's pain will pass but that the swelling will remain!"

NARRATED BY ELI GRATSIANI – 1992

Why Only Me?

Joha didn't have any work, and his wife said to him: "Go and look for work, because we don't have anything to eat."

One day he said to her: "Look, wife, I am going to such and such village to look for work. I'll stay there overnight and return tomorrow evening."

"All right!" said his wife, and thought: "If my husband is going away, I will invite my friends for a little while." And she called three of her neighbors.

One of them brought *borekas,* the second brought *raki,** the third a lute, and the four of them began to sing and dance, to eat and drink.

Suddenly . . . there was a knocking at the door—tak, tak.

"Dear God!" said Joha's wife. "My husband has come home!"

What did she do?

Very quickly she hid one friend under the bed, the second behind the door, the third she hid in the attic, and then opened the door to her husband.

"Goodness me, is it you, Joha? Are you back already?" she said to him. "Didn't you say that you were going to sleep there?"

"Yes . . . No . . . " Joha said to her. "I saw that there was no work there, so I returned home."

"Ah!" his wife said. "And when will you buy me the bracelets that I saw in the jeweler's shop window?"

* Turkish liqueur, similar to anisette

"When the One above gives to me," Joha said to her.

"And when will you buy me the fur you promised me?" said the wife.

"When the One above gives to me," Joha said to her.

"And when shall we move from this home and go to live in a better place?" his wife asked him.

"I told you already," Joha said to her. "When the One above gives to me!"

At that moment the one who was up in the attic emerged and said: "Why only me? There is one under the bed, another behind the door. Let them also give a little! Am I so rich?"

NARRATED BY MATILDA KOEN-SARANO – 1994

Semantics

Joha returned home suddenly and found his wife in bed with his best friend, who was a philologist.

Joha said: "I am surprised!"

His friend said to him: "No, no! You are not suprised! *I* am *surprised*! *You* are *stupefied*!"

NARRATED BY MATILDA KOEN-SARANO – 1992

Compensation

A rabbi gave a sermon in the synagogue and said: "Every woman must have a charm, in her laugh, in her walk, or in the eyes. Every woman has her *grasia*."*

* charm

Joha heard this, went home, and began to look at his wife. He looked at her this way, he looked at her that way . . . he touched her. He couldn't find the tiniest bit of charm in her.

"A plague on it! The rabbi said that you must have a little bit of charm. I can't find any!" he said. "On Sunday we shall go to the rabbi to get divorced!"

And she, the poor woman, what could she do? If her husband wanted to divorce her, she could do nothing!

The two of them went to the rabbi at the Bet Din.*

When they arrived, Joha said to the rabbi: "Our rabbi gave a sermon and said that every woman must have a charm. In the eyes, or in her walk, or her gestures, or whatever! I looked closely at my wife, and I touched her. . . . She doesn't have anything like that! I didn't find anything in her. Nothing!

The rabbi said to him: "What is your wife's name?"

"Grasia," Joha said to him.

"Well, what more do you want?" the rabbi said to Joha. "All the charm in the world is upon her!"

NARRATED BY MALKA LEVY – 1991

What Gratitude!

Joha was a very jealous man, and he had a very beautiful wife, named Grasia.

One day a guest came, a friend from his youth, and stayed with him a whole week.

At the end of the week, when the time came for him to return home, the friend turned to Joha's wife, without her husband seeing, and persuaded her to run off with him. And then

* religious court

he went away saying to Joha: "Thanks! *Grasias*! I am going off with your Grasia!"

NARRATED BY MATILDA KOEN-SARANO – 1991

What an Excuse!

Joha's wife bore him a daughter and . . . another daughter . . . and another daughter . . . and another. . . .

When she became pregnant again, Joha said to her: "If you bear me another daughter, I'll kill you! I'll kill you!"

She went, had tests, and said to him: "This time you have a son! A son!"

When the time of the birth arrived, Joha wanted to be at her side, to see what she would give birth to, and she gave birth to a daughter.

Joha said to her: "What? You have borne a daughter?"

She said to him: "No! No! This is the neighbor's. Yours hasn't come out yet. But he will soon come out! He will soon come out!"

NARRATED BY ALEX KORFIATIS – 2000

The Mirror

Joha lived in a remote village and was a bit backward.

One day he went to the city to buy something he needed.

As he was walking in the street, he saw a mirror in a shop window. He drew near and saw his reflection, but since he had never seen any mirrors in his life, he said: "Look at that man. Who can he be? He looks like my father."

He entered the shop and asked: "What is that there in the window?"

The shop owner said to him: "A mirror!"

Joha said to him: "Can I buy it?"

The shop owner said: "Certainly!" and, seeing him so attracted to it, sold it to him at a very high price.

Joha bought the mirror, took it home, and without showing it to anyone, carried it directly to the attic. And each day, when he came home from work, he took a cup of tea, climbed upstairs, and stood in front of the mirror, made faces, and stayed there, fascinated, for hours.

His wife, seeing this happen one day, two, then three, became suspicious and said: "What can my husband be doing there every evening? I'll go and see."

His wife waited until her husband was out of the house and then she went upstairs. But since she had never seen mirrors in her life, she looked at herself and said with rage: "Ah, now I understand!"

When her husband returned home in the evening, she seized him by the collar and said: "Ah, you son of a *mamzer!* Here you have a wife who is a real beauty, and you go to that rubbish you have upstairs there?!"

Then Joha and his wife began to fight and hit each other, and the neighbors, hearing all the noise, called the police.

A policeman arrived, and Joha's wife showed him the mirror. But since he, too, had never seen mirrors in his life, he looked at the mirror and said: "But . . . if you already have a policeman, why did you call me?"

The policeman went away, and Joha's wife took the mirror and ran to her mother.

She said to her: "Mother! My husband has a lover! What will I do?"

Her mother said to her: "Give it to me. Let me see!"

She took the mirror, looked, and said to her daughter: "Don't you worry, my daughter! From such a woman, you have nothing to fear!"

NARRATED BY MATILDA KOEN-SARANO – 1999

The Tassel of the Fez

Joha always came home furious and in a rage. It made his wife very upset, but what could she do, poor thing? Nothing!

Once she said to him: "Won't you ever come home like a normal person, so we can sit down and have a little talk?"

Joha said: "Look, when you see me come home with the tassel of the fez in front, it is because I am upset, and you must not say even one word to me!"

"All right!" his wife said.

At first, it was like this: Joha came home with the tassel in front; she wanted to ask him for money for cooking, to buy something in the shop . . . this and that. . . . But he was with the tassel in front. He was angry. She could not speak to him.

Once she said: "Now I am going to make him see reason!"

As soon as she saw him coming with the tassel in front, she put her apron on behind her and didn't look him in the face anymore.

He wanted to ask her something and could not.

This went on for one day, two, three, until he said to her: "Hey, what will be the end of this?"

She said: "If you have the tassel in front and I cannot speak to you, you won't be able to speak with me when you want me to cook this or that for you. I have my apron on behind me! So then let us sit down and make some order. If you won't put the tassel in front, I won't put my apron on behind, and we will be like a husband and wife should be!"

NARRATED BY MALKA LEVY – 1988

The Debt

The whole night long, Joha moaned and would not let his wife sleep. "Ay! Ay! What will be? What will be?" Finally, his wife could not resist asking: "What is it, Joha, what's wrong? You're not letting me sleep. Speak!"

"It's better that you shouldn't ask."

"You tell me, you'll see that I will find you a remedy."

"It is that tomorrow I have to pay a heavy debt to Moshon, our neighbor across the way, and I don't have a cent. How am I going to pay?"

"Don't you worry. Wait!"

His wife opened the window in the middle of the night and began to shout: "Moshon! Moshon!"

"Hey, are you crazy? Do you know what time it is?"

"It's nothing. He has got to wake up!"

Moshon's wife opened the window in a hurry: "Good Lord, what's the matter? You almost burst my gall bladder! Do you know what time it is?"

"Look, tomorrow Joha has to pay your husband a debt. You should know that he has no money and that he is not going to be able to pay him. Do you hear?" and . . . *trak* . . . she closes the window: "Now go to sleep, darling Joha. It's Moshon who cannot sleep!"

NARRATED BY BEKI BARDAVID – 1992

What a Difference!

Joha was a villager and lived in a village of peasant farmers who had sheep and cows.

One day Joha's cow died, and he was very sad. He didn't go to any celebrations, or anywhere he had been invited. He didn't go to any wedding, engagement party, bar mitzvah, or house consecration. He had no desire to speak. He was very sad. His friends didn't know what to say to him, and it took a long time for him to get over it.

One day Joha's wife fell ill. She was ill . . . ill. There was no hope. In the end, she died.

His friends said: "*Oy va voy!* Now he is not going to want to speak to us for as long as he lives. If he did what he did for a cow, what will he do for his wife?!"

What were they to do? How could they speak to him? They said: "Let us go to his house for a while; let us speak with him a little."

They went to his house and found him sitting at his table, drinking and eating. And he spoke about the world . . . he spoke about his children . . . he spoke about his work . . . he spoke of this and of that.

They stayed there a short while and then went away. They said to each other: "Isn't it amazing! Look! For his wife, he is already eating . . . as for the cow, remember how he behaved then!"

One of them said: "Tomorrow I am going to ask him."

The next day Joha came to work as usual. His friend said to him: "I want to ask you one thing, but don't be angry with me."

Said Joha: "No! Why should I be angry?"

His friend said: "When your cow died, for years you didn't go to any celebration! You didn't want to see anybody. And now that you have lost your wife, who was a fine woman, a fine housewife, the mother of your children . . . you are drinking *raki?*"

"Ah!" Joha said. "A cow—they will not bring me another. A wife—they will bring me another!"

Narrated by SOL MAYMARAN – 1987

Two Too Many

One day Joha's wife died. When the thirty days of mourning were over, Joha was consoled with a widow and married her.

The moment they were married, the joy vanished. Every night as they got into bed, his wife began to talk about her first husband.

At first, Joha told her to shut her mouth and to leave the dead man in peace, but she didn't listen and said: "My husband was handsome, a hero, a flower of manhood . . . a demon of intelligence."

And Joha felt humiliated, until he also began to talk about his wife—may she rest in peace!—about her beauty, what a fine housewife she was, about the blessed hands that she had.

All of this did not last long. One night, when his wife began to talk about her first husband, Joha lost patience and gave her a kick and threw her out of the bed.

His wife was furious and began to howl and weep, and did not stop until the the neighbors' faces appeared at the window.

"Joha, you criminal, you! Aren't you ashamed to beat your wife?"

And Joha replied: "Listen, good people, the matter is like this. When we go to bed, there are four of us: me, my wife, her first husband, and Fatma, my first wife. The bed is not big enough; it is narrow, it is not made for four, and my wife fell out of bed. That is all!"

The neighbors understood, and his wife did as well.

NARRATED BY SARA YOHAY – 1992

The Obvious Result

Joha was a little bit sad.

A friend asked him: "What happened to you, Joha? Why are you sad?"

Joha said to him: "I bought a very expensive fur coat for my mother-in-law!"

"Yes?" his friend said to him. "Really? So that she should be warm?"

"No!" Joha said to him. "To cover up her mouth! And now she has her mouth covered, but now my bank account is not covered!"

NARRATED BY ALEX KORFIATIS – 1998

Price Is No Object

Joha's mother-in-law was living with her daughter and her son-in-law.

Joha couldn't stand her anymore. He wanted to throw her out of the house and didn't know how to.

One day she said to him: "Do me a favor and buy me a television. I would give half a life for that TV!"

"Well, then!" Joha said to her. "I will buy you two, so that you should give your whole life!"

Narrated by ESTER LEVY – 1991

Appearances Are Deceiving

Joha's house was on fire, and his mother-in-law was inside.

Her son-in-law wanted to save her, but each time Joha entered the house, he came out with empty hands, without his mother-in-law.

And everyone was saying: "Ay, what a fine son-in-law that woman has. Look how he is taking risks to save her. He has already gone in three times, four times, into the flames, and he is going to get burned. He hasn't yet saved his mother-in-law, and he is still going inside."

A friend asked Joha: "Tell me, you who always said that you didn't like your mother-in-law very much, how is it that now you are making such a great effort to save her?"

Joha said to him: "What do you mean, 'save'? Every time I go inside, I turn her over next to the fire, so that she should be well toasted!"

Narrated by LEA AVIDAN – 1998

The Mother-in-Law

When he got married, Joha told his wife that he had one condition for living in peace with her. He said: "I don't want to see your mother in any shape or form in my house!"

His wife began to cry and said: "Look, how can I not see my mother? She bore me, she brought me up and wishes to be happy, to see me married in my own home. Why won't you let her come and visit me in my house?"

Joha replied that it was his condition, and if she could not be without her mother, then she should look for another husband.

His wife began to cry and moan and nag, until Joha agreed to let her go to an artist who would make her a statue that looked exactly like her mother. She could put this statue in a cupboard in the kitchen, and when she longed for her mother, she could raise her eyes to it and be consoled.

To cut a long story short, his wife kept her mother in the kitchen all the time.

Unfortunately, one day the lights went out, and Joha hurried to look for candles to light the light. Looking here and there, he found matches in the meantime. And when he opened the cupboard in the kitchen, the big statue of the mother-in-law fell on Joha's head and gave him such a blow that he fainted.

Joha cursed the whole world and especially his mother-in-law. Afterward he called his wife and said to her: "Now understand, I don't wish to see your mother in any shape or form. Neither alive nor as a statue! Even as a statue can you see what damage she has caused!"

NARRATED BY HAYIM TSUR – 1999

Cat or Fish?

It happened that Joha came on a Friday morning bringing a two-kilo fish, and he said to his wife: "Ah, my queen, may you remain so. Prepare me this jewel of a fish, which I bought because I fancied it. Look and see if you can cook it with this parsley and this sage, with a little bit of gravy."

"Yes, my king, don't you worry yourself."

Joha went off to work.

His wife began to cook the fish.

She said: "Ay, dear God, if Hanania my beloved were to come by! Perhaps I will give it to him instead of to my husband!"

When Joha came home at night he said: "Ah, my queen. Bring forth that fish, which I bought this morning."

Joha was thinking about the fish when his wife brought a plate with a burnt pie, burnt, burnt, and put it in front of him.

Joha saw this and said to her: "Ah, my queen, is this the fish? This is not fish!"

And she: "Yes, this is the fish."

He said: "No, this is not the fish!"

Joha kept insisting. Then she said: "Look, my king, forgive what I tell you, but look: I was preparing the fish. I left it for a little while; the cat came and ate it up."

Joha listened and looked at the burnt pie, which was so badly burnt that he didn't know what it was.

He said to her: "Bring me the cat. I will weigh it."

Joha weighed the cat and said to his wife: "This cat weighs two kilos, and the fish weighed two kilos. If this is the cat, where is the fish? If this is the fish, where is the cat?"

NARRATED BY MORDEHAY (MARCO) BENDELAC – 1998

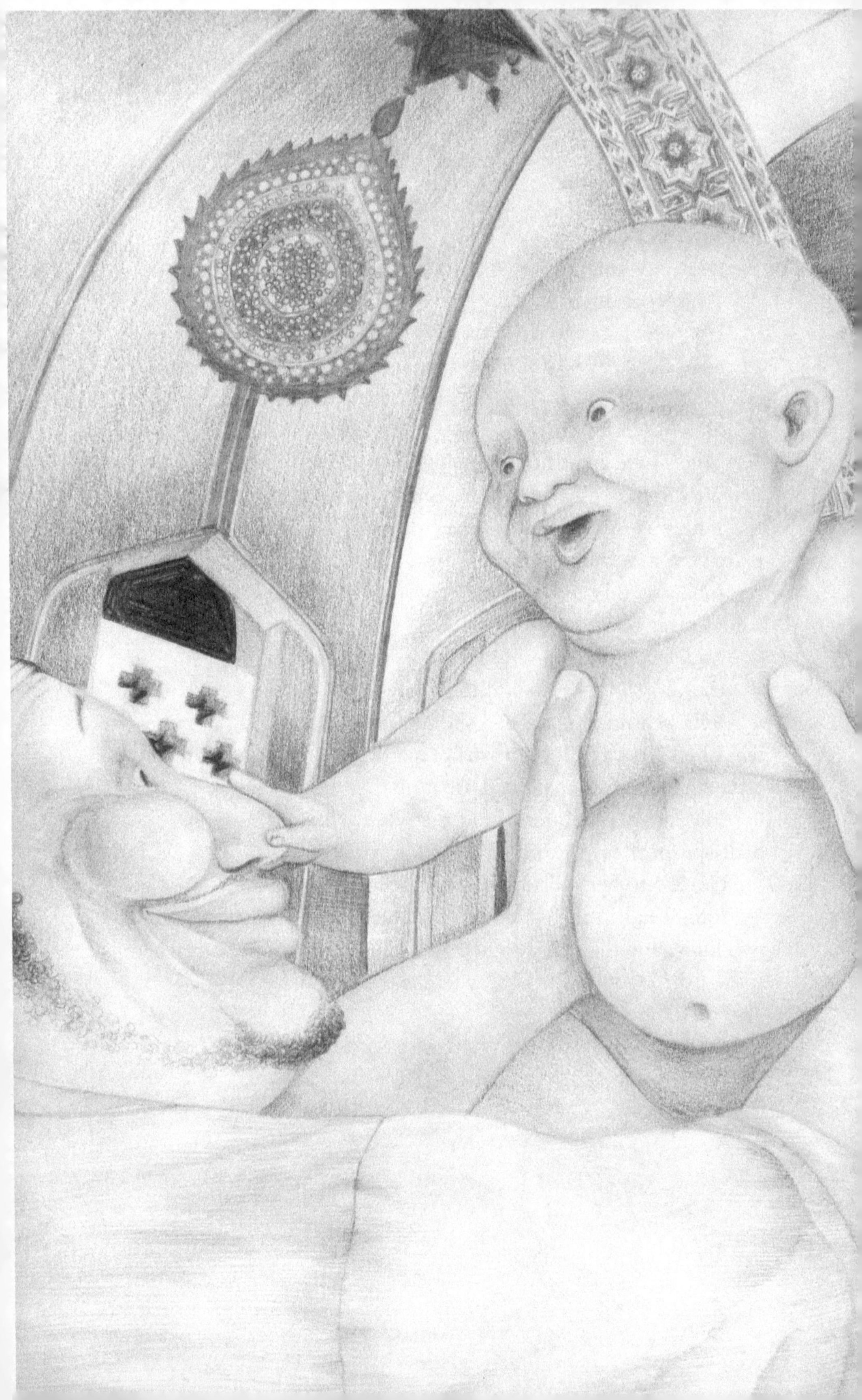

CHAPTER 7

JOHA, son, and grandson

"Like father, like son!
But what a grandson!"

What Prescience!

After a week of marriage, Joha's wife gave birth to a little boy. They came to where Joha was working and said to him: "Joha, a son has been born to you!"

He ran to the market right away, bought whatever he intended to buy, came home, opened the parcel, and began to put what he had bought next to the child's bed. There were books . . . notebooks, crayons . . . and the schoolbag.

His wife said to him: "What is this, Joha?"

Joha said to her: "One who traverses the road of nine months in one week, the following week can ask me to go to school! Now," he said, "while I have the money, I will buy him everything, because next week maybe I won't have the money!"

NARRATED BY RASHEL PERERA – 1987

A Preventive Slap

One day Joha called his son and said to him: "Go and bring water from the well." He put an earthenware jar in his hand and said: "Be careful not to break the jar on the way!" And he gave him a good slap.

The son began to cry and said: "Why did you give me a slap? What did I do? I didn't break the jar yet!"

Joha said to him: "Tell me, what good will the slap be after you have broken it?"

NARRATED BY JEANNETTE BEN-NAE – 1982

"Out of the Mouths of Fools and Babes . . . "

One day Joha took his little son to the market to buy a sheep.

When they reached the market, Joha began to feel the sheep, one after the other, until the son asked him: "Why are you doing that, Papa?"

Joha said to him: "I have to do this before I buy the sheep."

A few days later, when they sat down to eat, the son said to his father: "Do you know what? The neighbor was here, and it seems to me that he wants to buy Mama!"

NARRATED BY TSAHI HASDAY – 1999

Professional Matchmaker

Joha had a son who was very stupid. He was already grown up, and Joha wanted him to learn a profession.

One day Joha took him to a carpenter and said: "Look, teach my son one thing—I want him to earn a living . . . I am soon going to die—that he should earn a bit of money."

But the son said: "No, no, no! I cannot carry planks . . . nails. . . . I cannot!

Another time, Joha took him to a shoemaker. He said: "Please, teach my son. I will pay you whatever you wish!"

Joha's son stayed there one, two days, but he didn't like it. He said: "What? Hammer shoes the whole day long! This is not for me!"

What could he do? What could he do? His father took him to a matchmaker. He said: "Look, whatever you want, I will pay you. Teach my son to be a matchmaker."

The son said: "Yes, I do want to become a matchmaker!"

"Ah!" said the matchmaker, "being a matchmaker is very easy! We will go to a house. There, let us say, is a bride. I will say: 'The bride is beautiful! The bride is rich! She has hands of gold. She has a very fine dowry!' And you will assist me. You will say, 'What hands! What a dowry! What money!'"

When they went to the family of a bride, the matchmaker said: "Look, there is a very fine young man, quiet, respectable. He earns a good living. But," he said, "he has a little hump."

"What!!" said the matchmaker's assistant. "Such a hump! A really big, fine hump!"

NARRATED BY ESTER LEVY – 1998

Miserliness

Joha sent his son to study in America. But Joha was very miserly. The son was studying, but he had to pay rent; he had to pay for everything.

He sent a letter to his father: "Papa, I want you to send me money, to study more."

Joha didn't reply.

One day Joha's son wrote to him: "Papa, send me money, because very soon they will throw me into the street!"

His father sent him a letter, saying: "Take care that a bus doesn't run you over in the street!"

NARRATED BY ESTER BEN-YOSEF – 1999

Without Yogurt

Joha's son returned from the market and said to his father: "You don't know what happened to me in the restaurant! I entered, told the young girl there that I wanted *borekas* with cheese and yogurt. She said to me, 'We don't have yogurt!' I said to her: 'So be it! Then I want *borekas* with potatoes and yogurt.' You know what she said to me—'We don't have yogurt!' I said: 'Fine, so give me *borekas* with mushrooms and yogurt!' And she, the blackguard, had the effrontery to tell me, 'We don't have yogurt!'"

Joha said to him: "It's good that you have such strong nerves. I would have taken that yogurt and thrown it at her head!"

NARRATED BY ELIEZER PAPO – 1999

Everyone Does What He Can

Joha had a son and wanted him to study. He sent him abroad and said to him: "I will give you a lot of money, so that you should study."

The son said to him: "No . . . yes . . . OK," got up and went to America.

While he was there, from the day he began school, he got to know three, four girlfriends and spent time with them instead of going to classes.

His father sent him letters: "How are you progressing?"

"Don't ask!" his son wrote to him. "The teacher wants to recommend me for a distinction . . . (why I do not know!)."

And so a year passed. He sent a letter to his father: "The year is nearly over. I am coming back."

He came back, and Joha went to the market and told everyone that his son had done well at school abroad and that he wanted his son to give a lecture.

And as soon as the son came, Joha said to him: "My son, all my friends . . . the whole neighborhood is waiting for you. You will give a lecture about what you learned there."

"I am ready!" said the son. "Only," he said, "before I give the lecture here, make a podium for me, and I will climb onto the podium to give the lecture!"

The son went to the market, bought himself a brazier and a frying pan. He told nothing of this to his father.

When the time came, he climbed onto the podium in front of all the people and said to them: "Ladies and gentlemen, I open my little mouth and I say to you: The brazier climbed onto the podium, and the frying pan climbed onto the brazier! Hello, I'm back from abroad! And now I'm going to be fried in front of you!"

NARRATED BY ESTER VENTURA – 1999

Like Father, Like Son

Joha was on his deathbed. He gathered together all his children. He had ten sons.

He said to them: "When I die, I want each one of you to go to my grave, and each one put a hundred gold coins there. And say the Kaddish memorial prayer for me, OK?"

So, what did they do? When Papa died, the sons went to the grave, and nine of them each put a hundred gold coins on the grave. They said the Kaddish prayer.

But the youngest one didn't put anything down.

When his brothers went away, the youngest one wrote an IOU., took all the money, and put the IOU. in its place.

NARRATED BY MORDEHAY (MARCO) BENDELAC – 1998

. . . And Grandpa Too!

Joha went to board the train with his little grandson. He went up to the stationmaster.

"Tell me, how long is it before the train leaves?"

The man was a stammerer: "Twe . . . twen . . . twent . . . y . . . mi . . . min . . . utes."

A short time passed. Joha went up to him again.

"Tell me, how long is it before the train leaves?"

"Fif . . . fiftee . . . fifteen min . . . min . . . minutes."

Hardly any time passed. Joha went up to him once more and asked him the same question.

This time the stationmaster got angry. "Wha . . . what . . . do . . . you wa . . . want . . . ev . . . ry min . . . minute . . . as . . . king . . . ?

"It's not me," Joha said to him. "It's my grandson who likes the way you speak!"

NARRATED BY BEKI BARDAVID – 1996

CHAPTER 8

JOHA and the king

"I kill the king beneath my cloak!"

Providential Spaghetti

One day Joha came home very hungry: "Mama, I want to eat! Mama, I want to eat!"

His mother said to him: "Go and wander around for a bit, and I'll make you spaghetti in the meantime!"

She put the water on to boil, and he went off. He went off . . . walked around a bit, and then sat down outside. He was tired.

As he was sitting, he said, gesturing with his hands: "Now my mother has put the water on to boil. . . . The water is boiling. . . . Now my mother has put the spaghetti in the water. And now perhaps the spaghetti has already cooked. And now my mother is calling me—'Joha, come, come! Joha, come, come! The spaghetti is ready!'"

Meanwhile, the king and queen, who were sitting on their balcony, thought that Joha was calling them.

They said: "Let's go and see what Joha wants!"

They left their palace to go to him. At that moment, the whole palace collapsed and was destroyed.

The king and queen were saved, and they were very happy that Joha had saved their lives, otherwise they would have died in the destroyed palace.

They embraced him and said: "Why did you call us?"

Joha said to them: "No, no . . . I was thinking: My mother is calling me to come and eat the spaghetti."

The king said: "Let's go to your mother!"

They went to his mother, and she said: "What happened?"

Joha said: "Nothing, Mama! It happened like so and so . . . and look: The king and queen have come with me!"

The king gave him a purse of gold and said: "Take this purse, for having saved our lives!"

NARRATED BY SARA BEHAR – 1998

Seven with One Blow!

Joha was on his way to the city. He walked and walked, and was crossing a field. The flies didn't give him any respite.

Joha lashed out this way, and lashed out that way, and caught a fistful of flies.

He opened his hand and counted them: seven!

"Ah!" said Joha. "I killed seven with one blow!"

He wrote on his belt: "Seven with one blow!" and continued on his way.

All of those who met him read this on his belt and said: "What a strong man this is!" And they ran for their lives.

From one to the other, the news finally reached the ears of the king.

The king sent for Joha and said: "I heard that you killed seven with one blow. Since you are so strong, I want you to liberate my kingdom from this giant who is attacking us."

"All right!" Joha said to him. "But if I do it, I want your daughter in marriage!"

"So be it!" the king said to him.

The next morning, Joha went out to find the giant in the forest.

When he saw him from afar, Joha began to shout, "Run away, giant! Know that I eat 'slaughtered meat'! Know that I killed seven with one blow! Seven with one blow!" He ran from one part of the forest to another, each time hiding behind another tree.

The giant ran from one part of the forest to another, looking for Joha, but wasn't able to catch him or even catch sight of him.

And Joha was shouting and shouting, "I killed seven with one blow! Seven with one blow," until the giant fell down, dead from exhaustion and fear.

At that point Joha came out, took his knife, and buried it in the giant's heart.

Joha went to the king and said: "Lord King, I have killed the giant! Now give me your daughter as wife."

And so the king gave him his daughter. They made a great and beautiful wedding, and in the end Joha became king.

NARRATED BY MATILDA KOEN-SARANO – 1992

The Vinegar

The king sent Joha to buy vinegar.

Before he came to the bazaar where they sold vinegar, Joha passed in front of the fruit vendors, and he saw a beautiful bunch of grapes. He passed other shops and saw a more beautiful bunch.

Instead of buying vinegar, he bought grapes. On the way home he ate them.

He arrived at the king's palace, took off his trousers and exposed his buttocks to the sun. The king came and said to him: "Did you buy the vinegar?"

Joha said: "I saw that vinegar was very expensive and that the grapes were cheap. If you want vinegar, wait another two days. I am making it now. In another two days you will get it!"

NARRATED BY ALEX KORFIATIS – 1998

The Elephant

One day, to the city where Joha lived, there came a vizier who was a very unusual man.

This vizier brought an elephant to the city. The elephant entered here, entered there, destroyed one shop, destroyed another. Until one day the notables of the city, seeing that there was no other remedy except to go and ask the vizier to remove this evil from the city, decided to send representatives to the palace, to speak to him.

Ten people went, the notables of the city, and in front of them all was Joha.

They all went on their way to the palace, talking among themselves about what they would say to the vizier, how they would explain to him that this could not go on any longer, and so forth. . . . But as they drew near to the palace, one by one they began to disappear, because of the great fear they had of the vizier.

But Joha, being at the head of the group, did not see that the ones behind him had gone away, and so he entered alone and stood before the vizier.

The vizier said to him: "Why have you come?"

And Joha said: "We have come, I and these people, to ask you . . . "

And the vizier asked him: "Which people?"

And Joha turned around, and when he saw that the others had not come with him, he said to himself: Why should I risk my head for the city?

Joha turned around again to the vizier and said: "The thing that I wished to talk about is the elephant. The city sent me to ask you to buy another one, because this poor one is so lonely; the city can no longer bear its sadness!"

NARRATED BY ELIEZER PAPO – 1995

The King's Goodness

Joha stole an object of little value, and the king wanted to convict him of the theft.

Joha said to him: "Majesty, but why do you want to convict me?"

The king said to him: "Because I am a just person and must condemn the things that are unjust. If I do not convict you, they will say that I do not do justice."

Joha said to him: "Majesty, but if you do not convict me they will say, 'He is a good person, pious . . . a good-hearted person.' They cannot say otherwise! If you convict me for such a thing, then people will say that you are wicked, and even if many people say that you did well, there will be many others who will say of you, Majesty, that you are unjust, because Joha is a poor unfortunate who was convicted for stealing a bauble."

"Do you say that people will say that?"

"Yes, Majesty!" said Joha. "I assure you of it!"

"Well, then," said the king, "if that is the case, I pardon you!"

NARRATED BY MARIA BAHBOUT – 1988

All Donkeys!

The king said one day: "Every man who is afraid of his wife must give me a donkey. Joha, go and collect the donkeys and bring them to me!"

Time passed, and the king and the vizier saw a cloud of dust approaching.

"What is it?" said the king. "A revolution?"

"No," said the vizier. "It is Joha coming with the donkeys of all those who are afraid of their wives."

Joha came and said to the king, "Lord King, I am bringing you the donkeys, and I saw such a beautiful woman on the way!"

"Be quiet," the king said to him, "lest the queen hears you!"

NARRATED BY MATILDA KOEN-SARANO – 1998

The King's Chicken

One day Haroun al Raschid was walking incognito with his minister. They passed in front of two workers who were digging ditches in which to hide the garbage. One of them was Joha. It was winter, and it was cold.

The king said to Joha: "Won't the nine months of the year suffice to support the three?"

Joha answered: "No, because the thirty-two ate up everything."

The king said: "And if I should send you a chicken, would you pluck off its feathers?"

"Until the very last feather!" said Joha.

The king went off with his minister, and Joha finished his work and went home.

The king said to the minister: "Did you understand what I said to Joha?"

Said the minister: "No, Your Majesty, I didn't understand it."

Said the king: "All right, now go and have him explain it to you for me, because I didn't understand it, either."

"Very well, Your Majesty."

The minister went to Joha and said to him: "You know, yesterday the king and I passed by. . . . "

"Yes, I know," Joha said to him.

Said the minister: "Now, then, can you give me an explanation for what you said?"

"What do you think?" Joha said to him. "That I'll tell you without payment?"

"I will give you one hundred thousand ducats!" the minister said to him.

"I, for one hundred thousand ducats, wouldn't take a single step!" Joha said.

"Two hundred! . . . Three hundred! . . . Four hundred! All that I have—my home, my furniture . . . " said the minister. "Oh! I have nothing more to give, apart from the clothes I am wearing!"

"Hey!" Joha said to him. "Give me your clothes as well, otherwise I won't tell you!"

Then the poor man gave him his clothes as well.

Joha said to him: "The king asked me, 'Won't the nine months of the year suffice to support the three months of the year'—the winter. Then I answered him, 'The thirty-two ate everything! The teeth! The teeth.' And he said to me: 'If I send you a chicken would you pluck off its feathers?' Do you understand now? The chicken is you, and I have plucked your feathers, every last one!"

NARRATED BY MARIA BAHBOUT – 1988

The Substitute

One day the king called Joha and said: "Joha, I want you to make me a list of the stupidest people in the city, in the order of their stupidity, from the first to the last."

"Fine!" Joha said.

A few days later, Joha came before the king and showed him the list. And who was at the top of the list? The king!

The king saw the list and was astounded.

"How come," he said to Joha, "that I am the stupidest in the city? And why so?"

Joha said to him: "Lord King, is it not true that a year ago, you gave someone money to buy you horses, and until this day the man has not been seen?"

"Yes," said the king, "but I am certain that soon he will come and bring them to me."

"Fine," said Joha, "when that man comes, I'll remove your name from the list, Lord King, and will put his name there!"

NARRATED BY MATILDA KOEN-SARANO – 1998

The King's Horse

The king had a horse he adored, and he would always say: "If my horse should die, I will kill the one who comes to tell me that my horse has died."

One day, the prime minister found the horse dead. He said: "If I go and tell the king, he will kill me! The only thing to do is to have Joha tell the king that his horse is dead."

So he went to Joha and said: "Look, Joha, I'll give you a hundred ducats, and you go and tell the king that his horse is dead!"

Said Joha: "What? Am I crazy? He will kill me! And what use will the hundred ducats be to me then?"

The prime minister said to him: "But you know how to tell him!"

Said Joha: "All right, then give me the hundred ducats! Wait, no! Not a hundred! You must give me five hundred! Thus if I am going to die, something will at least remain for my children!"

Joha took the five hundred ducats, put them in his pocket, went to the king, and burst into tears.

The king said to him: "What's the matter?"

"Ah, Majesty!" said Joha. "How can I tell you, Majesty? I cannot tell you. It is too sad, Majesty!"

"But why can't you tell me?" said the king.

"Because it is sad for me!" said Joha. "It is sad for him as well, Majesty. But it is so sad for me! So terrible for me! How can I? How can I tell you?"

"Don't you want to tell me that my horse is dead?!" the king said to him.

"Majesty, I didn't say it!" said Joha.

NARRATED BY MARIA BAHBOUT – 1988

Neither in the Sky nor on the Earth

The king was angry with Joha once again. He said to him: "Joha, I don't want to see you either in the sky or on earth!"

Said Joha: "Where shall I go?" He set out and stopped in a wood, and made himself a swing. He sat on the swing and began swinging himself.

Then someone passed by. He said: "Joha, what are you doing here?"

Said Joha: "This is what the king told me to do!"

Another passed by and said to him: "Joha, what are you doing here?"

"I am here because the king sent me!"

All the people who passed, after a time reached the court, and the king asked them: "Tell me, did you see Joha?"

They said: "We saw him. He was in a wood. He was sitting on a swing and was swinging himself, and he said that you sent him."

"That I sent him?"

"Yes, that you sent him!"

"The son of a *mamzer*! Now I will go to see!"

Then they went there, and the king said to Joha: "Joha, come!"

"No, no! I'm staying here!

"Why are you going to stay?"

"I am going to stay because you told me to stay here!"

"I told you so? I didn't tell you anything!"

"Yes, you told me that you didn't want to see me either in the sky or on earth!!"

NARRATED BY RAFAEL VALANSI – 1992

When the Apology Is Worse than the Fault

The king said one day: "He who succeeds in making the apology worse than the fault will receive a prize from me."

Many people participated in the contest, but none succeeded.

One day Joha came before the king and said to him: "I can do what you ask, but I will have to dwell in the royal palace."

The king agreed and gave him a bedroom in his palace.

Joha stayed there, walking about, eating, drinking, having a good time, talking and laughing with everyone.

Two weeks passed in this manner. One morning, during the third week, the king was climbing the stairs.

Joha came up from behind and gave him a pinch on the behind.

"Ouch!" the king said to him. "What are you doing?"

Joha said: "Forgive me, Sire, I thought you were the queen!"

"What?!" said the king. "Are you mad?! Would you have the audacity to touch the queen?!"

"No, Sire," Joha said to him. "I only wished to show you that the apology can be worse than the fault, as you asked!"

The king laughed and gave him what he had promised.

NARRATED BY KOHAVA PIVIS – 1999

Face to Face

Joha was very friendly with the sultan, the king of the Turks. And the king was pleased when Joha made him laugh. One day Joha came before the sultan.

The sultan said to him: "I don't want to see your face! Get out of here!"

Ah! Joha was very offended and went away. He looked, looked, looked, looked, and found a house next to the sultan's palace. He entered and said: "I want to put a small window here in your wall."

"How so?" said the owner of the house. "Do you want to change the wall?"

Joha said: "I'll pay you whatever you want!"

"All right." the owner said.

Joha put in a small window. He knew when the sultan would go to the mosque to pray, and when he did Joha went and put his behind in the new window in the wall.

The sultan passed by and looked: There was a very interesting thing in that wall! He drew near . . . felt it . . . and gave it a pinch.

Joha let out a cry and came out.

"What is this?" said the sultan. "Are you making a laughing-stock of me?!"

"Why, Lord King?" said Joha. "There is no point in lying to the king! Didn't you say that you didn't want to see my face? I thought that you wanted to see my behind!!"

NARRATED BY VALENTINA TSOREF – 1987

Which of the Two?

Joha had no money left and didn't know what to do.

He went to his wife and said to her: "Look, I'll go to see the king, and I'll tell him that you died and that I don't have money to make a funeral for you. We will see what he will give me."

Joha went to the king and said: "Your Majesty, my wife has died and I don't have the money to make a funeral for her."

The king said: "Oh, your wife has died? Now, take this purse with money for the funeral for her."

Joha took the purse and returned home. He said to his wife: "You see?"

His wife said: "Very good! Now I will go to the queen and tell her that you died and that I don't have money for your funeral. We will see what she will give me."

Joha's wife went, crying, to the queen and said: "Joha has died. What will I do? I don't have the money to make a funeral for him."

"The poor thing!" said the queen. "Joha has died. . . . Take this, take this." And she gave her a purse with money, for Joha's funeral.

And Joha's wife returned home with the money.

Joha and his wife took two straw mats, stretched them out on the ground, and wrapped themselves inside them. They pretended to be dead and lay there.

The king came to the queen and said to her: "Did you see? Poor Joha. His wife has died!"

"No!" said the queen. "It is Joha who has died!"

The two began to argue. "No!" "Yes!" "It is him!" "It is her!" Finally, they said: "Let us go to their house to see which one has died!"

The king and queen entered Joha's house and saw the two of them stretched out on the ground, wrapped in the mats.

Said the king: "Who knows which one of them died first?"

Said the queen: "Yes, who knows?"

At that moment, the two of them stood up and said at the same time, placing their hands on their breast, "Me!"

NARRATED BY MATILDA KOEN-SARANO – 1999

King Midas

Many years ago there was a king called Midas, whose kingdom was in Thrace, in the north of Greece. Since Joha was well known as a magician, when he passed the palace, King Midas invited him to spend the night.

In those days it was not very easy to find an inn to spend the night at, so Joha accepted the king's invitation.

After they had had a good meal and gone to bed, the king came to Joha and asked him if it was true what people said, that he was a magician and could do anything he wished.

Joha said to him: "Yes!"

"If this is so," said the king, who was a great miser and who loved gold very much, "give me lots and lots of gold!"

Since Joha didn't have any gold, he said: "Very well! From now on, everything that you touch will turn to gold!"

And so it was: Everything that the king touched turned to gold. But there came a punishment from Heaven, because even the food that he touched turned to gold. And so it was that King Midas died of hunger.

NARRATED BY SARA YOHAY – 1988

The Three Questions

One day the king issued a decree: The Jews must answer three questions:

1. Who comes before God?
2. Who does God love the most?
3. Who will come after the king?

The Jews began to cry, as usual. What do they know to do, the Jews? To cry and to pray! Pray and cry!

Joha passed by and said to them: "What's new?"

They answered: "Only that the king has asked us three questions, and we don't know what to answer."

"Well, then, go and eat and don't worry! Me, I will take care of it!" said Joha.

Ten days passed. Joha said to the king: "I can only answer you, Sire, if you put yourself in a dark room, without any light, and hold the money in your hand." The king agreed.

Joha said to the king: "Count!" And the king counted: "One."

"No, no, you are wrong!" said Joha.

"But how? What comes before one?" said the king.

"Ah, that! Answer yourself! God is One, and before Him, there is no one!"

The king said: "That is good!"

"Now," said Joha, "take a box of matches and light a candle." He measured the room, put the candle in the middle, and said to the king: "The room is square. Now Your Majesty must tell me to which corner the candle gives the most light."

The king said: "It is the same everywhere!"

Joha said: "God is like that. He loves everybody in the same way. He has no preference."

Then the king said to him: "Now you must tell me who will come after me."

"Oh, that, I cannot answer, Your Majesty, unless you remove your garment," said Joha.

The king removed his garment. Joha gave him his own clothes, and put on those of the king. Then he opened the door and said: "Guards! Take away this ruffian who has not been able to answer my questions! Take him away!"

NARRATED BY MARIA BAHBOUT – 1988

The Best Meal in the World

Joha lived in a country where the king was very bad and very capricious.

One day the king got up from his throne and said: "I want to know what is the best meal in the world. Whoever gives me the best answer I will reward handsomely. But if the answer displeases me, I will throw him into prison!"

Everyone was afraid, but there was nothing they could do about it.

The king called Zebulun. Zebulun said: "The best meal is beans with rice."

"Throw him into prison!" cried the king.

After that came Solomon: "The best meal is meatballs with leek."

"Into prison!" ordered the king.

Then came Menahem. "The best meal is tuna fish."

"Into prison!" ordered the king.

Others said: "Zucchini pie . . . *borekas* . . . hard-boiled eggs . . . ," and all were sent to prison.

Finally, it was Joha's turn. He was already half dead with fright and went to see his poor father, who was a coal merchant.

He asked: "Papa, what am I to do? If I don't know the answer, the king will throw me in prison. What is the answer?"

Joha's father said: "Son, the best meal in the world is hunger.

If you are full, nothing satisfies you, but if you are hungry, even dry bread is tasty."

And so Joha went to the king and gave him the answer.

The king was so pleased with the answer that he took Joha and his father to the palace and made them rich, till the end of their days.

NARRATED BY ROZ DROHOBYCZER – 2000

The Proclamation

The king issued a proclamation that said that if the Jews could not prove to him that Jesus Christ was not the son of God, he was going to kill them all.

And so all the Jews went to pray in the synagogue. Joha passed by there and said, "What's the matter? Is it Yom Kippur today?"

"You don't know what trouble we are in!" the Jews said to him. "The king issued a proclamation saying that if we can't prove to him that Jesus is not the son of God, he is going to kill us all."

Joha said to them: "Go and eat! Don't worry. I will go to the king!"

And so the day arrived—the king had said eight days—and Joha had to present himself.

The ministers, seated and all of them rigid, with the king in their midst, were waiting for Joha. Waiting, waiting. He was to come at midday.

Midday passed. One o'clock passed. Half past one passed . . . two . . . three . . . four o'clock.

At half past four, Joha arrived on horseback, all sweaty and disheveled . . . very, very tired . . . out of breath.

"Eh!" the king said to him. "How do you have the audacity to make us wait such a long time?"

"Sire, I was in a place more important than your person!" Joha said.

"How dare you say such a thing?!" the king said.

"How? Of course—I dare to!" said Joha. "I was at a *brit*."

"The *brit* of whom?" said the king.

"Of the Son of God!" said Joha. "The Eternal Father invited me to the *brit* of His son. Should I not have gone?"

"Eh? What? Does God make sons and *brits*?!" said the king.

Said Joha: "Well, then, answer for yourself what I already knew!"

NARRATED BY MARIA BAHBOUT – 1988

Miracle à la Joha

Joha was a shoemaker. What he earned during the day, he ate or drank at night with his wife and his friends. Every night he made a big party.

One night a guard of the sultan passed by there. The next day he said to the sultan: "Look at that Jew! Every night he makes a party! Who knows how much he is earning!"

The sultan issued a decree closing all the shoemakers' shops. Joha came to his shop the next morning. It was closed. What was he going to do?

He stood in front of the shop and went into business cutting people's hair. At night he was once again partying with his friends. The same guard passed by once more and told the sultan about this. The sultan issued another decree: "All the barber shops will be shut!"

Joha saw that there was no work. What was he going to do?

Anyone who had no work became a soldier. Joha also became a soldier.

They put a sword in his hand, and he didn't know what to do. He made a wooden sword, put it in place of the real one, and sold the good sword. At night he was leaping and dancing about with his friends again.

The same guard passed by there and said: "How can this be?" He sent somebody to ask Joha.

Joha said: "I sold the sword and put a wooden one in its place, and with the money I got, we are eating and drinking!"

"Ah!" said the sultan. "Now we shall see." He took a man, called for Joha, and said to him: "This is a brigand! Cut off his head on the spot!"

What was Joha to do? He said to the sultan: "Good sultan, this is no blackguard. One sees it in his face. God will make it that I cannot kill him!"

And he took out his wooden sword.

Said the sultan: "This Jew is very intelligent! One cannot get the better of him. *Ayde,** go to your business!"

NARRATED BY SARA KENT – 1992

A Classic Reply

Hitler asked Joha. "If I were your father, what would you want to be? An engineer, a doctor?"

"An orphan!" Joha answered.

NARRATED BY BEKI BARDAVID – 1999

* Turkish for "Come on!"

CHAPTER 9

JOHA and his neighborhood

"People in glass houses shouldn't throw stones."

The Washtub

Joha said to his wife: "Go to the neighbor and ask him to lend us his big washtub. Tell him that we have a lot of laundry."

His wife went to ask for it, and they gave her the tub. After two or three days, Joha said to his wife: "Return the tub to the neighbor and also give him this little tub!"

So she gave him the big tub and the little tub.

The neighbor said: "What is this?"

"The tub gave birth last night!" Joha said.

"Oy!" said the neighbor. "How stupid that Joha is!" He said to his wife: "He gave us the little tub as well and told us that the tub had given birth to it! When he asks for it again, give it to him again."

A short time after, Joha again asked for the loan of the tub. The neighbor gave him the bigger tub.

Joha took the tub and said nothing. A week passed, two weeks, then the neighbor said to him: "Ha, Joha! I gave you the big tub! You didn't return it to me!"

"What big tub?"

"For the laundry!"

"Ah! It died!"

"How did it die?!"

"Just as it gave birth, so did it die!!"

NARRATED BY VALENTINA TSOREF – 1987

An Oven for All Seasons

As Joha was always without work, his mother said to him: "Become a baker!"

Joha built an oven with its door to the east. To dedicate it, he invited many people.

Among them were some jokers. They said to Joha: "Why do you have the door on the east side? Isn't the heat of the oven enough for you? The sun will come and burn you!"

"Ah!" said Joha. "You are right!"

"The wind from the west will come and will turn all the smoke back on you, and you will suffocate!"

What did he do? He destroyed the oven, built it anew, and put the door on the west side. Once again, he dedicated the oven. The guests arrived. Among them were other jokers.

They said to Joha: "How come you put the door on the west side? Isn't all the smoke sufficient for you!"

In short, whichever way Joha made it, the jokers always found a reason to criticize him.

In the end, what did Joha do? He went to a metalworker's shop, ordered a thick iron plate with wheels, and built the oven on top of it.

When the jokers came again and saw the door once more on the east side, they criticized him again. So Joha turned the oven on wheels to the west side.

Then he said to each and every one: "I will place it on whichever side you wish. You want it on the east side? Let it be on the east side. You want it on the west side? Let it be on the west side! I will turn it according to the season!"

Narrated by YAAKOV ELAZAR – 1990

A Diplomatic Answer

Joha's friend shouted to him: "Joha, are you sleeping?"
"No!"
"Lend me a hundred liras!"
"Now I'm sleeping!" Joha said to him.

NARRATED BY BEKI BARDAVID – 1992

"He Who Pays the Piper, Calls the Tune!"

One day Joha was on his way to the village. The little boys in the street began to ask him: "Joha, you are going to the village. Buy us little whistles!"

Joha said to them: "All right!"

One small boy jumped up and said: "Take five cents. Buy me a little whistle!"

Joha went to the village. When he returned, he gave the little whistle to the one who had given him the money.

They all began to shout: "Joha! What about us? Where are our whistles?"

Joha said: "The one who pays the money, gets the whistle!"

And that is how the saying "He who pays the piper, calls the tune!" came into being.

NARRATED BY RASHEL PERERA – 1987

What the People Say

Joha wanted to go into the city with his two children. He got on his donkey, and the children walked behind him on foot.

As he was passing through a small village, the people who were sitting in the café began to say: "Look at those poor children, walking on foot, and the father riding on the donkey! What a cruel father is that one!"

Joha, who heard this, felt that it was very true. He got off the donkey, put the two children on it, and followed on foot. They passed through another place, and on seeing them, the people said: "How badly educated are those children! The father is walking on foot, and they are riding on the donkey. What bad behavior!"

Joha took the children down from the donkey, and the children walked next to their father on foot, with the donkey by their side.

When the people saw them all walking on foot, they said: "Look, what stupid ones! They have a donkey, and they are walking on foot!"

Joha put the children back on the donkey and also got on himself.

They passed through another village, and the people who saw them said: "What a cruel person that one is! He and the children are sitting on the donkey! They will take away the soul of the poor donkey!"

Joha continued on his way in this fashion, until they reached the city.

The moral of this little tale is that people will find every kind of excuse for criticizing!

NARRATED BY JULIDE AVZARADEL – 1987

The Height of Diplomacy

A very honest and respected man died in his shop in the market at midday. Nobody knew how to break the bad news to his wife, a very thin and refined person, since they were all afraid that such a great sorrow would kill her.

Joha said to them: "I will tell her about it!"

They said to him: "No! She has to be told in a diplomatic way!"

In the end, however, since no one else wished to do it, they sent our good Joha to her.

Joha went to the home of the deceased, knocked on the door, and when the dead man's wife opened it, he asked: "Does the widow of Señor Salom live here?"

The woman said: "No!"

Joha said: "Do you want to bet?"

NARRATED BY ELIEZER PAPO – 2000

Sensitivity

Joha had a cousin who went to live in Germany and left his property in Joha's care. One day the cousin's cat died, and Joha sent his cousin a telegram, saying: "Your cat has died."

The cousin was overcome with sorrow; there were tears, wailings. . . . After the seven days of mourning, he sent a letter to Joha that said: "We Westerners are very sensitive. You should not have told me thus: 'Your cat has died.' You should have prepared me little by little. One week you should have written to me: 'Your cat, just like any cat, was jumping from one tree to another, but fell off the last one.' The following week you should have written me that its condition was worsening, and only in the third week should you have told me that it died."

A few years passed, and Joha's cousin received a new letter from him: "About your mother. Just like any mother, she was jumping from tree to tree . . . "

NARRATED BY ELIEZER PAPO – 2000

Everything Is Relative

Joha was walking in the marketplace with a friend.

Suddenly, a young man passed in the street with a big tray of *baklava* on his head.

Joha's friend said to him: "Look, Joha, what a tray of *baklava*!"

"Eh, what do I care?" Joha said to him.

"But they are taking it to your house!" the friend said to him.

"Eh, what do you care?" Joha said to him.

NARRATED BY MATILDA KOEN-SARANO – 1998

The Stammerer

A stammerer came and asked Joha: "Exc . . . use . . . me, Señ . . . or, where is . . . the . . . s . . . chool f . . . for . . . the staz . . . mmer . . . ers?"

Joha looked at him in amazement. "Why do you need a school? You are stammering perfectly!"

NARRATED BY ELIEZER PAPO – 1999

A Very Old System

One day Joha went to the coffeehouse and sat there. He took off his jacket and put it on the seat. Then he stood up and went off to the toilet.

The friends who had sat next to him said: "Let's play a game with Joha. Let's see what he will do!"

When Joha came back, he couldn't find his jacket. He said: "Where is my jacket?"

Nothing.

Said Joha: "Look, if someone took my jacket, he should tell me."

There was no reply.

Joha said: "Look, if you don't give me my jacket, I'll do to you what my father did!"

One said to the other: "What did his father do?"

"I don't know," said the other.

Then Joha said: "Look, give me the jacket. If not, what my father did, I'll do to you!"

The friends began to speak among themselves: "Who knows what his father did? Maybe he beat someone up, maybe he killed. Who knows?"

Finally, one said: "Come on, give him the jacket and get it over with!"

They took it and gave it back to him.

After they gave it back, his friends said: "Joha, on your life, tell us what your father did!"

"Ah, nothing!" said Joha. "He went and bought himself a new jacket!"

NARRATED BY SHMUEL BARKI – 1992

The End of the World

Joha had a sheep that was fat and beautiful.

His friends had their eye on the sheep: "What can we do to trick him so that he'll agree to slaughter it, and we can eat it all together and enjoy it?"

They made a plan, saying: "This is the way we will trick him!"

One of his friends approached Joha and said: "Do you know, Joha, that the end of the world is coming any day?"

"Who said?"

"Everyone is saying it!"

"But the end of the world, when it will be, only God knows such a thing!"

"Everyone is saying it! Since everyone is saying it, they must know something! Before the day comes, we will slaughter your sheep and have a fine feast!"

Joha met another friend, and he told him the same thing, advising him to take advantage of a good meal from the sheep.

Joha reluctantly agreed to make a feast with the sheep, to be rid of the remarks and advice of his friends, and his friends were very satisfied with Joha's decision.They went to the riverbank. They slaughtered the sheep, cleaned it, and said to Joha: "You know how to roast it on a good fire better than we do!"

They all noticed that Joha was very sad because he had been parted from the sheep he so loved. But Joha consoled himself, saying: "Today or tomorrow, since it is the end of the world, what importance does the sheep have?"

His friends, seeing Joha busy roasting the sheep, said: "We are going to swim in the river until the feast is ready. We want to enjoy our last day in the world!"

They undressed and gave their clothes to Joha to look after. But Joha couldn't stand it any longer. He realized that his friends had tricked him, and to take revenge, he threw their clothes and shoes into the fire.

When the friends returned to eat the well-roasted sheep, they asked Joha for their clothes. Joha told them that he had burned them.

They began to shout: "What did you do! Why did you burn our clothes? What are we going to do now?"

And Joha, very calm, replied: "Dear friends, tomorrow is the end of the world! You will not need your clothes or shoes anymore!"

NARRATED BY JULIDE AVZARADEL – 1987

Two Brothers

Joha had a Christian neighbor.

The Christian went each day to the bazaar to sell glass objects, which he loaded onto his donkey. Joha went to the synagogue, to pray.

Whenever the Christian and Joha met at the door of the synagogue, Joha said to him: "Good day!"

And the Christian said to him: "This donkey is your brother!"

Joha did not answer him.

One day, two days passed. . . .

The Christian said to him thus: "This donkey is your brother!"

Purim was approaching, and Joha said: "Now I will really teach this Christian a lesson!" When the donkey loaded with glass objects appeared, Joha began to smoke a cigarette.

His neighbor, the Christian, said to him: "This donkey is your brother!"

"My brother?" Joha said.

"Yes, your brother!" the neighbor said.

"Very well!" said Joha, and stood beside the donkey. He puffed on his cigarette, filled his mouth with smoke, and then filled the ear of the donkey with smoke.

When the smoke entered its ear, the donkey became very alarmed and whirled around, throwing to the ground all the glass objects that were on its back, and it began to run away.

The Christian took Joha to court.

At court the Christian said to the judge: "This is what happened . . . ," he said. "What did this person do to my donkey, that it ran off and broke everything?"

The judge summoned Joha and said: "Did this happen?"

"Yes," said Joha. "It is true that the donkey went wild, that it began to run and broke everything. But this donkey is my brother!"

"What do you mean," the judge said, "that he is your brother!"

"Ask him . . . ," Joha said. "I have been his neighbor for years. Every day, he has said to me, 'This donkey is your brother!' Tomorrow is the festival of Purim. I came and whispered in the donkey's ear, 'Dear brother! Tomorrow is Purim!' And he was so happy that he began to run!"

Narrated by VALENTINA TSOREF – 1987

The Storyteller

Joha loved to gather his friends, to make parties, to tell stories.

The whole world knew Joha.

Once he called his friends and said: "Come to my house. I want to tell you something."

"What are you going to tell us, Joha?" his friends said.

"I am going to tell you a story!" Joha said.

Well, the next day all his friends came to Joha's house.

Joha said: "Do you know what I am going to tell you?"

"Yes! We already know!" the friends said.

"Hey, since you already know," said Joha, "why should I tell it to you again?"

His friends went home.

A week passed, two. Joha once more called his friends: "Come to my house. I am going to tell you a story!"

His friends said: "This time we'll tell him that we don't know. So then he will tell us the story."

When they arrived, Joha said: "Do you already know what I am going to tell you?"

"No, we don't know anything!" his friends said to him.

"If you don't know anything," Joha said, "why should I tell you?"

Once again, the friends went home.

Time passed, and Joha called them a third time.

Well then, the friends said to one another on the way, "Look, if Joha tells us again that he is going to tell us a story, we'll tell him that some know it and others don't know it."

They came to Joha's house: "Ah, welcome!"

"Good to see you!"

"How are you?"

"How are you?"

Joha said to them: "Well, now I am going to tell you a story! Do you know it already?"

One of them jumped up and said: "Half of the friends already know it, and the other half don't!"

"Aha!" said Joha. "If that is so, those who know it can tell it to those who don't know it. That way, everyone will know it!"

NARRATED BY MALKA SHABETAY – 1987

A Strange Bathhouse

There was a woman whose husband went away, and she invited her friends to visit.

They were eating and drinking, having a good time. Suddenly, knock, knock at the door. The husband had returned. The woman hid them all in the coal storeroom. Among them was Joha.

Every night, this husband would play an instrument, and his wife would dance.

When Joha saw the wife dancing to her husband's music, he said: "I also want to go out and dance!"

"No! No!" his friends said to Joha. "Have you gone out of your mind? The husband will kill us!"

Joha is Joha. He said: "What do I care! I want to dance!"

"All right, my dear," they said to him. "Take my ring." "Take my watch!"

Joha took the ring, took the watch, and remained silent.

With the next dance he said: "I want to go out to dance!"

"No, my dear!" To get Joha to stay put this one gave him his shirt, the other gave him his trousers, until Joha stripped them naked and left them as on the day they were born.

The husband played again, and the wife danced.

Said Joha: "I am going to dance!"

"For mercy's sake, no! For mercy's sake, no!"

"I have to go out to dance!" And he went out with a huge bundle, this big!

Said the husband: "What is this?"

Joha said: "What? Don't you know there is a bathhouse here? I have finished washing and am going. Go and see: They're all naked. They are washing!" And he ran off.

NARRATED BY MALKA LEVY – 1991

All of Gold

An Englishman had a birthday.

He said to his friends, "Any present that you bring me, whether it be small or big, should be made of gold, okay?"

They all did as the Englishman wished.

The Scotsman brought a fish called "goldfish."

Joha brought a friend named . . . Goldenberg!

NARRATED BY BEKI BARDAVID – 1996

What Neighbors!

Joha came home very late one night. He climbed the stairs noisily.

The upstairs neighbor opened her door and said: "If you were my husband, I would give you poison to drink!"

Joha told her: "And if you were my wife, I would drink it with pleasure!"

NARRATED BY ESTER VENTURA – 1993

Ignorant Snobbery

Joha liked to mix French with his Judeo-Spanish.

He said: "My wife has filled the house with boxes of *conserves* (pickles). You should see the house; she has turned it into a *conservatoire*!"

Moshe replied: "That's nothing! My wife receives so many people that my house is already a *maison publique*."

Solomon then spoke: "My wife and I, we travel so much that we have not missed anyplace in the world!"

Joha was not at a loss as usual: "Then you must know the entire world *carte geographique*?"

"We didn't have time to go there yet! The next time!"

NARRATED BY BEKI BARDAVID – 1996

The Jewish Festivals

Joha and his friend, who was a Christian, were on their way to a conference and had a very long way to walk.

Said Joha: "You know what? We're getting very tired. Let's do this: Take me on your shoulders; I will count the festivals that we have. When I finish counting them, I will get down and you will climb up on me. This way, until we arrive, neither of us will get tired."

The Christian said to him: "All right, but first take me, because I am very tired!"

Joha took him, put him on his shoulders, and the Christian began to count: "Christmas . . . Easter . . . Pentecost." He finished and got down.

Joha climbed up and began: "Rosh Hashana, Yom Kippur, Sukkot, Hanukkah, Purim, Pesach, Shavuot, Nahamu."* He finished reciting all the festivals.

Then he continued: "Shabbat comes, Shabbat goes. Shabbat comes, Shabbat goes. Shabbat comes, Shabbat goes. . . . "

Meanwhile, they had already reached their destination.

NARRATED BY TUNA KOHEN – 1988

* Sabbath after Tisha B'Av

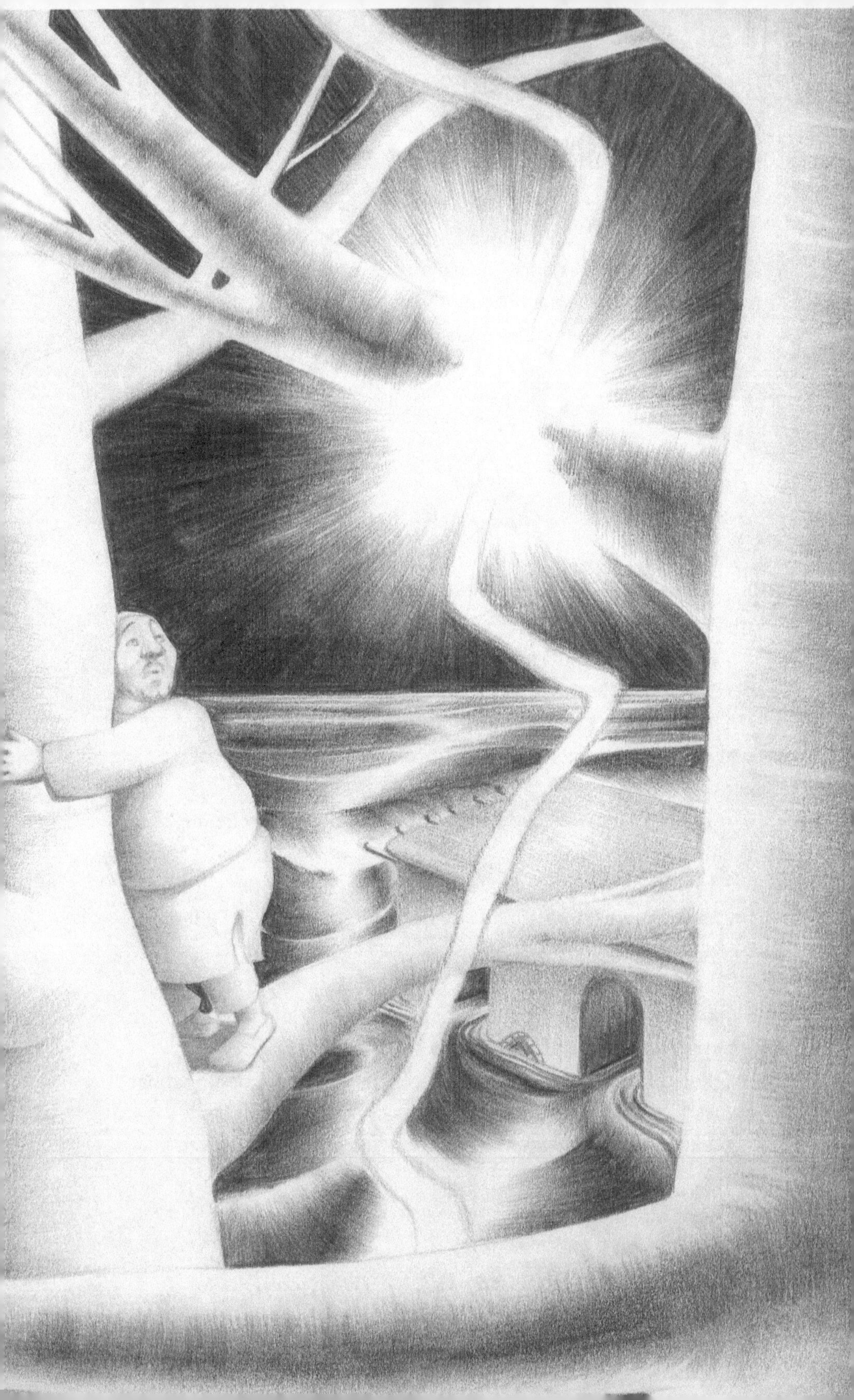

CHAPTER 10

JOHA talks about himself

"Joha went to the baths and didn't stop talking about it for years!"

The Left Ear

Joha is a very simple and cunning man. Once they asked him: "Joha, show us your left ear!" And Joha did like this: He passed his right hand over his head and said, "Here it is!"

NARRATED BY MAZAL STROCK – 1996

A Suitable Place

It was nighttime. Joha was outside in the street. He was looking for something on the ground, under the lamplight.

A neighbor passed and said to him: "Joha, what are you looking for? I will help you!"

Joha said to him: "I am looking for a ring that fell off my finger."

The neighbor began to look with him, but the two of them couldn't find anything.

After a while the neighbor said: "Joha, are you sure that this is where it fell? There's nothing here!"

"Ah, no!" Joha said. "The ring fell off in the house, when I went down to the cellar. But it is useless to look for it there, because there's no light. . . . Here there is light! That is why I am looking here!"

NARRATED BY MATILDA KOEN-SARANO – 1997

Easy Puzzle

Joha filled the pocket of his coat with grapes and went for a walk.

He met the neighbors' small children and said to them: "Children, if you can guess what I have in my coat, I will give you a bunch!"

"Grapes!" they said immediately.

"Goodness me!" said Joha. "How were you able to guess so quickly?!"

NARRATED BY MATILDA KOEN-SARANO – 1987

Each Unto His Own

Joha lived in a village far from the city. Once, twice a year he had to go and buy things to eat and to wear. He would take his little donkey and set out. The road was very long, so when he was alone and wanted to talk he would converse with the donkey.

One day, he said to it: "Do you know what we are going to do? Instead of taking the long way around, which will take us two or three hours, we will go along the railway track."

He took the donkey to the train track. A train was coming: "Ooo . . . ooo . . . ooo."

Said Joha: "Let it whistle. . . ."

"Whistle! Whistle!" he said to the train. "If you won't move aside, neither will I!"

The train went "Oooo. . . ."

Joha did nothing; he just stood in its path.

By chance, it happened that the train had to switch tracks.

It went onto the other track.

Said Joha to the donkey: "Didn't I tell you? It moved aside, I didn't!"

NARRATED BY NISIM ROFE – 1990

Premature Vision

Joha had never been on an airplane.

His friends said: "Let's see what will happen. Let's put him aboard an airplane."

They put Joha aboard, and he began to look through the window.

He said: "Oh! All the people down there look like ants!"

"Yes," his friends said. "It is true that when the plane takes off, they will look like ants down there—but the plane has not yet taken off!"

NARRATED BY VALENTINA TSOREF – 1990

Careful What You Say!

Joha was working in his shop with his assistant.

He said to the assistant: "Look out the window and tell me what the weather is doing."

The assistant looked and said: "Ah! We have rain. We won't have any customers!"

Joha looked him full in the face and said: "*We* have rain?! Since when are *we* partners?"

NARRATED BY MIRIAM RAYMOND – 1988

What a Voice!

One day, as he was washing himself, Joha began to sing. The bathroom was very small, and it had stone walls. In this small space Joha's voice sounded very beautiful, or so it seemed to him.

Ah! thought Joha. I sing well! I am going to sing in a place where other people can hear me. Who knows? Perhaps I can become a singer. Hey, hey! Perhaps everyone will want to hear me! Maybe they will like my voice! I will try!

When he finished washing, Joha went out onto the balcony of his house and began to sing very loudly. But outside, his voice went in all directions and did not please him. He said: "My voice is not the same here as when I was singing in the bath!"

Meanwhile, in the street next to his house, there passed by a man who said to him: "Joha, what are you doing? Can't you hear what a terrible voice you have? What a noise you make when you sing. Nobody is interested in listening to you!"

"Hey! Hey!" Joha said. "Do you think I don't know how to sing? I am a great singer, and I sing beautifully! But the problem is that my fine voice is heard only in the bath! Here, outside, it sounds horrible!! Come to my bathroom and you will hear a beautiful voice!"

Narrated by MIRIAM RAYMOND – 1987

"Eat, Coattails!"

Returning from work, Joha went to a party he had been invited to and presented himself just as he was dressed. But the waiters wouldn't let him enter because he wasn't dressed well.

Then he said: "I'll be right back!" He went and put on a very fine garment, all embroidered, with sleeves of gold, and when he entered again, they immediately said: "Ah! Please sit down!" And they began to bring him dishes.

One waiter brought him a dish, and Joha said: "Eat, sleeve!"

Another waiter brought him another dish: "Eat, coattail!" Another dish: "Eat, sleeve!" "Eat, coattail!"

The waiters said: "What's the matter with you?!"

Said Joha: "Eh! Before, when I came badly dressed, you wouldn't let me enter. It's to my sleeve, to my coattail, not to me, that you are bringing the food!"

NARRATED BY RASHEL CAPOANO – 1987

Ignorance Squared

Joha was in synagogue on a Friday night, and a stranger was there who had just arrived.

Well, as is the custom among Jews, he brought the stranger home to recite the Kiddush, the sanctification over wine. But in Joha's house there was a problem: The tradition was a very cherished one, but the master of the house didn't know how to recite the prayer. He was ignorant.

The time for reciting the Kiddush came. Joha, the master of the house, said to the stranger: "Please!"

"No, no, no!" said the stranger. "I am a visitor. Please—you, the master of the house, recite it!"

"No, no, no, I beg you! You are the stranger. You must do me the honor of reciting the Kiddush in my house!" said Joha.

And so it continued: first the one, then the other saying, "No, you!" "Not I!" "No, you!"

Then Joha raised the cup: "Before we were one ignoramus . . . now we are two! Amen!"

NARRATED BY NISIM MAYO – 1999

In War As in War

During the war in Israel, Joha would be given leave once a month from the commander, because he would bring back an Arab tank. They would give him medals and send him home.

This repeated itself for three months, one after the other.

Finally, the commander could not resist asking: "Look, Joha, I am not going to deprive you of your leave. Every time you bring an Arab tank, I will give you a week's leave. But tell me, I beg you, how do you manage to take a tank from the enemy? It isn't easy!"

Joha didn't want to tell him, but the commander was very insistent.

Joha said to him: "Look, I have a friend, Hussein, in the Arab army. He gives me his tank and I give him mine. One week he takes his leave and one week I take mine. He goes to his home and I go to mine."

NARRATED BY BEKI BARDAVID – 1999

Dangerous Haircut

One day Joha went to the barber for a haircut, but the barber wasn't there. So Joha asked the assistant to cut his hair.

The assistant, who didn't know his work too well, cut him and each time put a little cotton wool on his head.

When the assistant finished cutting half of his hair, Joha got up to leave.

The assistant said: "What are you doing? I haven't finished cutting your hair!"

Joha replied: "You have sown half my head with cotton. Now I want them to sow the other half with beans!"

NARRATED BY ISRAEL REGEV – 1998

An Eye for an Eye

Water was leaking from Joha's roof and he decided to mend it. He took a ladder and climbed up. When he was on the roof, doing the difficult and risky work, he saw an old man gesturing at him from down below.

Joha, very curious to know what the man wanted to tell him, descended the ladder and almost fell in his haste.

When he got to the bottom, the old man asked him for *tzedaka,** telling him that he was very poor.

Joha said: "Climb up to the roof with me!" And he helped the old man to climb the ladder.

When they both reached the top, Joha said: "And I am very poor and have nothing to give you! And now you go down like you made me do!"

NARRATED BY MIRIAM RAYMOND – 1984

* charity

Noblesse Oblige!

Three gentlemen, Joha, and a lady were traveling in a train. During the long journey the lady farted.

At that moment, one of the gentlemen stood up and apologized, saying: "Forgive me, it was me!"

Another two-hour journey passed, and the lady farted, like a lady.

The second gentlemen got up and said: "I beg your pardon, it was me!"

After another two hours, the same thing happened, and the third gentleman declared that it was him.

A half an hour later Joha stood up to drink a cup of coffee in the buffet and, leaving the compartment, said to those present: "I am going, but if this lady farts anymore, you may say that it was me!"

NARRATED BY ELIEZER PAPO – 1999

A Cheeky Question

Joha was sitting in a restaurant eating, when the person next to him at the table farted.

In order to cover it up, he began to make a noise with his chair and with his feet.

Joha said: "Hey! To cover the noise you are stamping your feet and banging your chair! But what will you do for the smell?"

NARRATED BY RASHEL PERERA – 1987

Where's the Beard?

Everyone wondered how it was that Joha, who was so religious, had no beard. Then one person took his courage in both hands and went and asked: "Joha, how is it that you don't let your beard grow?"

And Joha answered: "What can I tell you? Such and such happened: I had a big and luxurious beard, and it comforted me to stroke it all the time. Each day I would look in the mirror to see how much it had grown. It didn't have a single white hair in it. I was contented and proud. But one night, returning from the cafe, I met a friend who put the evil eye on my beard because his didn't grow, and the little one he had was white as snow."

"He put the evil eye on you?" said the other one. "Don't tell me that you believe in such things!"

"Why not?" Joha said. "Listen and you will see! This friend asked: 'Tell me, Joha, how do you manage to go to sleep at night? When you cover yourself up, do you put the beard outside the blanket or inside it?'

"I was silent for a moment and then I said to him: 'Well, actually, I hadn't thought about it until now. I will try tonight and answer you tomorrow morning.'

"At night I got into bed, turned off the light, and covered myself with the blanket. Right away the friend's question struck me. I put my beard outside, but it wasn't comfortable. I put it inside—once again the same thing. And so the whole night passed, putting it inside and outside, and I didn't sleep a wink the whole night.

"The next morning I met the friend, who asked me: 'Did you try yet? Tell me where you put the beard, outside the blanket or inside it?'

"I said: 'I don't know. I will tell you later.'

"The second night, the same thing happened, and so forth

for an entire week. In the end, my wife got very angry and began to shout: 'Well now, Joha, what's going on? You don't let me sleep the whole night! What happened to you?'

"I told her what had happened. Then my wife got out of bed, brought me a pair of scissors, and said: 'Come on, Joha, cut it off and let's get it over with!'

"I cut off my beard, hung an ear of garlic at my throat to ward off the evil eye, and from that day on, I have been sleeping in peace. Do you understand?" Joha said to him.

NARRATED BY SARA YOHAY – 1996

All Stand!

Joha boarded a bus in Tel Aviv and saw that there was no vacant seat.

Since he wished to sit down, he said: "Now I will make them stand up!"

He began to sing *Hatikva,* the national anthem!

They all stood up, at attention, and Joha sat down.

NARRATED BY RAHEL MIHAELI – 1994

The Origin of Joha

One day Issahar Avzaradel from Ashdod phoned and asked me: "About Joha—where does he come from? What is the origin of Joha?"

I said to him: "Look, Joha is known in Italy, in Turkey, in Egypt. I think that he probably originated in ancient Persia."

Issahar said to me: "I will tell you, I made a thorough investigation of my own, which took a long time, and I came to the conclusion that Joha was South African."

"How so?" I asked him.

"Because," Issahar said to me, "when Joha died, among the many tributes they paid him, they dedicated a city in his name."

"Which city?" I asked in amazement.

"Johannesburg!" Issahar replied.

NARRATED BY MATILDA KOEN-SARANO – 1996

The Latest Invention

Joha was walking in the street with two of his friends, an American and a Japanese.

Suddenly, the American stopped, looked at his watch, and said: "Wait . . . I have here an e-mail from New York."

"What?!" said Joha.

"Yes!" the American friend said. "In my watch I read not only the time, but I also have a radio, a TV, and a computer with e-mail. This is our latest invention!"

Meanwhile, the Japanese friend began to say something in Japanese to the air.

"With whom are you speaking?" Joha asked.

"I'm speaking directly with Japan," his friend said.

"What?!" Joha said.

"Yes!" the Japanese man said. "In one of my teeth there is a very small and sophisticated telephone, which enables me to do this. This is our latest invention!"

"I understand!" Joha said, and burped very loudly.

"At least say 'pardon me'!" the two friends said.

"What do you mean," Joha said. "This is the signal that I just sent a fax to my uncle in Johannesburg. This is my latest invention!"

NARRATED BY MATILDA KOEN-SARANO – 2000

Life Lesson

Joha was a porter in the market. One day, he was carrying a very heavy load and broke his shoulder. He came home in great pain and was bedridden for a whole month.

When he recovered and went back to the market, they took away his work, and he had nothing to do. Joha returned home, very sad and full of disappointment, and with an empty purse.

Joha's wife, who loved him very much, said: "Don't you despair, Johaiko, look! We have a bit of land here, a small garden. Go and plant tomatoes and cucumbers, and sell them in the market. I promise you that, with patience, you will get a good return."

Joha went to the garden and began to plant cucumbers and said to himself: "He who plants cucumbers, eats cucumbers."

Joha began to dig the ground to plant, and suddenly he came across a very big stone. He lifted it and found a sack filled with gold.

Joha began to shout to his wife to come and see the good fortune in the garden.

So Joha became very rich. He went with his wife to buy new clothes, and they bought a palace as well.

From that time on, Joha began to hold nightly parties at his home and invited the rich and famous of the city.

From time to time during a party, he took a little golden box out of his purse, went to a corner and opened it, smelled it, closed it, then put it back in his purse.

All the guests wanted to know what he was smelling. He would say: "Nothing! It's not important!" In this way, Joha continued to smell his little box.

One day, his close friend said: "I beg you, Joha, do me a favor. Let me smell, just once!"

"Very well," said Joha. "Come here. Take it and smell, if you want to so much."

The friend took the box, opened it with great ceremony, and when he smelled it, almost fainted from the smell—of excrement, mixed with ammonia.

"What is this, Joha? Are you mad?"

And Joha replied: "Listen, my friend! I smell this box to remind myself where I come from. And when I smell, I remember that this wealth is from the Almighty, blessed be He. I was only a porter!"

And so Joha lived and taught others how to live.

NARRATED BY HAYIM TSUR – 1999

The Strength of Age

Joha, who was already quite old, went for a walk with friends of his own age.

As they walked, they began to speak about the strength they had in their youth.

One of them said: "I, when I was a young man, was much

stronger than today. I could do twelve and a half miles in a day without stopping or getting tired!"

Another said: "When I was a young man, I was so strong that I could break a thick stick with one hand!"

Another said: "Ah! The strength of youth is not like that of old age!"

Said Joha: "What are you talking about? I am now as strong as when I was a young man!"

"Come on!" his friends said. "How can you say such a thing?"

"It's the pure truth," Joha said. "And I can prove it to you!"

"Prove it to us; we want to see!" his friends said.

Joha went over to a big stone that lay in the field, tried to lift it, but could not.

He said to his friends: "Did you see?"

"What did we see?" his friends asked. "We saw that you could not lift it!"

"Why?" Joha said to them. "Do you think that when I was a young man I could lift it?"

NARRATED BY MIRIAM RAYMOND – 1994

Who Needs Languages?!

Joha was with his son in the village square.

Suddenly, a stranger passed by and asked: "Do you speak English?"

"No!" the two of them said.

"*Parlez-vous français?*" the man asked.

"No!" the two of them said.

"*Parlate Italiano?*" the man asked.

And this time the two of them answered: "No!"

The man went away.

Joha's son said to him: "Papa, the time has come for us to learn some foreign language!"

"What for?" Joha answered. "What good did it do that man to know so many foreign languages?"

NARRATED BY MATILDA KOEN-SARANO – 1995

Untouched by Modern Life

Joha was living in Izmir. He noticed that all his friends were going on trips abroad, this one to Paris, that one to London, another to Rome.

He said: "Why shouldn't I go as well?"

One day he said to his wife: "Look, Grasia, now that the children are no longer at home, let us go on a pleasure trip. Let's go to Rome."

His wife was delighted.

Joha went, bought tickets for Rome, came home, and said to his wife: "Come on then, prepare the suitcase and don't forget to take the portable radio, because while I'm there, I want to hear what is going on in the world."

"Fine!" his wife said.

And so they arrived in Rome. They walked around, looked at everything. Every night Joha returned to the hotel, turned on the radio, heard Italian, and didn't understand a word.

One night he couldn't stand it any longer. He said: "Hey, what's wrong with this son of a *mamzer* of a radio? I can't understand a word!"

"Hey, shut it off then!" his wife said.

After that night he didn't turn it on anymore.

They walked around and around, and by now had seen all there was to see in Rome.

The day came for them to leave. As they were packing, Joha saw his wife take the radio and put it in the suitcase.

He said to her: "You can leave that here! What use will it be to us in Izmir?"

"Why?" his wife said.

"How why?" Joha said. "Didn't you see how it forgot Turkish and spoke only Italian?"

NARRATED BY MATILDA KOEN-SARANO – 1994

General Culture

Joha and his friend were discussing current events.

His friend said: "Did you hear that Agnon died?"

"Yes?" asked Joha in disbelief.

"Yes, yes, he has already died!" answered the friend.

"So Agnon has died," Joha repeated in a dramatic voice.

"Yes. How sad," the friend continued.

"Please help me to remember. Who was this Agnon?" asked Joha.

"Who was Agnon? Don't you know who Agnon was?" the friend asked indignantly. "Agnon was a famous writer."

"Writer?" asked Joha with great appreciation.

"Yes, writer!" replied the friend.

"And he died?"

"Yes, he died!"

"So who will be the writer now?" asked Joha, very pensively.

NARRATED BY ELIEZER PAPO – 1999

CHAPTER 11

JOHA and God

"God created him,
but He forgot to visit him."

A Brief Prayer

One day Joha got up in the morning, came into the kitchen, and said: "Mama, I want to eat! I'm hungry!"

His mother said: "First of all, go and pray."

Joha went to his bedroom and, after a few minutes, came out saying: "Mama, I have already finished. . . . Give me something to eat!"

His mother gave him the head and tail of a fish.

He said to her: "What? This is not fish!"

"Yes!" his mother said. "The *Shmone Esrei* prayer contains eighteen benedictions. You recited only the first one and the last one!"

NARRATED BY ESTER FELDMAN - 1999

The Nut and the Pumpkin

Joha was walking in a garden one day. It was terribly hot. Joha's head was boiling, when suddenly he saw a nut tree and decided to sit under it, to refresh himself in its shade. He took off his fez, raised his eyes, and gazed at this great tree.

"Just look!" he said. "What a curious thing: such a big and strong tree, and such small nuts!" To his right, he noticed a very big pumpkin growing from a plant as thin as a string. He was amazed and said: "What a curious thing: such a thin plant, and such a big pumpkin!"

But while he was resting, nature played a game with him: a nut fell off the tree and hit him on the head, making him dizzy, and he saw stars during the daytime!

Joha picked up his fez, put it on his head, and raised his hands to thank God for his wisdom, as he imagined what could have happened to him if a pumpkin instead of a nut had fallen from the tree.

NARRATED BY SARA YOHAY – 1991

A Virtual Miracle

Joha went to the synagogue on Sabbath morning and asked to be called up during the Reading of the Law, and he recited the *Birkat Hagomel.**

The other congregants asked: "What miracle happened to you, Joha?"

Joha said: "My robe was hanging out to dry on the terrace. A strong gust of wind came and threw it on the ground below."

"For goodness sake!" the congregants said. "Your robe fell down, and you are reciting the *Birkat Hagomel*?"

"Naturally!" said Joha. "Think for a moment what might have happened had I been inside it!"

NARRATED BY MATILDA KOEN-SARANO – 1998

If God Wills It!

One day Joha's wife felt cold. He said to her: "Wait! Near here is a field with some trees. I will go and cut some branches; then we will burn them and warm ourselves."

His wife said: "Say: 'If God wills it!'"

Joha answered: "What do you mean!? 'If God wills it!'?

* prayer of gratitude for being delivered from some peril

What does He care? Whether He wants it or not, I am going to cut!" And he went off.

As soon as he arrived in the field, he raised the axe to cut, but instead of cutting the branches of the tree, he cut his hand. And holding his hand, he returned home and rang the doorbell. His wife asked: "Who is it?"

And he answered: "If God wills it, it is me, Joha!"

NARRATED BY ESTER KOHEN – 1985

There Is No Sacrifice!

Joha went out with his sheep to graze and found himself all alone in a remote place in the midst of a very heavy rainstorm.

Seeing that the earth was being inundated, Joha climbed to the top of a very tall tree to save himself.

In the midst of the thunder and lightning and the hail, Joha began to pray to God: "Lord of the Universe, have mercy on me and save me! If I come out of here alive, I will give you a bull in sacrifice!"

The wind began to drop, and he descended to a lower branch and prayed to the Almighty: "Lord of the Universe, if you save me, I will give you a ram in sacrifice!"

A short while after, the rain stopped, and Joha said: "Lord of the Universe, save me! I promise you a cock in sacrifice!"

But when Joha saw that there was no longer any water on the ground, he got down from the tree and, raising his eyes to the heavens, said: "There is no sacrifice!"

NARRATED BY MATILDA KOEN-SARANO – 1980

The Same God

Joha went to the circus to earn money.
They dressed him as a lion.
Another lion came out to face him.
Joha was dying with fear. He began to pray: "*Shema Israel!*"
The other lion answered him: "*Adonay Echad!*"

NARRATED BY BEKI BARDAVID – 1992

"If They Give You, Take . . ."

Joha had an upstairs neighbor. This neighbor was rich. Every morning Joha got up, went to the front door, kissed the *mezuzah,** and said: "Ah, Lord of the Universe, give me one hundred gold liras! If you give me ninety-nine, I won't accept them!"

The upstairs neighbor heard him repeat this one day, two, three, five, ten.

One day he said: "Let us test Joha. We will see what he will do."

He went and put ninety-nine liras in a purse, and he threw it near Joha just as the latter was coming out in the morning.

Joha saw the purse, opened it, counted: One, two, three, fifty, seventy, ninety-nine! Ah," he said. "Merciful God, this time I forgive you, but next time I will not forgive you!" And he took the purse and put it in his pocket.

The rich man said: "Ay! He has put me in his pocket!"

NARRATED BY SHMUEL BARKI – 1992

* a decorative case attached to a doorpost containing verses from Deuteronomy

The Divine Opinion

Joha went to the market and there he saw three Arabs quarreling.

He said to them: "Why are you quarreling?"

They said to him: "Because we have seven camels and we want to divide them among three, and we don't know how to divide them."

Said Joha: "Listen, do you want me to divide them for you?"

"Yes!"

"According to the divine opinion, or according to the human opinion?"

"According to the divine opinion, naturally!"

"All right!" said Joha, and he gave two camels to one of them, one to another, and nothing to the third.

The rest he took for himself.

"But what are you doing?!!" the Arabs said to him.

"Excuse me!" said Joha. "One man has billions and doesn't know where to put them. Another has barely enough to exist. A third one has nothing. This is the division that the Lord of the Universe made!"

NARRATED BY MARIA BAHBOUT – 1988

Easier for God!

Joha is very honored in this story.

When he went out into the street, everyone paid him great respect.

One day he was walking in the street, and a man came up to him and said: "Joha, come quickly! I want you to give me a blessing: Ask that I should get well, because I am very sick!"

Joha said: "Tell me what you have."

Said the man: "Don't ask! I have headache, stomachache. I have pain . . . like stabbings in the head. My shoulder is bad. I can't bend over. My blood is not good. . . ."

Joha said: "Enough! Enough! Don't tell me anything else that is wrong with you. With all the ailments that you have, if I ask the Almighty to make you well, it will be easier for Him to make someone new!"

NARRATED BY LEVANA SASSON – 1999

Joha's Minyan

During the First World War Joha was at the front, fighting with the British forces against their enemies.

On Friday evenings the religious soldiers had difficulty forming a *minyan.**

Joha took it upon himself to form one and succeeded remarkably well.

When asked how he succeeded in forming a *minyan* every Friday evening, he replied: "It's very simple! I approach the enemy camp and I cry out, '*Minyan!*' In a second, all the Jews there cross the lines and follow me!"

NARRATED BY SARA YOHAY – 1996

* quorum of ten men for prayer

Everyone to His Own System

One day Joha was walking in the square—it was a delightful sunny day—when suddenly he heard a voice calling to him: "Joha, Joha, Joha!"

Joha, hearing this voice, turned around this way, that way, and saw the rabbi bent over double, one hand holding the wall and the other over his stomach.

Joha approached with great concern and said: "Señor Rabbi, what's the matter?"

"Ah, Joha," the rabbi said to him. "Don't ask!"

"What's wrong, Señor Rabbi?"

"Oh," the rabbi said to him, "you see me well dressed because I have been invited to the sultan. A great feast is taking place there, but I am not going. I have a very bad stomach pain!"

"So what are you going to do?" Joha asked him.

"Look," the rabbi said to him, "come and let us exchange clothes, and you will go there, as if you were the rabbi."

"All right!" said Joha. "If the rabbi so wishes, then I also wish it."

They went to a place where there weren't many passersby, and they exchanged clothes.

From the moment Joha put on the clothes of the rabbi, he already believed that he was the greatest rabbi in the world. He went, arrived at the palace, and they received him there with great ceremony.

In the middle of the feast, after they all had eaten and drunk, the sultan called one of his ministers. He said: "Look, I want you to bring to me in a separate room the rabbi, the Protestant and Catholic priests, and the Muslim cleric, the *hoja*. I want to speak to them."

"With great pleasure!" The minister went and called the representatives of the four religions, and gathered them in a room.

Shortly afterward, the sultan arrived. They all stood up and bowed.

The sultan said to the waiter: "Bring coffee, bring baklava . . . cakes." And they were conversing, drinking coffee.

The sultan said: "Look, if I called all four of you here, it is only out of curiosity. For a long time I have wanted to know something, and I have no answer for it. Only you can give me the answer."

They were all waiting to hear what the sultan would ask.

"Look, I already know," he said, "that the monthly salary you receive is not a sufficient salary, but it is all that we can give. More than that we cannot give. I want to know how you manage to subsist for the entire month." First he addressed the *hoja*.

The *hoja* said: "Lord Sultan, when I had two children, this salary was more than sufficient for me, and I could also save. Now God has given me six children." He said, "With six . . . one must buy schoolbooks . . . food . . . clothing." He said, "It is not sufficient for me."

"Aha, and how do you manage, then?" the sultan asked.

"In every kind of mosque, church, or synagogue, following the afternoon prayers, the faithful throw a few *grush** into a box. This is for charity. Then," he said, "what do I do? When I collect the money, I count what there is and take for myself fifteen to twenty percent, in order to manage the month. Otherwise, I could not live."

"And you?" the sultan asked the Protestant priest.

Said the priest: "Lord Sultan, I have eight children, and with the great economies that I make, I still cannot finish the month. And I also do the same thing as the *hoja*, although the salary that I take is a very just salary."

"All right!" said the sultan. "And you, Señor Clergyman, what do you do?"

* one cent

"I," said the Catholic priest, "as the sultan well knows, receive payment directly from Rome. I am unmarried, I have no children, I don't need clothes," he said. "They give me everything from Rome." He said, "But I have one or two small vices; I like to smoke and to drink a bottle of *raki* from time to time. Then I take a few *grush* to buy these things."

Joha was listening to all of this. What would he say, what would he tell, he who was unmarried, who didn't smoke, who didn't drink?

"And you, what do you say?" the sultan asked.

Joha stood up and said: "Lord Sultan, with the greatest respect I will tell you that I also have the same problem as the *hoja* and the Protestant and Catholic priests. The monthly salary we are given does not suffice me. I have, God be praised, ten children at home. I can give them neither food, clothing, nor schooling."

"Then how much do you take?" the sultan asked him.

"I," said Joha, "don't decide." He said, "He who decides is the Lord of the Universe. I take all the money, put it on a board, I climb to the roof, I look up at Heaven, I shake the board, and I say: 'Lord of the Universe, take what you wish and leave me the remainder.' And thus," he said, "I spend my life happy and content."

The sultan said: "Bravo, bravo! I am happy that each of you is talking with such honesty. I thank you very much, gentlemen," he said. "May God grant health and long life to all of you."

NARRATED BY ISSAHAR AVZARADEL – 1992

Incorrigible

One day Joha wanted to go to the market to buy a donkey. On the way, a friend of his saw him.

The friend said: "Where are you going, Joha?"

Joha replied: "I am going to buy a donkey."

It was market day—Wednesday.

His friend said: "Joha, say: 'God willing, I am going to buy a donkey'!"

Joha answered: "Whether God wills it or not, the donkey is at the market and the money is in my pocket, and I am going to buy the donkey!"

Joha arrived at the market. There were lots of people there, and they were all shouting: "Buy tomatoes!" "Buy lettuce!"

Joha saw a donkey that pleased him. He went over to the salesman and asked how much it cost. The salesman told him the price.

When Joha went to take the money from his purse, ouch! He saw that the money was no longer there!

He returned shamefacedly to his village. On the way he again met his friend.

The friend asked: "Joha, did you buy the donkey?"

Joha answered: "God willed it that they robbed me of my money, and I couldn't buy it!"

NARRATED BY KOHAVA PIVIS – 1994

Only One

It was Yom Kippur, the Day of Atonement, in the synagogue, at the time of the *Neila* concluding prayer. Everyone got up and said: "*Hashem Eloheinu, Hashem Echad!*" "The Lord our God, the Lord is One!"

Joha, who was standing there with all the rest, instead of "*Echad,*"* said "*Acher.*"†

The man next to him heard this. He immediately went to the *hacham* and said: "Rabbi, my neighbor is saying '*Acher*' instead of '*Echad*'!"

The *hacham* called Joha at once and asked: "Tell me, my son, what did you say, '*Echad*' or '*Acher*'?"

"'*Acher,*'" said Joha.

"No, my son," the *hacham* said. "We say '*Echad*'! There is only One God and no other!"

"Fine!" said Joha and went home, repeating to himself, "*Echad! Echad! Echad!*"

Suddenly, he forgot. He ran back to the synagogue, met the *hacham*, and said: "Señor Hacham, what was it you told me to say: '*Echad*' or '*Acher*'?"

"'*Echad'! 'Echad'!* I told you. There is only One God!" the *hacham* said to him.

"Fine!" said Joha, and went off, repeating in a low voice: "*Echad! Echad!*" But barely did he get home when he again forgot.

"Goodness me!" he said. "How does one say it: '*Echad*' or '*Acher*'?"

He again ran to the synagogue and looked for the *hacham*, but they told him that the *hacham* was an emissary, come from far away, and that he had left for Jaffa, to return to his place.

* One
† Other

Joha, in desperation, mounted a horse and rode the whole night long, so that he would finally reach Jaffa before the ship left that was taking the *hacham* back home.

The next morning, almost breathless, he reached Jaffa and asked where the Señor Hacham was.

They told him: "The Señor Hacham has already left! Look, the ship is already out at sea."

Without further ado, Joha began running toward the ship, running and running. He began to walk across the water. He reached the ship, saw the *hacham* on the bridge, and shouted to him: "Señor Hacham, Señor Hacham, tell me. How does one say it: '*Echad*' or '*Acher*'?"

"Ah, my son," the *hacham* said to him. "What does it matter, '*Echad*' or '*Acher*'? When one says it with a heart pure like yours, God lets you walk on the waters!"

NARRATED BY MATILDA KOEN-SARANO – 1999

Saving Souls

Joha had a donkey that he used for work. It carried everything from place to place. It did everything for him and was like a friend to him.

Joha didn't care whether he was a Jew or not, and he worked the whole week, including the Sabbath. One Sabbath, as they were walking down the street, they passed by a pit. The donkey fell into the pit. Joha went to a neighbor and said: "Give me a rope, so that we can pull the donkey out."

The neighbor said: "Excuse me! Today is the Sabbath. I cannot give you ropes. If you wish, go and ask the rabbi."

Joha went to Señor Hacham and told him everything: "The donkey is in the pit. We must pull him out!"

The *hacham* said: "No! It cannot be. It is the Sabbath!"

Joha said: "Señor Hacham! It is your donkey!"

"Get him out, get him out at once!" the *hacham* said. "It is a matter of saving a life!"

NARRATED BY SIMA BABANI – 1999

A Good Shamash!

Joha was made a *shamash*.* He had to check if anyone entered the syngagogue without having first reserved a seat during the Yom Kippur prayer service.

A man entered in the middle of the prayers.

Immediately, Joha accosted him: "Come here. Do you have a reserved seat?"

"Me? No."

"Then, out! Only someone with a reserved seat enters here."

"Look, I only want to have a word with my son-in-law."

"How long will you be staying?"

"Five minutes, no more."

"Very well, and then leave immediately. Do you hear?"

"Yes, yes, I will leave right away."

"Just make sure that I don't catch you praying!"

NARRATED BY BEKI BARDAVID – 2000

* a synagogue caretaker

Breaking the Fast

A friend asked Joha during the afternoon of Yom Kippur: "Joha, with what do you break the fast?"

"With ten olives"

"Don't you mean with one olive?"

"What do you mean? With ten olives!"

"When you eat the first, you are no longer fasting."

"Yes, it seems that you are right!" said Joha, and right away ran to a neighbor.

"As you live, Solomon, how do you break the fast?"

"With five olives."

"Ah!" said Joha to himself. "If he had said ten, I would have been able to make fun of him. What a shame!"

NARRATED BY BEKI BARDAVID – 2000

Religiosity

Once, when Joha got on the nerves of the entire world, the government threw him into the dungeon of a lunatic asylum.

One Sabbath day, Joha asked his guard to bring him kosher food.

He brought it for him. He ate, said the *Birkat Hamazon,** and then began to smoke.

The guard said to him: "Why did I bring you kosher food, if you are desecrating your Sabbath?"

"Señor! I am crazy!" Joha said to him, indignantly.

NARRATED BY ELIEZER PAPO – 2000

* Grace after meals

CHAPTER 12

JOHA and the law

*"Don't blame the thief,
blame the one who leaves the door open."*

"Joha, Pull the Door!"

You should know that this stupid Joha was always doing bad things, without knowing that they were bad.

Joha's mother was ill and was lying in bed. Joha wanted to go out for a walk.

His mother said: "Look, Joha, when you go out, pull the door," thinking that he was only going to give it a push to shut it.

But instead Joha pulled it . . . took it off its hinges and put it on his shoulders. Well, then he carried it off, and thieves entered the house and emptied the whole of it.

They didn't leave a thing behind. They took all the jewelry, all the rings that Joha's mother had, and a little money. They stuffed everything in a sack and ran off.

The house remained without a door.

That stupid Joha went off with the door on his shoulders and walked and walked . . . and came to a wood.

Just as he got there, night fell. He wanted to return home, but he couldn't see the road. He still had the door on his shoulders. Everything grew dark, and he remained there.

He climbed up a tree, placed the door on the branches, and thought he would go to sleep. He said: "Early in the morning I will wake with the birds and return home. What else can I do?"

Now, on this tree there were nuts. Every few minutes Joha took a nut, cracked it, and ate it, to pass the time.

As he was about to fall asleep, he suddenly heard people walking about down below.

"Good God!" he said. "What is this?"

Those who were sitting under the tree were talking: "This is for me . . . This is for you . . . This is for me . . . This is for you." They were sharing things among themselves.

Joha cast a glance, saw that they were holding a small lantern, and saw that they were dividing up the money, the jewelry, and the gems from his house.

He said: "Good God, what have I fallen into?" And without noticing it, he had spoken in a loud voice.

Hearing his voice, the thieves said: "What is this? Can it be that there is a *jinn** who is listening? . . . Woe to us!"

Joha was frightened and began to throw nuts on the thieves' heads.

They said: "Woe to us! Who knows! Perhaps there is a lion, a devil, a demon there?"

When Joha moved about, the branches and the door broke, and the door fell on the heads of the thieves.

Joha, from fear, clung to the tree, and the thieves ran away, running, running, running like madmen, so that this devil, this demon should not grab them.

Well, then, Joha began to climb down from the tree very slowly and cautiously, and under the door, he found the little lantern the thieves had brought with them.

He took the lantern and saw there money and jewels and all manner of fine things. He collected everything, put it in one big pot, and tied it all up well.

He said: "Son of a *mamzer*! Now I have the little light, I will begin to walk. Perhaps I will be able to get out of this wood."

He began to walk, carrying the door with one hand and, with the other, all the valuables.

And what should I tell you, to cut a long story short?

Walking, walking . . . the dawn came. And when the birds began to fly and sing, at the time of the morning prayer, Joha arrived home and saw his mother standing in the doorless doorway, crying, "Everything is gone!"

Joha said to her: "Look, Mother, I have brought you the door. Take it! And take this as well!"

* Arabic for "evil spirit"

His mother saw all the riches—because the thieves had robbed the whole neighborhood—and said: "This is not mine! *Ya, haboub,** this is not mine!"

Joha said to her: "Look, Mother, I brought everything I found there. Take it, and may you only enjoy good things, God be praised!"

He put the door back in its place. "But, Mother, next time, please don't tell me: 'Pull the door!' Say to me only: 'Close the door!'"

NARRATED BY HAYIM TSUR – 1996

How to Bring Food Home

Joha was not born to be a worker. Still, he had to bring food home. One night he decided that, early the next morning, before the birds woke up, he would do something.

No sooner thought than done. And really, before the birds woke up, he entered a garden with a sack this big and filled it with all manner of good things he could find, with cucumbers, tomatoes, vegetables, and fruit.

As he was about to put the sack on his shoulder, a guard accosted him. And what a guard! Six and a half feet tall, with the face of an assassin and bulging eyes as big as eggs.

Joha's legs trembled; his bowels turned to water.

The guard stood in front of him and said: "What are you doing here?"

And Joha replied: "I'm not doing anything! Do you remember how, two days ago, there was that strong wind? The wind lifted me up and and threw me here!"

* "No, my friend"

"All right," said the guard, "maybe it is as you say. Tell me who picked all these things." He pointed to the sack, which was now completely full.

Joha feigned amazement: "Do you remember how strong the wind was? So when it threw me this way and that, I caught hold of one thing after another. And so they were picked."

"All right," said the guard, "supposing that this was the case, who put them inside the sack?"

And Joha would not have been the Joha we know had he not answered thus: "You are right to ask that question, Señor Guard. And I am standing here and watching and marveling . . . " and his voice was full of sweetness. His eyes were like those of a child. And walking slowly, ever so slowly without turning his head, he made for the exit.

"Hey!" cried the guard laughing. "Take your sack! You earned it!"

NARRATED BY SARA YOHAY – 1992

A Noisy Blanket

One very cold winter's night, Joha's wife woke up, hearing shouting and talking in the street. She woke up Joha and told him to go and see what the shouts in the street were about.

Joha was cold. He didn't want to get out of bed.

He said: "Let them shout there! They will grow tired of it and will go away!"

But his wife grew insistent because she could not get to sleep.

Finally, Joha got up. He wrapped the blanket around his shoulders and went out.

After a few minutes—the street was already quiet—Joha returned and said innocently to his wife: "You know what all the shouting and noise was about? It was our blanket! When they took it, everything became quiet!"

NARRATED BY SHABETAY HAKIM – 1992

What a Shame!

Joha was very poor and very cowardly.

One day he was sitting at home by himself. Suddenly, there was a noise. Thieves were entering the house.

Oh my God, he surely was going to die! What could he do? What could he do?

Quickly he ran upstairs and hid in the cupboard.

The thieves, after taking all there was downstairs, climbed upstairs. And what was the first thing they did? They opened the cupboard and saw Joha there.

They said: "What are you doing here?"

"I am ashamed that you didn't find anything downstairs. Out of shame I came up here and got into the cupboard!"

NARRATED BY ESTER LEVY – 1999

The Lucky Shirt

Once Joha hung up his shirt. Then thieves came and fired at his shirt and made bullet holes in it.

When he got up in the morning, Joha said: "What good fortune! Had I been inside the shirt, they would have killed me!"

NARRATED BY ITZHAK SIMHA – 1987

Whose Fault?

One night a thief came to Joha's house and took everything of value that was in it.

Suddenly, Joha began to shout: "Thief! There is a thief here! A thief here! A thief!"

Joha's neighbors came and said: "Hey, Joha, you didn't attach an iron door!"

"You didn't put a barbed wire fence in front of your house."

"You should have put iron bars on the windows."

"You didn't put in anything!"

"You are right, I agree," said Joha. "It is all my fault! The thief is not to blame, is he?"

Narrated by JAK ASAYAS – 1996

Fifty-Fifty

Thieves entered Joha's house.

Joha already knew that he was poor and had nothing in the house.

The thieves were searching very slowly.

Joha got out of bed and started to search behind them, slowly, slowly.

When they reached the corners, he said: "Look, if you find something . . . fifty-fifty!"

Narrated by KOHAVA PIVIS – 1997

Sweet Revenge

Joha was living in a neighborhood where there was a policeman who was always starting something with him. Whenever he saw Joha, he would say: "Joha, don't stand here! Joha, go over there! Joha, what are you doing?"

Joha would say to himself: "What am I going to do to this fellow, so he shouldn't talk to me this way again?"

One day he got up early in the morning and said to his wife: "I am going off to work." He didn't eat at home because his wife was still in bed. He said: "I'll go and eat at the market."

Joha went off. All the shops were closed. But Joha wanted to eat, and then he saw that the soupmaker's shop was open. Joha said: "I'll go in there."

He entered: "Shalom, shalom!"

The man said to him: "Oh, shalom, shalom! How are you? What are you doing at such an hour?"

Joha said to him: "I have a bit of work. I'm going to work. I'm hungry; I came to eat."

The man, who already knew Joha, said to himself: "At such an hour there is no food. I have a little soup left over from yesterday. I will give it to Joha."

He said: "Joha, I have soup. Do you want it?"

Said Joha: "All right!" and the man poured out the soup for him.

Joha ate and left. He began to walk, to walk, to walk, but could not stop . . . his insides were churning over . . . the soup had given him diarrhea.

Now, there were no toilets; there was nothing there. He said: "What am I going to do?" There was no alternative. He lifted up his garment, sat down in the middle of the street, and as he was sitting, who should he see? The policeman, coming his way!

"Ugh!" he said. "Now he is going to say to me: 'Get up!' He will see the dirt on the ground and will give me a fine. What am

I going to do? What am I going to do?"

Before the policeman reached him, what did Joha do? He took off the cap he had on his head and put it over the dirt and held it there.

The policeman came and said: "Joha, what are you doing?"

"Ah! Don't speak to me now!" Joha said to him.

"Why?"

"My wife got up in the morning to feed the birds, and the bird escaped from the cage. Now I have caught it here . . . and I can't leave it. If I lift the cap, it will fly away. Now I have to bring the cage here."

The policeman said: "You know what? I'll stand here and hold it, and you go and bring the cage from home."

"Fine!" said Joha, and let go of the cap.

The policeman put his hand over the cap and waited for Joha to return with the cage, to put the bird in it.

He waited half an hour, one, two hours. . . . Joha didn't come. Finally, he said: "And I will go home also. . . . Now I will show Joha. I'll take the bird and won't give it back to him."

Slowly, slowly, ever so slowly, he lifted the cap, so that the bird should not escape, put his hand there . . . and drew it out. "Oy!" he said. "From now on I shall leave Joha in peace!"

Narrated by SHMUEL BARKI – 1992

Stamp of Servitude

There were 40 thieves who liked to make Joha angry and make fun of him. Joha's mother had a little hen. One day the thieves stole the hen and fried it and ate it, each one taking a piece.

And they said to Joha: "Here is your hen, look!"

Joha said to them: "Now I will buy a sheep. I want to see how you eat it!"

He bought a small sheep, brought it home, and let it grow big.

A week later, the thieves stole it.

"Look, Joha!" they said to him, licking their fingers. "We are eating a piece each!" They said, "If you should die, we will come and defecate on your grave!"

Said Joha: "Fine!"

He said to his mother, "Look, I am going to buy a stamp. I will pretend that I am dead. Make me a small window in the grave. When they come to defecate, I will show them!"

"Very well!" said his mother.

Joha pretended to be dead. His mother wept. The gravediggers came; Joha's mother gave them money to leave the little window open. Joha took the stamp.

The thieves came, saw that the gravediggers had buried him, and said: "We will defecate on his grave." One came and defecated. Joha stamped him on his behind with the stamp. He did the same for the second one. He said: "Just as they made me eat it, now let them eat it!" And he stamped the behinds of each of the 40 thieves, but none of them told the other.

Joha rose from the dead and said: "I did not die! Now I will show the lot of you!"

He went to the *kadi* and said: "Those forty thieves were servants of my father."

"Your father's servants?!"

"Yes!" he said. "They were my father's servants!"

"Have you got proof of it?"

"Look," said Joha, "take down their breeches and make them all stand there. Look on the behind of each of them!"

They all had the stamp on their behind.

The *kadi* came and said: "You are the servants of Joha!"

Joha took them as his servants. He made them work in the garden. He would give them beatings: "Work in the garden! You are my servants! Didn't you eat the hen? Didn't you eat the sheep?"

Joha was the victor.

NARRATED BY REBEKA COHEN-ARIEL – 1989

Heavenly Cake

The story goes like this: There were three thieves who, one night, stole a big cake from a shop. The three of them ran off with the cake and sat down to eat it.

As they were about to cut it, one of them suggested: "Why should we cut it? Instead let's give it to the one who tells the story with the biggest lie in it."

"All right!" said the others.

And when were they going to tell these stories? They said: "Tomorrow morning, when we wake up, each one of us will tell the biggest lie he can."

One of them was a Christian, one was a Muslim, and the third, Joha, was a Jew.

They got up in the morning and the Christian told his story: "I dreamed that holy Jesus came to me and invited me to sit in a chair beside him in the Seventh Heaven. And I went up and had the honor of spending the entire night sitting next to holy Jesus!"

The Muslim said: "It appears that we were not far from one another, because I dreamed that Mohammed said to me: 'You will come to me at the Eighth Heaven.' And so I spent the entire night with Mohammed, and I spent it sitting beside him with great honor!"

Said Joha: "And I dreamed that an old and very simple man came and said to me: 'Listen Joha, seeing that your Christian friend is sitting in the Seventh Heaven, and that your Muslim friend is sitting in the Eighth Heaven, I suggest to you that you should eat the cake, because neither of them will return from there!' So I got up in the middle of the night and ate the cake, and now there is no more of it!"

NARRATED BY HAYIM ARZI – 1992

What a Watermelon!

Joha was very poor. He had nothing. Life was hard.

One day he said: "I will divert a channel of water from the river so that it passes by my house, and then I will be able to grow vegetables in my garden."

The government only allocated to each person a little bit of water, but Joha didn't listen. He took his mattock and began digging, digging. Suddenly, he found a box.

He took it home, put it on the table, opened it and saw—gold!

Suddenly, his neighbor entered and said: "Oh! What is this? Gold? I want half of it!"

"But . . . I haven't counted it yet!" Joha said to him.

"If that is so," said the neighbor, "then I want two thirds! If not, I will go to the sultan and denounce you, and you will be punished!"

"All right, all right!" Joha said. "Maybe you are right, but wait a bit. I will bring a watermelon from the kitchen. We will eat watermelon, and afterward we will divide up the treasure."

Joha went into the kitchen, opened a watermelon, took out all its insides, threw it away, and filled the green watermelon with *kubbe*. He closed up the watermelon and came back into the room with it. He cut it open, and suddenly the watermelon was full of *kubbe*.

The neighbor marveled at this and said to him: "How can it be? This is a watermelon!"

Joha said: "But it is full of *kubbe*. What do you care? Eat *kubbe*!" They both ate.

Joha took a stick and said to the neighbor: "Get out! Neither a half, nor a third, nothing! Go to the sultan if you wish!"

The neighbor went to the sultan and denounced Joha.

The sultan sent for Joha. He said to him: "I heard that you found gold!"

Joha said: "Who told you so?"

"I heard it from this man," the sultan said.

Joha said to him in his ear: "My Lord Sultan, he will tell you that inside the watermelon we found *kubbe*. Ask him, and you will see!"

"Tell me," said the sultan to the neighbor, "what did you find inside the watermelon, when you opened it?"

"Kubbe!" said the neighbor.

Joha said: "Do you see, Lord Sultan? This one is a little crazy! Just as he said he found *kubbe* inside the watermelon, so did he say that I found gold in a box!"

NARRATED BY ALEX KORFIATIS – 1993

Born Unlucky

Joha was not rich—he was poor—he worked by day and ate at night. One day he received a letter saying that in such and such village he had an uncle. This uncle had died, and he had been left an inheritance.

Said Joha: "My luck has changed! I will go and see." And he got up and went.

They said to him: "Yes, here is everything that belonged to your uncle. It is yours."

Joha took the money, returned home, and bought a big building. He had two friends; he married them off. He bought clothes for the family. He did everything. He bought fine clothes for himself and every day went out beautifully dressed.

One day a neighbor met him and said: "Joha, everything you have done is very good. You have already bought everything for yourself and your family, but you haven't bought yourself a pair of shoes."

Joha said: "You are right, but these shoes are very comfortable on me."

"But it doesn't add up," the neighbor said. "It's not smart. . . . You are so well dressed. Buy yourself some new shoes."

So Joha got up, went to the shop, and bought himself a new pair of shoes. They were rather tight on him, but there was no alternative. In the end, he would have to get used to them. He put them on.

Now, what he had been wearing before was a pair of sandals. He took the sandals and carried them home.

"Now," he said, "what am I to do with these sandals?"

He thought, thought, thought. "What will I do now?" he said. "Now I will go to the baths. I am wearing my new shoes. I will take my sandals as well, leave the sandals there, and come back home."

Joha went to the baths, soaped himself, washed, put on the new shoes, and came home.

The next morning . . . knock, knock at the door: "What is it?"

"Listen, Joha," said one man. "You forgot your sandals at the baths. Look, I have brought them for you."

Joha now thought, thought, thought what to do. He took them and threw them in the river.

"Now," he said "I have got rid of them!" He came home.

The next morning: knock, knock on the door. Who is it? The

fishermen. They said: "You threw these sandals away. Our net slipped! We didn't catch a single fish!"

They gave him back the sandals. But they were soaking wet.

Joha put them on the balcony to dry. His dog came and playing, playing, threw the sandals down into the street, where they split the head of a passing woman.

She came upstairs, shouting: "Joha, what did you do? Look what happened to my head!"

Joha said: "Take some money, be quiet, and go away! (He had a lot of money now.) The woman went away.

Finally, Joha said: "These sandals are not going to remain here. I have already decided what to do." He said, "When night falls, I will dig a pit in the field opposite; I will bury them, and that will be the end of it."

When it was nighttime, he saw that there were no people around. He went and dug a pit, put the sandals in it, and returned home.

The next morning—police! "Joha," they said, "at night you went and dug in the field. The government treasure is buried there—all the money of the government. You took it!"

"I took it?" said Joha. "What are you talking about!"

"Yes . . . No . . ." They were going to try him!

He was put on trial. They said: "Look, he is the one who stole all the money of the government!"

"I stole?" said Joha. "Now I will tell you what happened." He said, "I received a big inheritance. And so I tried to get rid of the sandals, and I went and buried them."

"A likely tale," the judge said to him. "You stole everything!"

They went to his home, took away all the money from the inheritance, and he was left penniless.

NARRATED BY ESTER VENTURA – 1993

"Two Grush for You!"

Joha was walking through the market, smelling the *shashlik** and the kebabs. Since he did not have a *grush* in his pocket, he contented himself with smelling.

Suddenly, a person he didn't know approached him and hit him in the face.

Joha felt himself falling and saw stars, in the middle of the day. He didn't know how he managed to get to his feet! He seized the one who had hit him and said: "You villain! Idiot! You scum! What did I do to you? Son of a donkey, why did you hit me?"

"I beg your forgiveness!" said the unknown man. "I made a mistake! I took you for someone else!"

Joha was not convinced. He brought him before the *kadi*. The *kadi* listened to Joha but looked at the other man, and what did he see? The other man was making gestures to him and pointing to his pocket, where he had his money.

The *kadi* understood that he could expect *bakshish*† and said to Joha: "The man was mistaken! He will pay you two *grush,* and so he will compensate you." And he gave the unknown man permission to go and get the money.

Joha waited for an hour and then realized that a trick had been played on him by the *kadi* and by the one who had hit him. He approached the *kadi,* lifted his hand, and hit him in the face. And as the *kadi* was coming to his senses, after seeing stars in the middle of the day, Joha said to him: "I have no more time to wait: When that man brings the two *grush*, *you* take them!"

NARRATED BY SARA YOHAY – 1991

* roasted meat

† a bribe

Caught by a Coat

Joha had no money. So he took out loans. He did this for one month, two, three. Finally, the moneylender said: "Give me back the money!"

"Very well! Next month I will give you back the money!"

The month passed. Joha didn't give the money back. Another month passed, and the moneylender said to him: "You don't want to give me back my money? Then come before the judge."

"But I can't go!" said Joha.

"Why not?"

"Because it is very cold and wet. I don't have a coat. I can't go!"

"I will give you my coat!"

They went to the court. During the trial the judge said to Joha: "What do you have to say?"

"This man is mad! He doesn't know what he is talking about! Ask him whose coat this is. He will tell you that it is his."

The judge asked the moneylender: "Whose is the coat Joha is wearing?"

He said: "It is mine!"

"You see!" Joha said to the judge. "Everything that is not his, he says is his! Can you see that it is all lies?"

And so they acquitted Joha.

NARRATED BY LEA COHEN – 1990

Piece by Piece

Joha was in prison. One day he asked to see the warden.

"What is it, Joha?" the warden said to him. "What have you come to ask?"

"Don't ask, Señor Warden! I cannot breathe!"

"Well, let them take you to the infirmary." And they took Joha to the infirmary.

"You will need a nose operation. We will make an appointment for you." And Joha had the operation to remove his adenoids.

Shortly afterward, Joha again asked to see the prison doctor.

The doctor told him that he would need an operation on his tonsils. And they removed his tonsils, and he recuperated.

Barely a month passed, and Joha was writhing in pain.

They carried him to the infirmary at once. Joha had appendicitis. He had an infection, and they took out his appendix the very same day.

In the end, the warden came and said to him: "Listen, Joha, if you think that you will leave the prison piece by piece, you are very much mistaken. There will be no more operations, even if you burst! Do you hear?"

NARRATED BY BEKI BARDAVID – 2000

Planting Camels

Joha was walking through the market when he stopped in front of a stall selling many varieties of seeds: for roses, for fruits and vegetables, for mint and watercress.

He was looking about when suddenly he saw a small pile of large balls . . . dry and yellow. He asked the vendor: "What is this?"

The vendor said: "They are camel seeds!"

"Camel seeds!" said Joha. "Is it possible?"

"Certainly, Señor Joha!" said the vendor, who had already recognized him.

"How much are they?" Joha asked.

"Each one half a ducat, a special price for you!" the vendor said. "To anyone else, I sell them for double the price!"

"All right!" said Joha. "Give me thirty. But you assure me that they will grow into camels?"

"Absolutely, Señor Joha! Trust me!!" said the vendor, giving him the seeds and taking the ducats.

Joha went home, went into the garden, prepared the ground, and planted the camel seeds. And every day he went into the garden to see if camels were sprouting from the earth. One morning he went into the garden and saw that thirty little green leaves had sprouted.

"Ah!" he said. "That son of a *mamzer* of a vendor has cheated me!"

He left everything and ran straight to the market, looked for the seed vendor, and seized him by the collar. He shouted: "You have cheated me! What camels? Green leaves are sprouting!"

The vendor said to him, calmly: "But Señor Joha, you have no patience! This is how the camels begin to sprout. The green leaves are the ears of the camels, which emerge first."

"Really?" Joha said.

"As I do live!" the vendor said. "Would I deceive a gentleman like yourself?"

"Very well, very well!" said Joha, and he left to go home.

As he arrived there, he saw that his garden was full of camels.

He entered the garden and saw thirty camels, fat, beautiful, with bells at their throats.

"Ah!" said Joha, full of joy. "And so it is true! They have already grown for me!"

He took the camels, put them in his stable, and locked the door.

But those camels had an owner. They belonged to a caravan master who was passing that way. He had seen the little leaves in

Joha's garden and said: "I will put my camels here, so that they should eat the grass, and I will go to the café to drink a carafe of *raki.*"

When the caravan master came out of the café and went to collect his camels, he saw that they were no longer there. He asked around, here and there, and they told him that it was Joha who had stolen his camels.

The caravan master knocked on Joha's door.

Joha came out and said: "What do you want?"

The man said: "Give me back my camels!"

"Your camels!" Joha said. "Those camels are mine! I planted them, and they grew for me!"

"Are you crazy?" the caravan master said. "You planted them? . . . You stole them from me! Give me them back to me, right away!"

"No!"

"Yes!"

The two of them began to quarrel, and the neighbors brought them before the judge.

Each of them gave his version of events to the judge.

The caravan master said: "I passed by the garden of this man, I saw green leaves, I left my camels there to eat the leaves, and I went to the café. When I returned, the camels were no longer there. This man stole them from me!"

Said Joha: "I bought thirty camel seeds. I planted them, and the camels grew for me. They are my camels! . . . They are mine! . . . They are mine!"

As he said, "They are mine!" Joha banged his hands on his chest.

It appeared to the judge that Joha was giving him a signal, indicating that he had a wallet full of money on his person, which he would give to the judge if he said that the camels were Joha's.

The judge said: "The question is clear. This man bought

thirty camel seeds, planted them in his garden, and thirty camels grew for him. The camels are his!"

And so they sent the caravan master away without his camels, and the camels remained with Joha.

After a while, the judge, who was expecting that Joha would bring him what he had promised, decided to go to Joha himself.

He knocked on the door, and Joha opened it and said: "Good day! To what do I owe this honor?"

The judge said: "I came to take what you promised me during the trial about the camels. . . ."

"What do you mean, 'promised' you?"

"What, don't you remember?" the judge said. "You gave me a signal—beating your chest with your hand—to indicate to me that you had a wallet full of money there, which you would give to me if I said the camels were yours."

"No!" Joha said. "I was giving you a signal to make you understand that I had a big stone there, to break your head if you did not say that the camels were mine. And look, I have the stone right here!"

The judge was so frightened that he took to his heels, and as far as we know, he is still running.

NARRATED BY MATILDA KOEN-SARANO – 1997

All Right!

Joha was the judge in his village. One night he was at home when two neighbors who had been quarreling came to ask him to say which of them was right.

Said Joha: "I will have to listen to each one of you separately."

The first neighbor came in and told Joha the whole of the case from his point of view.

Joha said to him: "You are right!"

The first neighbor left, and the second neighbor came in and gave his version of events.

Joha listened to him attentively and said: "You are also right!"

At that moment Joha's wife, who had been listening, came out of the kitchen. "But, Joha, how is it possible that both of them are right?"

"And you are also right!" Joha said to her.

NARRATED BY MATILDA KOEN-SARANO – 1993

The Cross-Eyed Judge

Joha was a judge, and he was cross-eyed. They brought three witnesses before him.

He asked the first: "What is your name?"

The second one answered: "Moshe!"

Joha said to him: "I didn't ask you anything!"

The third one said: "I didn't say anything!"

NARRATED BY ESTER GONEN – 1995

Small Consolation!

There was a young man who was very, very poor. He stopped one evening in front of a chestnut vendor. The smell was overpowering . . . his soul was ready to leave him. But he didn't have the money to buy.

He just stood there, stood there . . . and one came and bought, then another.

The vendor came and said to the poor young man: "Aha! You are not buying, but the smell is consoling you. You must pay me right away!"

They quarreled and then went before the judge, who was Joha.

Joha took a lira in his hand and said to the vendor: "Look, he was consoled by the smell, and you, now then, look, look, look . . . be consoled by the sight of the lira he should have given you!"

NARRATED BY ESTER LEVY – 1987

The Case of the Hard-Boiled Eggs

A young fellow got up one morning and decided to set out from his village to the city, in order to get to know the country. When night fell, he saw a light in the distance. He drew near and found himself in front of an inn.

The innkeeper welcomed him and seemed to be a very amiable man. He set the table and served him a roast chicken and two hard-boiled eggs.

"Please," the innkeeper said to the customer, "eat, drink, and sleep here. The hyenas come out at night, and it is dangerous to be out on the road."

And so he did stay at the inn. In the morning the young fellow took out money from his pocket to pay, but the innkeeeper said to him with a voice full of sweetness: "Don't you worry now. Take it easy. When you return safely, come by here and give me the money."

Marveling at meeting such a good-hearted man, the young fellow bade him farewell and set out, deeply moved.

Two months passed, and the young fellow returned to the inn. He entered and said: "Señor innkeeper, now make up my bill. I wish to pay my debt."

"Look, young man," said the innkeeper, "the debt is a bit complicated. Come now, let me see. . . . Give me two hundred *grush,* and we will clear your debt."

"For goodness sake!" cried the young man, beating his forehead. "For one chicken and two eggs . . . two hundred *grush?*"

"It's like this," said the innkeeper. "A hen lays one egg each day, so many eggs per month. Each egg produces one chick. What do you want, that I should give you a hen that makes chicks every day so cheaply! Are you mad? Hand over the money and . . . have a good journey!"

The young fellow said that he wanted to go to the *kadi* and the innkeeper agreed. Now, he knew that the *kadi* was a man susceptible to bribery. What did the innkeeper do? He took a sack, filled it with the hens, which poked their heads out from it, and went to the *kadi.*

The *kadi,* seeing the hens, rejoiced in his soul and said to the young fellow: "The innkeeper is right! Pay, and if you have witnesses, bring them," and he fixed an hour for him.

The unfortunate fellow, pulling at his hair, went outside and at once found himself face-to-face with Joha.

Joha asked: "What's the matter?" And when he heard what had happened, he said: "I am here. Don't you worry. I will be your witness. Just wait a bit!" and he disappeared.

The young fellow waited and waited, but Joha didn't appear. The hour set by the *kadi* passed. More hours passed, until in the distance he saw Joha come running, drenched with sweat.

"Come on, let's go to the *kadi*!" he said, and they went.

The *kadi* asked why they were late, and Joha spoke: "Don't ask, Señor Kadi. I had to prepare wheat for planting, and as I don't have the money to buy it, I took boiled wheat that was in my house and it took me several hours to count every grain of it."

It seemed to the *kadi* that he had caught Joha trying to play the wise guy, and he said: "Don't you fear God, Joha? How can boiled wheat become wheat to plant?"

And Joha replied: "Just a minute, Señor Kadi. If from your boiled eggs come forth chicks, why shouldn't plants come out of my boiled wheat?"

The *kadi* reflected a little, gave a just sentence, and the innkeeper exploded with rage.

NARRATED BY SARA YOHAY – 1991

No Use Arguing!

Two neighbors were quarreling continually over a plot of ground that lay between their two properties.

One of them said: "It's mine!"

The other said: "No, it's mine!"

In the end they began to hit each other and had to go before the village judge, who was Joha.

Joha listened to both their arguments and said: "Wait a little. I will go and ask the ground itself to which of you it belongs."

He went to the plot, stretched himself full length over it, put his ear to the ground, and began to listen with the utmost attention. Afterward he got to his feet and gave his sentence: "The ground gave me its answer. It said: 'I don't belong to the one or to the other. It is they who belong to me!'"

NARRATED BY MATILDA KOEN-SARANO – 1997

CHAPTER 13

JOHA the glutton

"Once you start to eat, you won't stop."

The Unmixed Salad

Joha said to his mother: "Mama, I want salad! But I want it now, right away!"

His mother said to him: "Take, cut, eat!"

So he took the salad, cut it up, and put it into his mouth.

"But you don't eat it like that!" his mother said to him. "First you cut it up. After that, you put oil in it, and salt, and lemon juice . . . you also put—"

"Everything will be put in it!" Joha said to her. "You do what you have to do! Everything will be put in it!"

Joha put a bit of salad in his mouth, and in his hand he put a bit of oil and lemon juice and salt. He put a bit more again and again, three, four times. Mmm! He was so full, he couldn't speak anymore.

And in the end, his mother said: "What is this? The salad has to be mixed! Now how will you go about mixing it?"

"Now I am mixing it!" said Joha and threw himself out of the window.

NARRATED BY MARIA DE BENEDETTI – 1987

Too Literally

Joha went one day to visit his bride-to-be, and her family gave him meatballs to eat. He began to eat them whole.

The bride-to-be said to him: "Joha, not like that! Something that is round, one has to cut at least into four!"

"Aha, all right," said Joha. "I didn't know that!"

When he returned the next day, they gave him a dish of lentils, which are small and round.

Joha began to cut them into four and so never ever finished the dish.

NARRATED BY VIKTORIA MISISTRANO – 1999

Irresistible Pastries

Joha's mother sent him to buy three pastries.

Joha went to the patisserie, bought three pastries, and on the way home, felt inclined to taste them. He tasted one and said, "Mmmm! These pastries are really good!"

He said, "I will eat another one!" And he ate the second as well. Only one pastry was left.

When he came home, his mother said: "Joha, did you buy the pastries?"

"Yes, Mama!" Joha said and showed her the one remaining pastry.

"Where are the others?" his mother said.

"I ate them!"

"How did you eat them?"

"Like this!" said Joha, as he took the third pastry and ate it.

NARRATED BY HADAR ARZI – 1999

A Fishy Tale

Joha was very poor, and once in a while he was invited to a Sabbath evening meal at the home of the local rich man.

One Sabbath evening, entering the rich man's house after the synagogue prayers, Joha glanced into the kitchen to see what they had prepared for the meal. And what did he see?

On the table he saw two dishes. In one there was a big fish and, in the other, a little fish.

Joha said to himself: "Oh, I hope they give me the big fish! I am dying from hunger!"

Well, they recited the *Kiddush* over the wine, recited the *Netilat Yadaim* blessing for washing the hands, and the *Hamotzi* over the bread, and they sat down to eat.

A waiter entered and placed the dish with the little fish in front of Joha.

Joha put on a sad face and did not eat.

The rich man said: "Come on, Joha, why aren't you eating? What's the matter?"

"Nothing!" Joha said. "I have no appetite. I am very sad."

"But why?" .

"Because I remembered my son. . . . I had a son who went to sea and did not return," Joha said.

"Come on, eat now!" the rich man said. But instead of eating, Joha lowered his head onto the plate and muttered something very quietly in the ear of the little fish. Afterward, he put his ear next to the fish's mouth and made out that he was listening to what the fish was telling him.

"What did you say to the fish?" the rich man asked.

"I said to it: 'You, who have just come out of the sea, did you perhaps hear something concerning my son?'"

"And what did the fish tell you?" the rich man asked.

"The fish said to me," replied Joha, "'I am still very young, and I cannot know anything. But in the kitchen is my father, who is much bigger than me. He will surely know something. Let them bring him to you here, and ask him.'"

And so they brought the big fish before Joha, and Joha . . . he ate it!

NARRATED BY MATILDA KOEN-SARANO – 1994

Just Like My Mother's

Joha's wife was an excellent cook, but every meal that she made, Joha would say to her: "Ah, where is the meal my mother made? . . . She really knew how to cook!"

The poor wife, who cooked very tasty meals, always tried to cook even better, but to no avail. Joha tasted the meal and said: "Ah, where is the meal that my mother made?"

One day she was so sad that she put the food on the flame and forgot about it.

The food was burned.

What should she do? There was no time to cook another meal.

When Joha came, she put a dish in front of him with the burnt food, fearful of what her husband would say.

But no sooner did Joha taste a spoonful of the food than he said: "Ah! This is the meal my mother made!"

Narrated by MATILDA KOEN-SARANO – 1992

Invitation to a Feast

Joha had nothing to eat.

His wife said to him "Joha, *effendi,* are we always going to remain without food? The children are crying."

"Don't you worry," Joha said.

"You prepare the oven. We are going to eat of all good things. Such as we have never eaten before," he said.

Joha went out into the street and called all those who were there to come and eat. He said: "Come to my house to eat! Come to my house to eat!"

They said: "Joha, have you become rich?"

"I haven't become rich," said Joha, "but today is my day. I

want you all to come to my house to eat."

They all came inside. The Turks are accustomed to taking off their shoes at the door.

When they had all entered, Joha collected the shoes, put them in a sack, went to the bazaar, and sold them cheaply. For twenty pairs of shoes he received, let us say, thirty liras.

He went to the butcher, bought a sheep; went to the fishmonger, bought fish; bought vegetables for a salad; bought everything. . . .

He went home and gave them all something to eat.

They said: "Ah, Joha, where did you get all of this? What day is it today?"

"I cannot tell you that!" said Joha. "Eat! It is yours!"

He gave the children something to eat, he gave his wife something to eat. They ate and drank.

"Eat!" said Joha.

"Joha," they said to him, "we have no room left!"

"Eat!" Joha said. "It is all yours. It is all your property! Eat it!"

They had all eaten and drunk. They went outside, looked: Their shoes were not there!

They said: "Where are our shoes?"

"Ah," said Joha, "did I not already tell you that you were eating your property. It's with your money that you ate!"

NARRATED BY LEA BENABU – 1993

Free Cake . . .

One day Joha's wife sent him to buy a cake for the Sabbath.

Joha went to the market, entered a patisserie, saw the cakes close up, and asked the shop assistant for a chocolate cake.

The assistant gave it to him.

Joha waited a few minutes, addressed the shop assistant again, and asked him to exchange the chocolate cake in his hand for a cheesecake.

The assistant exchanged it for him, and Joha left the shop.

Since Joha had not paid before leaving, the assistant ran after him, crying: "Hey, señor! You left without paying!"

Joha turned around and said in amazement: "Excuse me, señor shop assistant, for what do I have to pay you?"

And the shop assistant answered him, very astonished: "How 'for what'? For the cheesecake, naturally!"

And Joha: "Excuse me, señor, I gave you the chocolate cake for this cake!"

"But," said the shop assistant, "then you have to pay me for the chocolate cake!"

"Excuse me, señor shop assistant, but I didn't take the chocolate cake!" Joha said to him. "Why should I have to pay for it?"

NARRATED BY EYTAN ARZI – 2000

How to Make Meatballs

Joha was walking in the bazaar. He saw a shop where they were selling *kiftes.** He asked how they were made.

They said: "We mince the meat, we mix it with chopped parsley, we make the meatballs, and we fry them."

Joha went off, bought what was necessary, but forgot the name "*kiftes.*" He returned to the shop and asked: "What do you call this?"

* meatballs with pita

They said: "*Kiftes,* meatballs!"

Joha went off, but after a while he forgot again. So he went and asked again.

Finally, he went home and said to his wife, showing her the meat and the parsley: "Make me this!" without mentioning to her the name of what he wanted.

His wife said: "What should I make for you?"

"This! This!" Joha said to her.

His wife did not know what to make for him. Finally, Joha grew angry and began to beat her.

His wife went to the police, told them everything, and said: "In the end he made *kiftes,* mincemeat, out of me!"

Joha said: "You wicked woman. If you already knew what they were, why didn't you make them for me?"

NARRATED BY DORA SASSON ZUARES – 1992

Optional Participation

Joha and three of his friends arranged to have a meal together.

The friends were an Englishman, a Frenchman, and a German.

The English friend brought cigars.

The French friend brought a bottle of wine.

The German friend brought beer.

Joha brought his little brother.

NARRATED BY BEKI BARDAVID – 1996

Baklava Pastry for Purim

Joha was poor, and he had a rich upstairs neighbor. Very frequently he saw them bringing trays with fried chicken, tarts, and pastries, up to the neighbor. . . .

When Purim was near, Joha saw that they were bringing a tray of Turkish pastry, *baklava,* up to his neighbor.

He said to his wife: "We must taste that *baklava*. You'll see. I am going to do something, and we will taste it!"

And so, what did the two of them decide? They decided that on the day of Purim, they would stage a very big quarrel between themselves. The neighbors, on hearing that Joha was beating his wife, would come to separate them, and so he would manage to find the way to go upstairs.

And so it was. They began to quarrel, and she shouted, "Help!"

The neighbors came down and said: "Joha, what is this? Are you beating your wife?! No, no, no! Come, come upstairs to us for a little while!" And they made him come upstairs to them.

On the table was the enormous tray of *baklava.*

The neighbors said to Joha: "Sit down, Joha, sit down and eat!"

He sat down and began to eat the *baklava* from one side and then finished the section in front of him. He wanted to eat from the other side as well but was embarrassed. So what did he do?

He said: "You know? When my wife makes me angry . . . When she doesn't do what I want, I take her . . . thus . . . by the ear, and I throw her out!" And he took the tray, turned it rapidly to the side that was still full, and began to eat very rapidly from that side as well.The neighbors, seeing that there would soon be nothing left for them, said: "Look, Joha, we will give you a piece of *baklava* for your wife. Go, take it to her, and *Purim Sameach*! . . . A happy Purim! . . ."

Joha took the plate with the *mishloah manot,** went down to his wife, and said: "Do you see how successful our quarrel was?"

NARRATED BY MATILDA KOEN-SARANO – 1995

How Many Borekas?

It happened that Joha went to buy *borekas*.

The *borekas* vendor was standing there with a big tray.

Joha said: "Well, how much do they cost?"

The vendor said: "Look, for one dollar you can eat what you want."

Joha began to eat and had already eaten six, seven, eight, ten, twelve *borekas*. . . .

Feeling sick, the vendor and said: "Oh! Tell me, Joha, don't you want to stop and have a drink of water?"

And he said: "Yes, but in the middle of my meal, no!"

NARRATED BY FELIX ROMANO – 1999

Key Soup

Joha had no work, and his wife said to him: "Go, find some work, to bring us something to eat! The children are hungry!"

And he said: "I have been looking, and I haven't found any work!"

And so it was she who cooked here and washed there, and she always brought something home to eat. And that is how they spent their lives.

* the Purim gift of sweetmeats

One day she couldn't find anything to do. She said to her husband: "Joha, today there will be nothing for us to eat!"

Joha said to her: "Don't you worry, wife, you will see what I will bring back for you at noon."

He took a big saucepan, stuffed the key to the house into his purse, one of the old kind, and went off to the market. There he stood himself in a corner, collected some boards, and lit a fire.

Joha filled the saucepan with water, threw the key into it, and put the saucepan on the fire. The water began to boil, and Joha started to stir the pot with a ladle.

An itinerant vendor passed by and said: "Joha, what are you making?"

"Key soup!"

"Key soup?" said the man. "And how does it taste?"

"Marvelous!" Joha said. "But if it had a little onion, it would be even better!"

"A little onion?" the vendor said. "I sell onions. . . . I will give you one!" And he gave him the onion.

Joha put it in the saucepan and went on stirring, stirring.

Another vendor passed by and said: "Joha, what are you making?"

"Key soup!" Joha said to him.

"What?!" the other man said. "I never heard of . . . But is it tasty?"

"And how!" Joha said. "But if it had a little tomato, it would taste even better. . . . "

"I will give you one!" the man said. "I sell tomatoes. . . . "

And so it went, on and on. One by one, all the vendors in the market brought him a carrot, a potato, some parsley, a little pumpkin, a piece of meat, a bit of rice . . . until the soup was cooked.

When Joha saw that the soup was ready, he drew out the key, cleaned it, and put it in his purse. He hoisted the heavy saucepan onto his shoulder, saying: "Thank you, my friends!

May God bless you!" and went off home to feed his family, who were waiting for him impatiently.

And all those in the market who had been preparing to eat "key soup" remained with their tongues hanging out.

NARRATED BY MATILDA KOEN-SARANO – 1992

Venison or Bulgur Pilaf?

Joha loved venison, and when he found some, he didn't miss the opportunity to buy it. But every time he bought some, he wasn't able to enjoy it because the cats ran after him.

He would bring it home and give it to his wife to cook, but when he sat down at the table, he found himself with just a plate of bulgur pilaf.

One day he lost patience and said to his wife: "How is it that I don't find even a small piece of venison on the plate? I am sick and tired of this rice dish!"

"Ah, well now, my dear *effendi,*"* his wife said, "don't you know who eats the venison meat? Our black cat!"

As soon as he heard this, Joha got up from the kitchen, entered the living room, seized his wife's fur coat, and put it in an iron cupboard. He locked it with two locks.

His wife, curious, asked him: "Well, my dear *effendi,* what is the cat going to do with the fur? Why did you hide it?"

And Joha, as if expecting the question, answered thus: "My precious, if the cat drools over something that cost only two *grush,* how much more so will it lust for something that is costly?"

From that day on, the bulgur pilaf turned into venison.

NARRATED BY SARA YOHAY – 1992

* sir

Dinner at the King's Table

Joha was very hungry. One day as he was walking in the street he saw a big sign. On the sign was written: "Food and drink and one ducat in the hand."

He knocked on the door. They opened it for him. He went inside. They said to him: "Welcome!"

It was the king, who said that he was giving food to everyone.

Joha went inside. He found himself in a big room. In the middle of the room there was a very big table, completely empty. The king sat down at one end and, at the other end, Joha.

The king clapped his hands to the servant, saying: "Bring in the first course!"

Joha was watching how the servant entered, pretending to hold a tray in his hand—a tray groaning with food—and placed it on the table.

Joha looked at the king, began to taste, pretending, as it were, and said: "Lord King, in my entire life I have never eaten such a quantity of delightful fish. How tasty it is!"

The king said: "Our cooks are famous. They cook dishes such as exist in no other city. . . ."

Well, Joha made out that he was cutting with his knife and fork and all, and ate away with gusto. He finished and said: "Ah, it was very tasty, Lord King!"

The king clapped his hands, and the servant entered again: "Bring me the second course!"

The servant came and brought the second course. Joha looked: There was nothing to eat. He took his fork, said: "What is this?"

"This is wonderful lamb. We roasted it!" the king said.

"Very tasty meat!" said Joha. "Lord King, in my life I have not eaten such a quantity of succulent meat. It is the first time in my life!"

And he ate and ate, as it were, that is to say, he pretended to be eating.

"Fine!" said the king. "Now the servant will bring a very beautiful thing!"

The servant brought ice cream like the Turks make. And he was eating, as it were, the ice cream with pudding. There was neither ice cream nor pudding there.

"Now," said the king to the servant, "from the cellar down below bring up a bottle of wine . . . of the vintage wine that I like."

"Ah, Lord King," said Joha, "everything is wonderful, but I don't drink wine."

"You will drink!" said the king. "We will drink to our health together."

Well, the servant went down, as it were, and brought a bottle of wine. There was no wine, nor was there any bottle.

Joha took the cup, said: "Lord King, don't force me! Afterward I do crazy things!"

"No!" said the king. "You won't do anything crazy! We will drink together!"

Joha filled the cup and said: "Lord King, do you want some as well?"

"Yes!" said the king, and Joha, as it were, filled the cup for him. *"L'chaim!"**

They both took and drank.

Joha had already drunk one cup, and then two. . . . The bottle was empty, as it were.

Joha said: "Lord King, the wine is delicious. The bottle is already empty."

"Go, bring another bottle of wine!" the king said to the servant.

The servant brought, as it were, another bottle of wine. Joha

* To life!

drank and drank. He got up, as if drunk, gave the king a punch, and threw him down off his chair.

"What are you doing?" the king said to him.

"Lord King," said Joha, "It is not my fault. It is the wine's fault. I drank wine and lost my senses. Didn't I already tell you that I don't drink wine? You forced me to do it."

Joha made to rise and the king went to help him. Joha raised his hand, gave him another punch and knocked him off his chair.

The king said to him: "What are you doing?"

Joha said to him: "I am drunk, Lord King. I do not know what I am doing!!"

The king said to him: "You are the first one to get the better of me in all my life. Until now," he said, "I gave to all of them to eat in this way, as I gave to you, and they all were weeping." He said, "You gave me such blows as I will remember for the rest of my life."

"Now," the king said to his servants, "bring him everything that you should have brought him. Let him eat and drink. And I will give him not only one ducat but a purse of gold ducats."

They brought things for him to eat and drink. . . . And he ate, drank, and left with the gold ducats.

As he left, one of the servants said to him: "I saw you when you entered. What did you eat?"

"What do you mean, what did I eat?" Joha said. "I ate fish, I ate meat, I ate ice cream. . . . "

"You ate real food?"

"Hey," said Joha, "I will tell you the truth: At first it was not for real, but the second time it really was for real."

And so it was that Joha got the better of the king and left well satisfied.

Narrated by LEA BENABU – 1993

Spicy Dish

A wealthy man was marrying off his daughter and invited the whole neighborhood to the wedding. Among all the guests were two poor souls who lived at the end of the street, Joha and his friend Yakob.

The tables were laid . . . and they were there.

"Joha, look!"

"What, Yakob?"

"That yellow thing. What is it?"

"It looks just like egg. . . ." There was a time when eggs were scarce there. . . .

"Look, I'm going to take a bit with my teaspoon. Cover me so that they won't see me. I will taste it."

He took the teaspoon, tasted. He began to shed tears, tears, tears. . . .

"Why are you crying, Yakob? Is this a time for crying?"

"Don't ask. I remembered my wife, who drowned at sea!"

"Ah . . . and how was what you tasted?"

"Wonderful!"

"Good! Now I am going to take a big spoonful!

Joha took a big quantity with a big spoon, put it in his mouth, began to cry . . . to cry . . . to cry. . . .

"What's the matter, Joha?"

"I am crying because you didn't drown at sea with your wife!" Joha said to him.

NARRATED BY LORA HAZAN – 1990

What an Appetite!

Joha was invited to dine at the home of a rich man.

They sat him down at a table filled with fine fare: meat, fish, cakes, fruit.

The rich man said: "Bon appetit, Joha! Eat as much as you wish!"

Joha set about eating with gusto everything they put in front of him. And so he was eating . . . eating. . . .

When he had well and truly gorged himself, he suddenly exclaimed, "Just look! The strangest thing . . . I don't know why they say that the appetite comes with eating. I have already been eating for three hours nonstop, and I am still not hungry!"

NARRATED BY MATILDA KOEN-SARANO – 1986

The Blood-Red Soup

Joha's wife loved to cook and was always looking for new recipes. One day a little boy, not a Jew, who was curious and was looking through her window, saw that the pot on the fire contained something red. Blood!

Very scared, the boy ran to his parents and told them what he had seen in Joha's house. The whole village armed itself with sticks and advanced toward Joha's home crying, "Death to the Jews! Death to the Jews!"

Joha opened the door and asked calmly: "Why this pogrom?"

"There is blood in your saucepan!" the neighbors cried.

Joha lifted the saucepan off the stove, brought it outside, and said: "Look! It is borscht, which my wife learned to make from an Ashkenazi friend!"

His neighbors, who were famished, seized the saucepan from him and ran away. Joha turned to his wife and said: "You see what happens when you take recipes from the Ashkenazim. . . . One catches their misfortunes! From tomorrow, we will eat only bread and cheese!"

And he kept his word.

NARRATED BY SARA YOHAY – 1996

The Real Reason

A Turk got very angry with the Jews and told Joha: "Everywhere you are the best. . . . You have beautiful homes . . . you are fruitful . . . you wear fantastic clothes. How is it that you are so intelligent?"

"It is very simple," Joha replied. "We eat fish heads."

"Really? If I eat the heads of fish, will I also become intelligent?"

"Undoubtedly!"

"Well, then, come on!" said the Turk. "Take me to a restaurant, and we will see. I am inviting you."

The two of them went to a fancy restaurant and ordered fish.

The Turk began to eat the heads, and Joha ate the fresh fish.

After three or four heads, the Turk grew angry.

He said: "What is this? I am paying and eating the little heads. And you are eating the delicious fish!"

"Can't you see, can't you see?" Joha said to him. "With three heads, you have already become intelligent. But you still have a long way to go. Eat more, and you will see!"

NARRATED BY BEKI BARDAVID – 1992

Advice in Payment

Joha was sitting in a restaurant. He ate, finished eating, and said: "I am already full. I will go home." And he got up to leave without paying.

The restaurant owner said to him: "Why aren't you paying me?"

Joha said: "Because I don't have even a shekel!"

"What!?" the restaurant owner said. "So what will be?"

"Instead of money I can give you some advice."

The restaurant owner, realizing that he was not going to get any money, said to Joha: "All right! Give me this advice!"

"Always take the money first, before you give people something to eat!"

NARRATED BY HADAR ARZI – 1999

Military Strategy

Señor Mehmet invited Joha to come and drink *raki* with him.

They sat down by the seashore and ordered a delicious meal. In the salad were fat, shiny olives.

Joha had already tried everything. This time he wanted to taste a little of the olive. He tried ever so hard with his fork, again and again, but didn't manage to catch hold of the olive. Realizing that he couldn't stab it with his fork, he gave up trying to eat it. He went on to something else.

Señor Mehmet—*tik*—extended his fork, stabbed the olive, carried it to his mouth, and ate it.

"You see, Señor Joha, I, in a flash, caught it. You spent hours trying, and nothing!"

You would think that Joha got annoyed, but he said: "It is indeed so, Mehmet *effendi,* but do not forget that if I had not tired it out so, you would never have managed to catch it!"

NARRATED BY BEKI BARDAVID – 1996

Encore!

Joha went to Paris. He walked around a little, visited a museum, and then felt like eating.

He went into a restaurant, sat down at a table.

A waiter came, brought him the menu.

Joha looked at it. It was in French, and he didn't know French. Joha was ashamed to say that he couldn't read, so he pointed to a dish and showed the menu to the waiter.

The waiter went away, brought him a plate of beans.

"Now then!" Joha said to himself. "Did I come to Paris to eat what I eat every day at home? I want something better! But how to tell this to the waiter?"

At that moment he saw the man sitting at the next table finish his roast beef, call the waiter, point to the plate, and say, *"Encore!"*

Joha thought that this was the name of what the other person was eating, so he also called the waiter and said to him: *"Encore!"*

But what did the good waiter bring him? Another plate of beans!

Joha was astounded. He called the waiter and said, pointing to the other man: "Tell me why my *encore* is not like his!"

NARRATED BY MATILDA KOEN-SARANO – 1995

Fasting the Joha Way

Joha didn't fast on Yom Kippur. He quickly recited the *Shofar* service to himself, ran to the synagogue, and after he had drunk water and eaten two small olives, sat down at the table with the members of his family, who had all been fasting. And he began to eat with them, and eat more than they.

His wife got very upset.

She said: "What a strange fellow you are, Joha! You don't fast, and you sit and eat like the rest of us, as if you had fasted. Shame on you!"

"Why are you so upset? I couldn't keep the fast. . . . But at least I am breaking it!"

NARRATED BY BEKI BARDAVID – 1999

The Conditional Sukkah

Joha used to make *sukkah** booths, to rent out for the Sukkot Festival and so earn a bit of money. But he rented them out on one condition: to be invited during the entire festival to eat with the family who rented the *sukkah*.

The family who rented the *sukkah* said: "Let him come! Why not? Where five eat, six can eat. . . . Where seven eat, eight can eat. . . ."

But on the first day of Sukkot, Joha came to the family who had rented one of his booths and began to eat and eat and eat. He ate everything, without leaving anything for the others.

Very enraged, the family said: "Who put Joha in our *sukkah*?

* small booth covered with branches during the holiday of Sukkot

We don't want him there any longer! Let him take his *sukkah* and never come back!"

They gave it back to him and sent him away.

The second day of Sukkot, Joha went to eat with another family who had rented one of his booths, and the same thing happened. Joha began to eat and eat and eat . . . until they sent him away with his *sukkah*.

This is how Joha spent all the seven days of Sukkot, every year. Until there spread from family to family the expression, "Who put Joha in my *sukkah*?" which has remained until our day, and which is said by one who does not wish to enter a business deal, who does not want under any circumstances to know about something, and does not wish even to hear about it.

NARRATED BY MIRIAM RAYMOND – 1999

A Glutton Even in Dreams

There were two friends, two very good friends. One of them was Joha.

One day they met. Joha's friend said to him: "I had a dream last night."

He said, "I dreamed that I got on a train and went to the very end. I took another train and came back. I took the train again and went to the very end. I took the other train and came back again. And so on until this morning."

"Fine!" Joha said.

"And you, what did you dream about?" his friend asked.

"I dreamed there was a marvelous wedding. What clothes, what dancing, what singing! Really beautiful. And afterward they brought delicious food: chicken, meat, fish, salads! It was a marvelous wedding! We finished the food, then they brought sweetmeats: baklava, marzipan, honey, and nutcake."

"For pity's sake!" his friend said. "Why didn't you call me?"

"Well," Joha said, "you were on the train!"

NARRATED BY SOL MAYMARAN – 1995

The Chicken

Joha's neighbor brought him a chicken. He said to Joha, "Now, cook it and enjoy it."

"How nice that you brought me a chicken!" said Joha. "Come in, enter, we shall eat it together."

And his neighbor came inside.

Joha cooked the chicken. They sat down and ate it, but not all of it. They ate a little and left some for another day.

The next day two people came to Joha and said: "We are the neighbors of the one who brought you the chicken yesterday. We want to taste it."

Joha said: "Well then, come in! There is a little bit left."

They ate, and they finished the chicken.

On the third day another three came. They said, "We are the friends of the neighbors of the one who brought you the chicken. And we want to taste it."

Joha brought a pot with watery soup and put it on the table.

They smelled a most terrible smell. "What's this, Joha? Aren't you ashamed to give us this kind of thing to eat?"

He said to them: "Look, this is the soup of the soup from the bones of the chicken that the friend of the neighbors of your friends brought me!"

NARRATED BY LEVANA SASSON – 2000

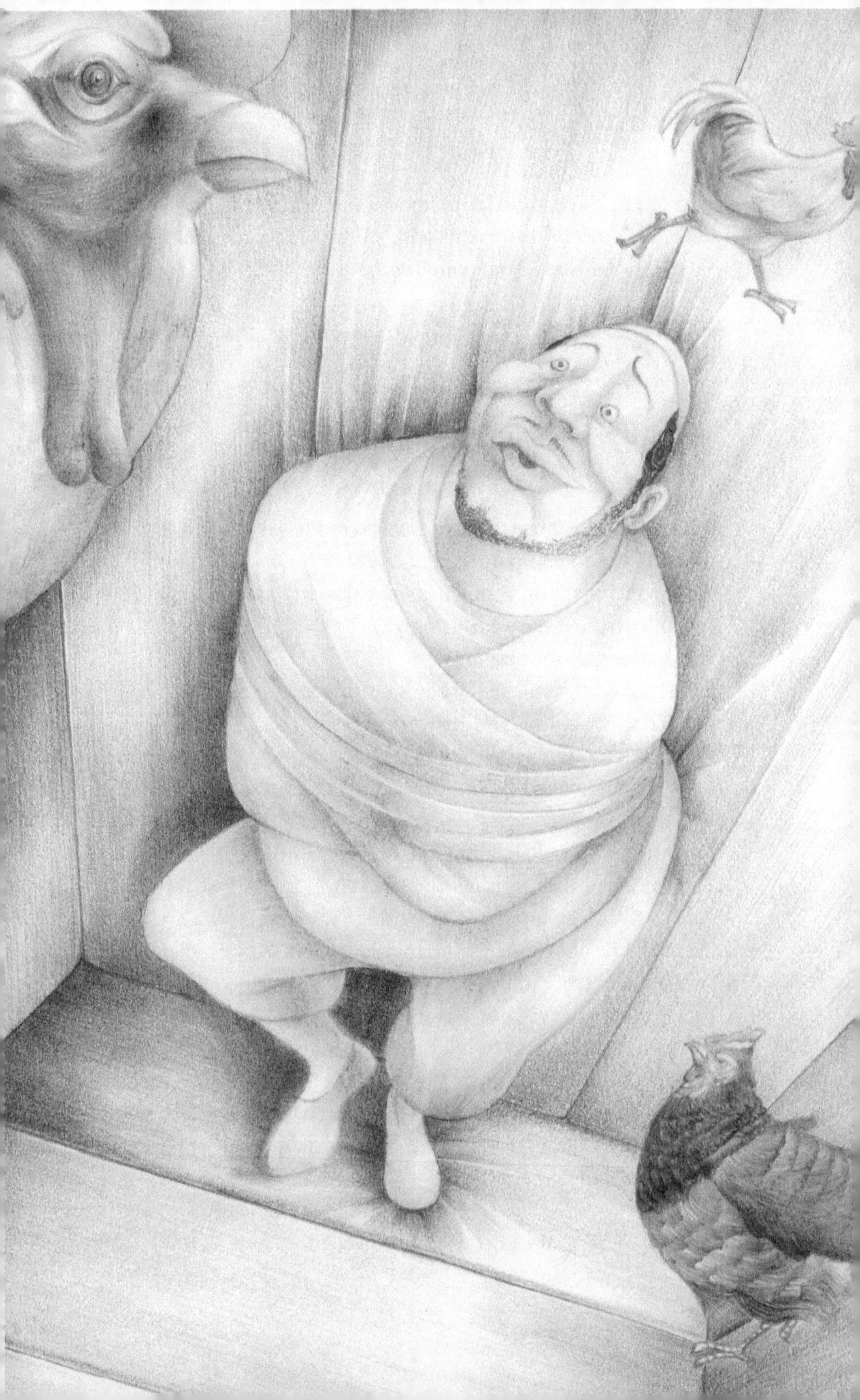

CHAPTER 14

JOHA in the hospital

"One is born with luck and good fortune, and another with a double hernia."

What about the Interest?

One day Joha went to the doctor. He said: "I can't hear in this ear."

The doctor looked, found a coin inside it, and extracted it.

He said: "How long have you been like this?"

Joha said: "It's been five years already."

The doctor said: "Why didn't you come earlier?"

Said Joha: "Because I didn't need any money."

NARRATED BY ESTER GONEN – 1999

The Obstinate Patient

One day Joha went to the dentist. He said: "I have a very bad toothache."

The dentist said: "Which tooth is hurting you?"

Joha thought to himself: He doesn't understand! Isn't he a dentist? And he didn't answer.

The dentist took his pliers and extracted a tooth. He asked: "Has the pain gone?"

Joha didn't answer.

And so it went on, until the dentist had extracted all his teeth. Afterward, he asked: "Which was the tooth that was hurting you?"

Joha said: "Aren't you a dentist? You're supposed to know! Do I have to tell you?"

NARRATED BY MATILDA KOEN-SARANO – 1993

A New Method

Joha was a doctor. There was one patient who had a sore throat and couldn't speak, eat, or drink. They summoned all the doctors, and they could do nothing. Finally, they called Joha.

Joha came with a box full of slips of paper and told the patient's wife that her husband should come and take a slip.

The man came and took one. Joha said to him that before he did anything else, he wanted ten ducats, and he would cure him. Afterward he took the slip of paper and read it and told him that he must take an enema every night.

"An enema for a sore throat!?" said the patient.

"Yes!" said Joha.

The patient began to laugh. . . . He laughed and laughed, laughed and laughed, until he was cured.

NARRATED BY LEA COHEN – 1990

A Cure for Depression

A very famous and distinguished Jew—Señor Cuencas, let us call him—began one day to suffer from depression. He began to act strangely and was completely transformed. His smile vanished, and he wore a Tisha B'Av* fast-day face.

The gentleman's wife consulted with doctors throughout the city without finding one who could solve the problem.

One day Señora Cuencas met her friend Madame Rashel and told her about her troubles. After Madame Rashel heard the whole story she said: "Listen, I know a doctor who is

* a day of mourning, the anniversary of the destruction of both holy Temples in Jerusalem

recently arrived in our city. I could ask him to take a look at your husband.

"Excellent!" said Señora Cuencas.

Now I will tell you that the doctor was Joha himself.

This little Joha had no work, and his wife was always saying to him: "Go and look for some work, and earn money to bring us something to eat!"

Foolish Joha went and saw that a doctor dressed in a white gown was giving some advice and filling his purse with money. So he made himself a doctor, and they called him Joha the Wise.

And then . . . to make a long story short . . . Señor Cuencas sent her husband to this doctor.

"What's the matter with you, Señor Cuencas?" Joha the Wise asked him.

"I am suffering from depression and have no wish to live," the man said.

Joha the Wise took his hand and felt his pulse. Then he said: "Look, Señor Cuencas, you go home, take a hammer, put your hand against the wall with the fingers open on the wall, and with the other hand begin to pound your fingers with the hammer. Each time the hammer hits the wall and not the fingers, you will rejoice, and so you will be cured of your illness. *Ayde,* so then, Señor Cuencas, put down the ten liras and go home to your little wife."

Now, believe it or not, Señor Cuencas was cured of his sickness, and Joha grew rich.

NARRATED BY HAYIM TSUR – 1999

Who Is the Crazy One?

Joha had a friend who had a son in the Istanbul mental asylum. His friend said: "You are going to Istanbul. Please go and see how my son is getting on . . . if he needs anything. . . . "

And Joha, who was such a close friend, said: "I will certainly go!" And he went to see his friend's son.

Joha entered the room and said: "I came from Izmir. I am a friend of your papa. I came to see how you are and if you want anything."

His friend's son said: "No, I don't want anything. I only want you to get me out of here. I am already well!"

Joha said: "All right! I can see that you are well. I will tell your papa. We will see how to get you out of here. *Au revoir, au revoir!*" And he started to leave.

Suddenly the son called him: "Monsieur Joha! Please tell my father that I have become a human being again!"

"Fine! I will tell him," and he made to leave.

The son called him again: "Please be sure not to forget. Tell my father that I am already well." And he called him in this manner five or six times.

Finally, Joha became angry and said: "Don't you worry! I will tell your father that he should get you out of here and put me in your place!"

Narrated by ESTER KOHEN – 1990

Mistranslation

There were two Jews, one of whom was ill with stomach pains. The other was Joha.

The doctor there was French. The sick man did not know

French. How was he going to explain his ailment?

Joha said to him: "Don't you worry, I am here. I know French very well."

They went to the doctor.

The doctor said to the sick man: "*Qu'est que tu as?*" (What is wrong with you?)

"Stomach pains . . . in the intestine. How does one say it?"

"Aha!" Joha already knew what to say: "*Il a mal aux saucisses.*" (His sausages hurt.)

"*Depuis quand?*" (Since when?), the doctor asked.

"Since when have you had this pain?" Joha asked his friend.

"Since Tisha B'Av!" said the sick man.

"Ay, ay, ay . . . " said Joha. "How are we going to say 'Tisha B'Av'?"

He thought, thought, thought about it. "Ah," he said, "*Docteur, il a eu mal aux saucisses depuis la destruction du Temple de Jerusalem!*" (Doctor, he has had a sausage ache since the destruction of the Temple of Jerusalem.)

"*Ayde,*" said the doctor, "your place is not here! *À l'Hôpital de la Paix!*" And he sent them to the lunatic asylum.

NARRATED BY BEKI BARDAVID – 1996

"Better to Be Struck by a Sane Person than Saved by a Madman"

One day Joha was leaving his house when he saw a group of children shouting at a man, "You are bald! You are bald!"

Joha also said: "You are bald!" without knowing the meaning of the word.

Hearing Joha say that he was bald, the man seized an axe and began to chase him.

Joha ran, and the man ran. Joha soon was out of breath from so much running. He saw a tree and climbed up it.

The man with the axe said: "Come down, come down. I am going to cut down the tree with the axe and throw you off it!"

"No!" said Joha. "Do what you want. I am not coming down!"

Just then a lunatic passed by and said: "What's the matter?"

"Joha told me that I am bald and climbed up the tree. He refuses to come down," said the man. "When he comes down, I will forgive him."

Said Joha: "I'm not coming down!"

The lunatic took out a razor blade and said: "Look now, Joha, if you don't, I am going to cut down the tree and you will fall below!"

Joha came down. The man exclaimed in amazement: "How is it that he wouldn't come down when I threatened him with an axe, but with the razor blade he agreed to?"

To Joha he said: "Don't speak to me like that again, but tell me why you didn't want to come down when I held the axe in my hand, yet you did when he held the razor blade?"

"He said he was going to cut the tree down!" said Joha.

"Can one cut down a tree with a razor blade?"

"Yes!"

"How so?"

"He is crazy; he can do it. You are not crazy. You cannot!" Joha said to him.

NARRATED BY SHMUEL BARKI – 1992

Corny Story

They locked Joha up with the lunatics because he thought that he was corn and that the chickens would gobble him up.

Every year the director of the asylum called him and asked if he knew that he was not corn.

To which Joha would reply that he was afraid of the chickens because he was corn. And so they would lock him up again for another year.

The years passed, and one day Joha saw the director and said: "Señor Director, I am no longer mad! I know that I am not corn!"

"Ah, bravo, my son!" the director said. "Go, fetch your suitcase, and come to me. I will give you a paper that says you are well now!"

Joha went and returned with his suitcase, dressed like a bridegroom. He shook the director by the hand, thanked him, took the paper, and went out into the street.

Suddenly the director saw that he had returned. "What is it, Joha?" he said. "What are you doing here? Are you crazy?"

"No!" said Joha. "I told you that I am certain that I am no longer corn, but do the chickens know it?"

NARRATED BY SARA YOHAY – 1991

A Crazy Joke

All the lunatics were asleep in their beds. Joha and two others could not shut their eyes. Among those who were asleep was one who was snoring in such a manner that the curtains were trembling.

"For goodness sake!" said Joha. "The noise he is making is deafening! You know what?"

"What?" the others said to him.

"Let's play a trick on him. Let's cut off his head and throw it on top of the cupboard, and when he wakes up he will go crazy searching for his head!"

And the others agreed.

Narrated by SARA YOHAY – 1991

They Are Crazy

Hitler went to visit the lunatic asylum.

All the lunatics had been taught that when Hitler arrived, they had to salute him by raising their hand.

They all raised their hands. Only the guard, who was Joha, didn't raise his hand.

Hitler got angry: "You! Come here! Why didn't you raise your hand!"

"Am I crazy?" Joha said to him.

Narrated by BEKI BARDAVID – 1999

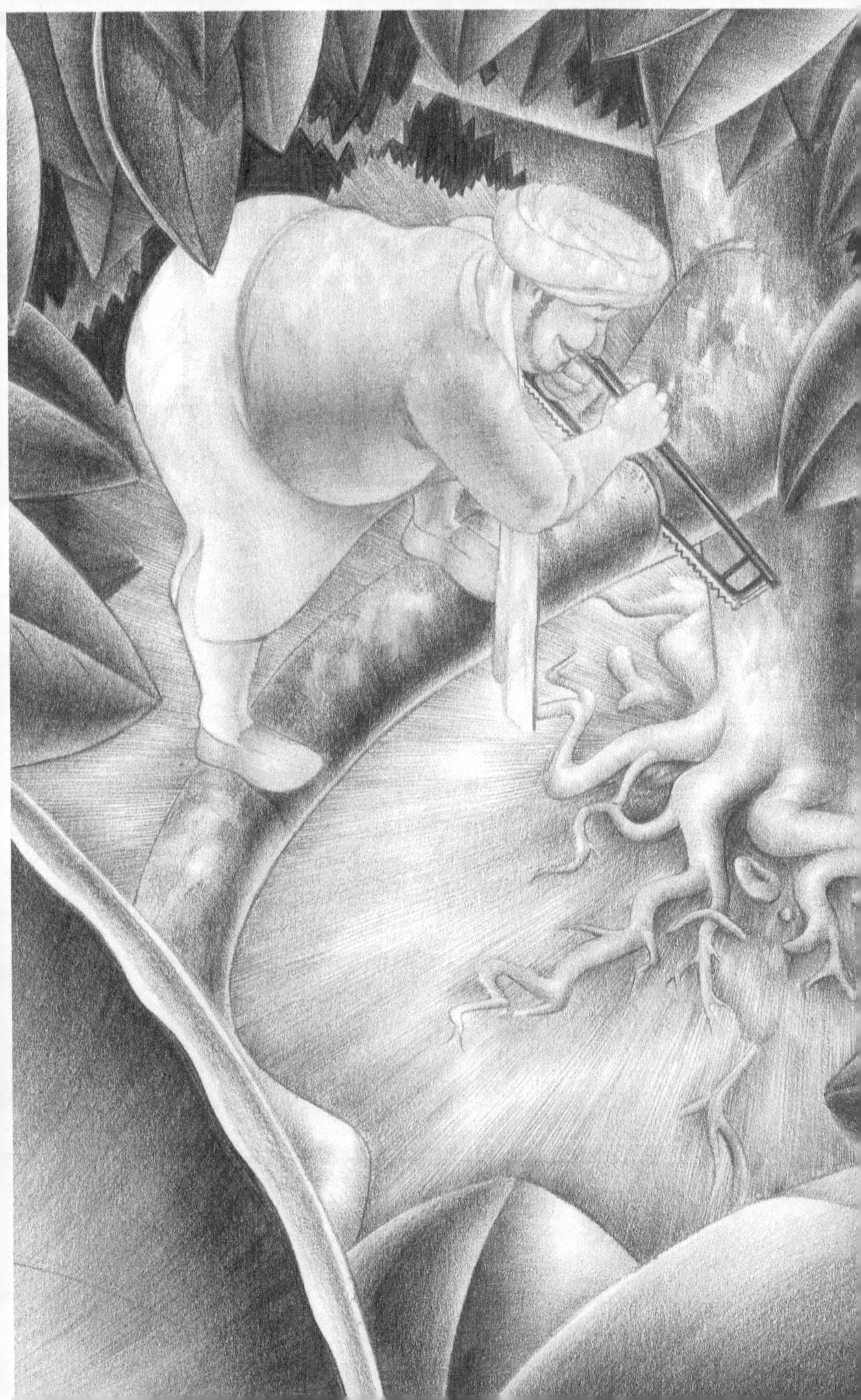

CHAPTER 15

JOHA and death

"Joha died, but his fame endured."

Levi Is Leaving

Once Joha saw a crowd of people following a coffin. "What's going on?" he asked himself.

He went with them, listened. They were all talking about a Señor Levi who was a civil servant, a man who loved people and always gave to charity, and how ". . . today he is leaving us forever . . . " and all have come to pay him their last respects.

"Very well," said Joha. "I will place myself here, to see when this person, the one who is always giving to charity, will come, and how much more he will give me now that he is leaving for good."

Well, the funeral cortege continued on its way, and our good Señor Joha walked with them, as he looked for Señor Levi to arrive. Joha looked and looked, but Señor Levi didn't appear.

At the very moment they began to lower the coffin into the ground, Joha cried out in a despairing voice: "Where is that Levi? It is as if the ground has swallowed him up!"

NARRATED BY ELIEZER PAPO – 1999

None of Their Business

One day Joha dressed himself entirely in black. People asked: "What happened to you? Why are you dressed like that?"

Said Joha: "The father of my son has died. For this reason I had to dress myself in black!"

NARRATED BY SUSY ATTIAS – 1988

What a Sweet Death!

Joha was traveling on a hot summer's day and came to a neighboring town. There he met an acquaintance who invited him to his home to drink a cold sherbet drink and refresh himself.

They stood in front of a saucepan full of iced sherbet. The friend gave Joha a coffee spoon and he took a soup spoon.

Poor Joha! How was he going to quench his thirst with that small spoon? He sweated even more with the effort.

The other one swallowed with the large spoon, and said: "Ah, dear God, I am dying! Ah, dear God, I am dying!" And this was repeated each time the spoon entered his mouth.

Finally, feeling terrible, Joha could stand it no longer. He groaned like a wild beast and said: "For pity's sake, brother, pass me the big spoon so that I should also die just once!"

NARRATED BY SARA YOHAY – 1992

Cause of Death

Joha was the king's jester. Once, the king got angry with him and said: "You may drink *raki,* but you may not take an appetizer."

"Oh no! Why?" said Joha.

"You may drink *raki,* but you may not take an appetizer, I tell you!" the king repeated.

The good Joha sat down on the balcony and watched the people passing by.

At that moment, a funeral cortege passed. Joha said: "Stop! Let none pass!"

The king said to him: "Why?"

"I wish to speak with the dead man!" Joha said.

"You are going to speak with the dead man?"

"Yes, I wish to speak with the dead man!"

Joha went, lifted the lid of the coffin, and came back, making a gesture as if to say that he certainly had been right.

Then the king said to him: "What did you say to the dead man?"

"Don't you worry about it. Nothing!"

"No! You are going to tell me!"

"Very well. I asked him what he died from."

"And what did he die from?"

"From drinking *raki* without an appetizer!"

NARRATED BY RAFAEL VALANSI – 1992

Has He a Head?

Joha decided to hang himself. He took a rope, went to a bridge. He tied the rope to the bridge. He put the rope around his neck and jumped. The rope broke, and Joha fell into the water.

And although he did not know how to swim . . . this way, that way, this way, that way . . . finally . . . somehow, he managed to come out of the water.

He said: "To hell with it! With such a hanging I could really have lost my head!"

NARRATED BY ELIEZER PAPO – 1995

Something to Be Afraid Of

Joha and his wife were looking out the window. A funeral cortege was passing by.

The wife of the dead man, dressed in black, was walking beside the coffin. She was crying and shedding tears of grief.

She was saying in a loud voice: "Ah, my dear husband! You are going to a place where there is no light . . . where it is cold . . . where there is no food. And who will look after you when you are hungry . . . when you are cold . . . when you are in the dark? Ah, ah, ah!"

On hearing this, Joha turned to his wife and said: "Close the door! They are coming to our house. They want to leave him here!"

NARRATED BY MIRIAM RAYMOND – 1994

A Real Bargain

Joha was in court and they were judging him.

The judge asked: "Joha, I have understood everything, but explain to me why you killed your wife!"

Joha said to him: "Your Honor, what could I do? I was passing the cemetery, and a grave was being sold there at a bargain price. Shouldn't I have bought it? . . ."

NARRATED BY HAYIM ARZI – 1998

A Very Strange Tomb

When his father died, Joha made him a *kever.** He made a gate, put a big lock and key on it.

He said to the people: "Now I am sure that no one is going to steal my father!"

At the back, however, all was open. But the important thing was that there was a gate and a lock.

NARRATED BY SHMUEL BARKI – 1992

A Very Good Reason

At the funeral of Rothschild, Joha was crying, crying, crying.

Those who were present asked him: "Are you a relative of the deceased?"

"No!" he said. "That is the reason I am crying!"

NARRATED BY LEVANA SASSON – 1992

Back from the Grave

Whenever Joha was depressed he would go for a walk to the cemetery. There he forgot everything, became philosophical, and said to himself: "Well now, my dear fellow, life is short! Now then, my dear fellow, don't worry! Everything will be all right. You are a good soul! You are in a bad mood! *Ayde,* out with all your complaints! Here they all will listen, and none will say a word."

* tomb

And in so doing, he would get rid of his depression and return home.

One morning, burdened with anxieties, he went to the cemetery. It happened that, at the same time, a band of horsemen was approaching.

"Mighty God!" he said, clutching at his heart, "they must be the Forty Thieves of Ali Baba!" and he was about to flee. But not finding anywhere to hide, he undressed, put his clothes under a stone, and threw himself into an open grave.

When the horsemen drew near, their blood turned cold with fear on seeing a naked man poking his head out of the hole and looking this way and that, with a face as white as paper, trembling, and opening and shutting his eyes, which were filled with earth.

One of the horsemen breathlessly asked him: "Are you alive or 'better than us' (a dead person)?"

Joha, half sitting up so as not to show that he had soiled himself with fear, answered in a faraway voice: "I am dead and better than you! I was seized by a yearning for this world, and I came out to take a look and to see what was going on."

On hearing this, the band of horsemen fled and never returned there.

NARRATED BY SARA YOHAY – 1991

The Last Possible Place

Joha lent money to Moshon. After a week, he began to look for him. He wanted him to repay the debt.

Joha went to his house. Moshon's wife said to him: "Moshon isn't here! I don't know where he is!"

Joha went to the café to look for him. He didn't find him there, either.

He went to the market. He looked among the stalls. But he wasn't there, either.

Finally, the unfortunate one went to the cemetery, and there he sat down at the entrance.

People passed and asked: "Joha, what are you doing here?"

Joha said: "I lent money to Moshon. I looked for him everywhere, that he should return the money, and I didn't find him."

They said, "Hey, so why are you waiting here?"

"Aaah!" said Joha. "Everyone passes by here. In the end, he also has to pass by here!"

NARRATED BY KOHAVA PIVIS – 1999

Celestial Orchestra

One day Joha decided to become a *hacham* and was very successful. Everyone admired him for his wisdom and his good advice.

One day a man who had been waiting for him during the prayers approached and said: "Joha, you, who are a man of God, will be able to find a solution to the problem that I have. I earn my living as the conductor of an orchestra, and one thing is now preoccupying me: I want to know if they have a philharmonic orchestra in Heaven so that I won't remain idle when my time comes."

Joha said: "How can I know such a thing?"

"You ask God and He will give you an answer." And the man returned every day with his request, to see if Joha had received an answer.

Finally one day, Joha called the man and said: "Look, I have an answer for you. They told me that up there on high they have a philharmonic orchestra and a symphony orchestra. And so now you can sleep peacefully."

The man got up to leave, thanked Joha, and went out into the street.

One minute later, Joha ran after him and said: "Forgive me, I forgot to tell you the most important thing."

"What thing?" the man asked.

"That tonight you have your premiere there!"

NARRATED BY SARA YOHAY – 1995

The Death of Joha

Joha had a little donkey. He would go and cut wood from the trees, load it on the donkey, and then go and sell it. One day he climbed a tree and was cutting a branch. A little old woman passed by and said: "Joha, what are you doing? Can't you see that you are going to fall?"

She said: "You are cutting the branch you are sitting on!"

"Have you become a fortune-teller already!" said Joha.

"No! No!" the old woman said and went off.

One minute passed . . . five . . . Joha fell to the ground. "Good God! That old granny is a fortune-teller!"

And Joha went running after her: "Granny! Granny! Granny! Come here!"

"What's the matter?"

"You predicted that I would fall off the tree! Predict for me when I am going to die!"

"You want me to predict when you are going to die?" said the old woman. "You have a little donkey. . . . When it farts three times, then you will die!"

"Now I already know it—I know on which day I will die!" said Joha. He gave the little donkey a big load of wood. The donkey, as it was now well loaded, began . . . *pum!*

"I am already a little ill!" said Joha.

A short while later, *pum!* . . . the second!

"I am already very sick! . . . very sick!" he said.

Then came the third . . . *pum!* . . . Joha fell to the ground and died!

In the meantime, some children were passing by. They said: "Look at Joha! He is sleeping! Let's take away his donkey! Let's steal it from him!"

Joha jumped up and said: "If Joha were alive and would see you taking away the donkey, look what he would do to you!"

NARRATED BY NISIM ROFE – 1998

At Life's End

Joha was already on his way to the other world. He called to each of his children by name.

"Rebeka!"

"Yes, Papa, I am here."

"Izak!"

"Yes, Papa, I am here."

"Leah!"

"Yes, Papa, I am here."

"David!"

"Yes, Papa, I am here!"

"Eliezer!"

"Yes, Papa, I am here."

"You wretches!! Who has remained in the shop?!"

NARRATED BY BEKI BARDAVID – 1996

Instead of Him

Joha was very ill and was about to die. He said to his wife: "Put on your most beautiful dress. . . . Wear all your jewels. . . . Put on rouge and powder, and sit down beside me!"

His wife, to please him, did as her husband requested. She put on her most beautiful dress. She put on her necklaces and bracelets. She applied rouge and powder and sat down beside Joha.

After an hour, two, his wife was growing tired of sitting like that. She asked Joha: "But why do you want me to be seated next to you, dressed up and made up?"

Joha answered her: "In a few minutes the Angel of Death is going to come here. He will see me so thin and pale, and you so beautiful, that he will take you away and leave me here!"

NARRATED BY AHARON COHEN – 1999

With One Leg Outside*

My mother, Esther (Ganon) Ascher, *en ganedre este,*† may she be in the Garden of Eden, used to say: "Joha said that when he died, they should bury him with one leg outside." But why?

Why did Joha say that when he died
They should bury him with one leg outside?
Three little tales I'll tell you
Then you decide which one is true!

* This is an original poem in the Spanish ballad style.
† may she rest in peace in Paradise

1. *Joha's friends told him that when he was dead*
He'd be eaten by worms from toe to head.
"But what's left free in open air
Is safe—no worm would venture there!
So when you come to bury me
Leave me one leg outside and free!"

2. *"If the Messiah comes some day*
We'll go to our Holy Land to stay.
Even the graves will open, and Jews
Will all arise and hear the news."
Joha heard the rabbi's every word
And thought about what he had heard.
"How to get out of that heavy earth-bed . . .
You're not even alive and strong, but dead! . . .
With one leg outside, how easy it'll be
I'll be the first the Messiah to see!
With one leg outside, wings will grow from my feet
I'll be the first the Messiah to meet!
With one leg outside, through the air I'll flit
And beside the Messiah I will sit!"

3. *"It doesn't matter when a person dies*
Whether he was foolish or wise.
You can't tell who's lying under the ground."
So spoke the sage. Said Joha: "I've found
A way. If they leave me one leg free
They'll say: "That was Joha!" That's me!
My tales of Joha I've told to you.
No good? Let's see what you can do!

NARRATED AND TRANSLATED BY
GLORIA J. ASCHER – 1999

Narrators' Circle: "The Ladies of Ladino"

When my previous book was published, in 1986, I asked the late Yaakov Bonano, who was on the Ministry workers committee, to send a notice to all the employees saying that the book was available and that I wished to sell it to them at a reduced price.

He said to me: "Look, anyone here who has written a book never sold more than two or three copies."

I said to him: "So let there be only two or three. It doesn't matter. I want them to know about it. Perhaps a few will be sold."

Yaakov went to see the head of the committee, and they sent out a circular. More than a hundred of my books were sold at the Ministry alone!

I sold one book to Rachel Yosefov, who came the following day and bought another and said to me: "Look, my mother has a neighbor who knows many tales. I want you to come and interview him."

"Of course." I went right away with my tape recorder and interviewed the late Sol Maymaran, who knew dozens of tales.

While interviewing Ester Levy, the mother of Rachel, who

had invited me, I asked: "And you, don't you know how to narrate tales?"

"No," she replied, but gradually as she listened to Sol, she felt the urge to tell tales, and she came out with some very beautiful ones that she had remembered from her childhood.

In the end, she said to me: "Come again next week, this time to my home."

I went to her home, and there were five women there who told me some very fine tales. Two of them were so enthusiastic that the following week they invited me to the home of Ester's sister, Shoshana (Rosa) Elboher, and there I met a group of twenty Jerusalemite women who had the tales in their hearts and on their lips: among them, Malka Palti, Shoshana Rosenthal, and Yvon Sitton.

A month later, at Yvon Sitton's home, there were thirty women and a buffet full of marvelous food, like at a wedding.

At this point I said: "Next time you will come to my home!" And I added my other informants to these narrators.

From week to week the group grew, with Levana Sasson, Malka Shabetay, Lea Basson, Lea Cohen, Renée Arochas, Malka Simha, Ester Ventura, Ester Ben-Yosef, Susy Salem . . . each one of them from a different origin but all of them Ladino-speaking. Among these gifted narrators and singers were Ester Levy and Julidé Avzaradel from Ashdod, and the late Valentina Tsoref and Malka Levy, who appeared in the theater and on radio programs.

The news spread even beyond the borders of Jerusalem. And so members from the Tel Aviv area joined the circle: Naama Hillel and Mali Geva, Kohava Pivis and Sara Meshulam (who studied in the course for narrators at Bet Ariela), the late Sara Yohay from Netanya and Maty Bar-Shalom and Sima Babani and Sara Saadon from Maalé Adumim. And among them were lovers of the theater and song, like Rina Luria and Tikva Ben-Tzvi. And these are only some of the names of the narrators, who today number over fifty.

As the years passed, the circle received visits from researchers and singers wanting to get to know this special group that narrated tales and fables in Ladino, that sang, danced, and laughed, and that ate choice foods from our tradition and came away with the recipes. And from which came books of tales and songs. There came to us Professor Tamar Alexander, Dr. Judith Cohen from Toronto, Hilary Pomeroy from London, Dr. Wendy Smith and Jill Kushnir from Los Angeles, Professor Gloria J. Ascher from Quincy, Massachusetts, and many others. The singer Betty Klein has belonged to the circle from the beginning, making it rejoice with her beautiful voice and learning from the members' ancient songs, which were new to her.

The meetings are held once a month, sometimes in the homes of the narrators, even outside Jerusalem, and sometimes in the office of the National Authority for Ladino and Its Culture, with the help of its secretary, Dolly Burda, who also belongs to the circle. The Authority has contributed to the group's enlargement with some of its pupils from teachers courses, like Ella Gros-Gefen, Mazal Linenbeg, Dr. Livnat Bitty, Robina Levinsky, and Rivka Sternfeld, and it gives the narrators the opportunity to participate in the Festival of Narrators of Tales, held in Israel each year during the Festival of Sukkot.

And now, as a final marvel, Michal Held, a young researcher and teacher at the Hebrew University of Jerusalem, is doing her doctoral thesis on the circle itself.

Informants

ADDADI Nella - Born in Tripoli (Lybia) (1927). Studied in the Italian School and in the school of the Alliance Israélite Universelle. Immigrated to Israel in 1973. Lives in Tel-Aviv. p. 28.*

ALBUKREK (Kohen) Lina - Born in Çorlu (Turkey) (1898). Lived in Istanbul and died there in 1985. Her stories were recorded by Beki Bardavid. p. 110.

ARZI Eytan - Born in Jerusalem (Israel) (1969). Studied industrial management. Lives in Modiin. Son-in-law of the author of this book. p. 238.

ARZI Hadar - Born in Jerusalem (Israel) (1993). Is the great-grandson of a Sephardic family. Lives and studies in Modiin. Son of Eytan Arzi. pp. 235, 251.

ARZI Hayim - Born in Alexandria (Egypt) (1938), to an English father and a Sephardic mother. Immigrated to Israel in 1949. Studied in Alexandria, in Bath Yam and at the Hebrew University of Jerusalem (M.A.). Academic teacher of Hebrew literature and history of the Jewish people. Lives in Jerusalem. Father of Eytan Arzi. pp. 217, 271.

ARZI Maor - Born in Jerusalem (Israel) (1992). Is the great-grandson of a Sephardic family. Lives and studies in Modiin. Son of Eytan Arzi. pp. 80, 82

ASAYAS Jak - Born in Istanbul (Turkey) (1945) and lives there. Studied at the Jewish Elementary School, in the B'nai Brith School, and at the Turkish School of Accountancy. p. 213.

ASCHER Gloria J. - Born in New York (USA) (1939) to parents from Izmir (Turkey). Studied at the Bronx High School of Science, Hunter

* book page(s) on which the informant's tale appears

College, the University of Bonn (Germany), and Yale University (M.A. and Ph.D in Germanic languages and literatures). Teaches Germanic languages and literatures, Judaic studies, and Judeo-Spanish at Tufts University. Lives in Quincy, Massachussetts. p. 277.

ASSERAF Yehuda - Born in Algeria (Oran) (1935). Immigrated to Israel in 1957. Studied in Algeria and in Israel. Lives in Jerusalem. p. 77.

ATTIAS Susy - Born in Istanbul (Turkey) (1940). Studied at a Turkish School. Immigrated to Israel in 1979. Was member of the Lady Narrators Circle. Lived and died in Jerusalem. p. 268.

AVIDAN (Shaul) Lea - Born in Izmir (Turkey) (1947). Immigrated to Israel in 1949. Studied in Israel. Lives in Netanya. p. 125.

AVZARADEL Issahar - Born in Rhodes (Aegea) (1923). Studied there at the Alliance Israélite Universelle. Emigrated to the Belgian Congo in 1939 and worked in Lomela from 1942 to 1946. Went to the United States in 1947 and lived in Brazil from 1947 to 1950. Returned to the Belgian Congo until 1960 then immigrated to Israel. He is a poet and storyteller. Lives in Ashdod. pp. 47, 96, 106, 198.

AVZARADEL (Israel) Julidé - Born in Milas (Turkey) (1931). Studied at the Lycée Kuz in Izmir. Immigrated to Israel in 1950. Lived in the Belgian Congo from 1952 to 1960. She is a singer. Wife of Issahar Avzaradel. Lives in Ashdod. pp. 161, 165.

AZULAY Smadar - Studied Judeo-Spanish at the Ben-Gurion University of the Negev under the author of this book during the academic year 1999–2000. Lives in Livne. p. 42.

BABANI Sima - Born in Israel (1953). Studied in Jerusalem at Beit Hinuch School. Member of the Lady Narrators Circle. Lives in Maale Adumim. p. 203.

BAHBOUT (Zard) Maria - Born in Tripoli (Lybia) (1909). Lived in Rome from 1953. Died there. pp. 29, 32, 141, 143, 145, 151, 153, 196.

BARDAVID (Albukrek) Beki - Born in Istanbul (Turkey) (1936) and lives there. Studied French philology and linguistics at the University of Istanbul. She is currently working on her Ph.D. in philology. She is a collector of Judeo-Spanish folktales and proverbs. pp. 39, 42, 53, 57, 59, 60, 62, 65, 67, 121, 135, 155, 160, 170, 179, 195, 204, 205, 223, 240, 250, 251, 253, 261, 265, 276.

BARKI Shmuel - Born in Izmir (Turkey) (1924) and studied there at the Turkish School and at the B'nai Brith School. Immigrated to Israel in 1949. Lived in Jerusalem and died there in 1993. pp. 81, 103, 164, 195, 214, 262, 272.

BARZILAY (Hanan) Matilda Mazaltó - Born in Rhodes (1914). Studied there and immigrated to Israel in 1935. Lived in Jerusalem and died there in 1993. p. 89.

BEHAR Sara - Born in Beirut (Lebanon) (1928) and studied there. Immigrated to Israel in 1968. Moved to Mexico in 1974 and lived there until 1995. Now lives in Israel. pp. 22, 138.

BEN-NAE (Afumado) Jeannette - Born in Istanbul (Turkey) (1937). Lived in Paris from 1946 to 1960, the year she immigrated to Israel. Studied at the Maimonides School in Paris and received a degree in French and Judeo-Spanish literature from the Hebrew University of Jerusalem. Lived in Jerusalem and died there in 1992. p. 130.

BEN-YOSEF (Ben Sasson) Ester - Born in Istanbul (Turkey) (1939). Immigrated to Israel in 1944. Studied in Petah Tikva. Member of the Lady Narrators Circle. Lives in Jerusalem. pp. 41, 132.

BENABU (Cohen) Lea - Born in Istanbul (Turkey) (1932). Studied at the B'nai Brith School there. Immigrated to Israel in 1948. Member of the Lady Narrators Circle. Lives in Jerusalem. pp. 237, 245.

BENDELAC Mordehay (Marco) - Born in Tangier (1939). Lived in Kiriat Shemona (Israel) in 1956. Returned to Tangier where he lived until 1964, the year of his emigration to Canada. Studied in Tangier and in Toronto. Is an accountant. Lives in Toronto. pp. 126, 134.

BURDA (Sarfaty) Dolly - Born in Istanbul (Turkey) (1948). Lived in Havana (Cuba) from childhood to 1971, the year of her immigration to Israel. Studied in Havana and in Jerusalem. She is the secretary of the National Authority for Ladino and Its Culture in Jerusalem. Member of the Lady Narrators Circle. Lives in Jerusalem. p. 30.

CAPOANO Rashel - Born in Marseilles (France) (1909). Studied at the Institute of the Franciscan Sisters in Piraeus (Greece) and in the "Scuola Media Comunale" in Naples. Lives in Turin (Italy). p. 178.

COHEN Aharon - Born in Tel-Aviv (1934) to a Sephardic mother. Studied at Kfar Haroe Yeshiva, and at the Hebrew University of Jerusalem (M.A. in literature and education). Israrli emissary to Italy (1957–60) and to Ethiopia (1976). Principal of the Midreshet Amalia

High School for 25 years. Now director general of the National Authority for Ladino and Its Culture. Husband of the author of this book. Lives in Jerusalem. p. 277.

COHEN (Cohen-Yohananov) Ester - Born in Jerusalem (1913) to a mother from Monastir. Studied at the Spitzer School. Lives in Jerusalem. p. 46.

COHEN (Levy) Lea - Born in Jerusalem (1934). Studied at St. Joseph School and at the evening high school in Jerusalem. Member of the Lady Narrators Circle. Lives there. pp. 223, 259.

COHEN Yosef (Mordo) - Born in Buenos Aires (Argentina) (1934). Immigrated to Israel in 1957. Studied at the Naval Lyceum in Buenos Aires and at the Institute for Youth Leaders from Overseas in Jerusalem. Lives in Yahud p. 73.

COHEN-ARIEL (Cohen) Rebeka - Born in Jerusalem, in the Shama neighborhood, at the foot of Mount Zion (1910). Studied in the Old City and at the Evelina de Rothschild School. Lives in Jerusalem. p. 215.

CORDOVA (Ben-Ezra) Hana - Born in Izmir (Turkey) (1935). Immigrated to Israel in 1948. Studied in Israel. Lives in the Tel-Aviv area. p. 17.

DE BENEDETTI (Capoano) Maria - Born in Istanbul (Turkey) (1904). Studied at the French Institute in Piraeus (Greece), at the Municipal School in Naples (Italy) and at the Ecole Superieure in Marseilles (France). Lived in Turin (Italy) and died there in 1987. p. 234.

DROHOBYCZER (Kohen) Roz - Born in Istanbul (Turkey) (1949). Studied at the Jewish High School and at the American School. Lived from 1969 to 1974 in Jerusalem and studied at Bezalel School of Art. Lived in Istanbul from 1975 to 1981. Moved to the United States in 1981. Lives in St. Louis (USA). The author received her folktale via Internet. p. 153.

ELAZAR Yaakov - Born in Jerusalem in the Jewish Quarter of the Old City (1912). Studied in the Talmud Torah of the Sephardim in Jerusalem and finished the Mizrahi Teachers Seminary. Continued his studies at Sephardic yeshivas and studied *shechita* (ritual slaughtering). Author of books about Sephardicc life in Jerusalem. Lives in Jerusalem. p. 159.

ESKENAZI (Sarano) Vittoria (Vitto) - Born in Milan (Italy) (1940) to parents from Turkey. Studied in Milan at the Jewish Community School, and at Brera Academy of Art. Immigrated to Israel in 1963. Author's sister and owner of an Italian restaurant in Tel-Aviv. Lives in Tel-Aviv. p. 71.

FELDMAN (Ouliel) Ester - Born in Jerusalem (1928) and lives there. Studied in the Seminar Lebanot Mizrahi. Member of the Lady Narrators Circle. p. 192.

FERRERA Vitali - Born in Istanbul (Turkey) (1941). Immigrated to Israel in 1956. Studied on a kibbutz and at the School of Dramatic Art. Poet, actor, storyteller, and stand-up comedian. Lives in Kiriat Ono. p. 94.

GONEN (Behar) Ester - Born in Egypt (1945). Immigrated to Israel in 1947. Studied at the Hebrew University of Rehovot (dietetics). She is a dietician. Member of the Lady Narrators Circle. Lives in Rehovot. pp. 228, 258.

GRATSIANI Eli - Born in Tsur Moshe (Netanya) (1945) to a mother from Hebron and a father from Greece. He studied and lives there. For many years was the principal of the local school in Tsur Moshe. p. 115.

GREGO Pola - Born in Cairo (Egypt) (1932) to a family from Izmir. Studied there at the Bon Pasteur School. Moved to France in 1972. Immigrated to Israel in 1974. Lives in Holon. p. 22.

HAKIM Shabetay - Born in Russhuk (Bulgaria) (1936) and studied there. Immigrated to Israel in 1948. Lives in Tsur Moshe. p. 211.

HALEVA Itzhak - Born in Istanbul (Turkey) (1940) and lives there. Studied at the Jewish School in Istanbul and the Porat Yosef Yeshiva in Jerusalem. Today he is the chief rabbi of Istanbul. p. 83.

HALEVA (Nafi) Naftali - Born in Istanbul (Turkey) (1943) and lives there. Studied at the Alliance Israélite Universelle School. Brother of Rabbi Itzhak Haleva. p. 106.

HASDAY Tsahi - Born in Rishon Lezion (Israel) (1974) and lives there. Studied Judeo-Spanish at the Ben-Gurion University of the Negev under the author of this book, during the academic year 1999–2000. p. 131.

HAZAN (Selanikió) Lora - Born in Izmir (Turkey) (1920). Immigrated to Israel in 1943. Studied at the B'nai Brith School in Izmir. Member of the Lady Narrators Circle. Lives in Jerusalem. p. 248.

KENT (Baruh) Sara - Born in Istanbul (Turkey) (1925), and studied there. Immigrated to Israel in 1972. Lives in the Tel-Aviv area. p. 154.

KOEN (COHEN)- SARANO (Sarano) Matilda - Born in Milan (Italy) (1939) to parents from Turkey. Studied in Milan at the Jewish Community School. Immigrated to Israel in 1960. Received a B.A. in Italian literature, Judeo-Spanish, and folklore from the Hebrew University of Jerusalem. She is a professional storyteller and the author of many other books including this book. Has lived in Jerusalem since 1962. Grandmother of twelve. pp. 27, 31, 37, 53, 55, 61, 72, 95, 102, 106, 107, 109, 113, 116, 118, 119, 140, 142, 144, 149, 163, 174, 175, 183, 184, 187, 188, 193, 194, 203, 224, 227, 231, 235, 237, 241, 242, 249, 252, 258.

KOHEN (Malki) Ester - Born in Izmir (Turkey) (1923). Studied at the "Istituto Centrale Italiano" and at the American College in Izmir. Lived in Istanbul until 1965, the year of her immigration to Israel. Lived in Kfar Yona B and died there in 2000. pp. 193, 261.

KOHEN Tuna (Fortuna) - Born in Istanbul (Turkey) (1945). Studied there at the B'nai Brith School. Immigrated to Israel in 1968. Lives in Tel-Aviv. p. 171.

KORFIATIS Alex - Born in Jerusalem (1947) and lives there. Studied at the Geula High School. Studied art in Germany and Greece. pp. 33, 36, 50, 51, 118, 124, 140, 218.

LEVY (Ifrah) Ester - Born in Jerusalem, in the Yemin Moshe neighborhood (1920). Studied at the Alliance Israélite Universelle School. Professional storyteller. Member of the Lady Narrators Circle. Lives in Jerusalem. pp. 24, 104, 109, 124, 131, 212, 228.

LEVY (Dasa) Malka - Born in Jerusalem, in the Yemin Moshe neighbourhood (1918). Studied at the Alliance Israélite Universelle School. Was member of the Lady Narrators Circle. Lived in Jerusalem and died there in 1994. pp. 116, 120, 169.

MAYMARAN (Cohen De Habaton) Sol - Born in Jerusalem (1921), lived there and died in 2000. Studied at the English School. Was member of the Lady Narrators Circle. pp. 25, 36, 108, 123, 254.

MAYO Nisim - Born in Argentina (1934) to parents from Orla and Magnasia (Turkey). Studied in Argentina and lives in Buenos Aires. p. 178.

MEYUHAS (Levy) Simha - Born in the Old City of Jerusalem (1904).

Studied Judaic studies at the Gimnasia Ivrit and at the Hebrew University. Lived in Jerusalem and died there in 1989. p. 27.

MIHAELI (Mizrahi) Rahel - Born in Jerusalem (1942) and lives there. Works at the Ministry of Foreign Affairs. Studied in Jerusalem. p. 183.

MISISTRANO (Mizrahi) Viktoria - Born in Istanbul (Turkey) (1924). Family moved to Buenos Aires when she was nine months old. Studied in Buenos Aires and lives there. p. 234.

MODIANO Alberto - Born in Salonika (Greece) (1928) and studied there at the Italian School. Has lived in Lausannne (Switzerland) since 1953. p. 64.

PAPO Eliezer - Born in Sarajevo (Yugoslavia) (1969). Rabbi and lawyer. Immigrated to Israel in 1992. He is now studying for his M.A. in Ladino at the Hebrew University. Teaches at the Ben Gurion University of the Negev and at the Midreshet Amalia in Jerusalem. A storyteller and author of a book. Lives in Jerusalem. pp. 23, 59, 63, 64, 66, 77, 82, 86, 93, 110, 133, 141, 162, 163, 181, 189, 205, 268, 270.

PERERA (Israel) Rashel - Born in Izmir (Turkey) (1928) and studied there in the Turkish School. Immigrated to Israel in 1949. Lives in Azor. pp. 103, 105, 130, 160, 181.

PEREZ Yoel - Born in Jerusalem (1945). Studied in the Rehavia Gymnasium, at the Hebrew University, and at the Sorbonne (Paris). Has an M.A. in biology. He is working on his Ph.D. in folklore. Professional storyteller and manager of a storytelling school in Tivon. Lives in Yodfat. p. 76.

PIVIS (Chikurel) Kohava - Born in Izmir (Turkey) (1943). Immigrated to Israel in 1949. Studied at the Givat Washington Seminary. Studied at Beit Ariela School of Narrators in Tel-Aviv. Professional storyteller. Member of the Lady Narrators Circle. Lives in Petah Tikva. pp. 23, 105, 147, 201, 213, 273.

RAYMOND (Sarano) Miriam - Born in Milan (Italy) (1945) to parents from Turkey. Studied at the School of the Jewish Community in Milan. Immigrated to Israel in 1967. Author of a books on dreams. Sister of the author of this book. Lives in Ramat Gan. pp. 176, 177, 180, 187, 253, 271.

REFAEL Hayim - Born in Salonika (Greece) (1924). Studied there in the Italian School. Deported to Germany during the Second World War, was in eleven concentration camps. Immigrated to Israel in 1946. Lives in Tel-Aviv. pp. 54, 55.

REGEV Israel - Born in Beit Shean (Israel) (1972) and lives in Arad (Israel.) Studied economics. Studied Judeo-Spanish at the Ben-Gurion University of the Negev under the author of this book, during the academic year 1998–1999. p. 180.

ROFE Nisim - Born in Istanbul (Turkey) (1902) and studied there at the Alliance Israélite Universelle School. In 1920 went to Barcelona, where he lived until 1944, the year of his immigration to Israel. Lived and died in Jerusalem. pp. 176, 275.

ROMANO Felix - Born in Argentina (1935). Studied in Buenos Aires. Lives in Buenos Aires, where he practices law. p. 242.

SAADON (Goldenberg) Sara - Born in Jaffa (Israel) (1952). Studied in Holon, at Bar Ilan University (philosophy, education, and Judaism) and at the Michlelet Minhal College of Administration. Member of the Lady Narrators Circle. Lives in Maale Adumim. p. 43.

SALINAS Roza - Born in Turkey. Interviewed in the Jewish Hospital of Balat in Istanbul, July 1984. p. 74.

SASSON (Saba) Levana - Born in Jerusalem (1942) to a mother from Turkey and a father from Greece. Studied at the Seligsberg School. Member of the Lady Narrators Circle. Lives in Jerusalem. pp. 49, 79, 196, 255, 272.

SASSON ZUARES Dora - Lives in Rome. Tale recorded by Aharon Cohen. pp. 114, 239.

SHABETAY (Behar) Malka - Born in Bursa (Turkey) (1934) and studied there in the primary school. Immigrated to Israel in 1948. Studied at the Hebrew ulpan in Ein Karem. Member of the Lady Narrators Circle. Lives in Jerusalem. p. 168.

SIMHA Itzhak - Born in Salonika (Greece) (1905) Immigrated to Palestine in 1914. Exiled by the Turkish government to Syria and brought to Istanbul along with 300 other exiles. Returned to Palestine in 1918. Studied at the Jewish School in Salonika, Jerusalem, and Istanbul. Lived and died in Jerusalem. pp. 104, 212.

STROCK (Brami-Lumbroso) Mazal - Born in Tunis (Tunisia) (1940). Studied in Tunis, Marseilles, and Paris. Immigrated to Israel in 1988. Lives in Jerusalem. p. 174.

TOKATLY Pinhas - Born in Jerusalem in the Yemin Moshe neighborhood (1921). Studied in Doresh Tzion, at the Alliance Israélite Universelle School and at the College des Frères. Lived in Jerusalem and died in a suicide bomb attack in Jerusalem in 2002. p. 48.

TSARUM (Sanes) Aliza - Born in Bursa (Turkey) (1921). Immigrated to Israel in 1925. Studied at Beer Yaakov. Member of the Lady Narrators Circle. Lives in Jerusalem. p. 102.

TSOREF Valentina - Born in Sliven (Bulgaria) (1910). Studied at Tzaritza Eleonora Girls School. Immigrated to Israel in 1945. Was member of the Lady Narrators Circle. Lived in Jerusalem and died there in 1991. pp. 29, 75, 148, 158, 166, 176.

TSUR Hayim - Born in Jerusalem (1938) and lives there. Studied at the High School and at the Academy of Music of the Hebrew University. Also studied in the United States. Violinist, composer, and music teacher. Director of the Folklore and Music Division in "Kol Israel," the Israel Broadcasting Authority. pp. 70, 126, 185, 208, 259.

VALANSI Rafael - Born in Entrerios (Cordoba) (Argentina) (1925), to a mother from Izmir (Turkey). Studied in Buenos Aires and lives there. pp. 146, 269.

VENTURA (Romano) Ester - Born in Izmir (1930). Immigrated to Israel in 1949. Studied at the Katznelson Ulpan in Jerusalem. Member of the Lady Narrators Circle. Lives in Jerusalem. pp. 40, 57, 73, 133, 170, 219.

YOHAY Sara - Born in Barcelona (Spain) (1937). Her grandparents came from Turkey and lived in Kavala (Greece). From 1939 she lived in Athens. Studied in the Greek School and in the Saint Joseph French School, until the end of high school. Studied classical dance at the Royal Academy in London. Lived in Milan from 1959 to 1967, the year of her immigration to Israel. Ran a dancing school in Netanya. Member of the Lady Narrators Circle. Lived in Netanya and died there in 1997. pp. 52, 58, 124, 150, 182, 192, 197, 211, 222, 229, 244, 264, 249, 265, 269, 272, 274.

www.ingramcontent.com/pod-product-compliance
Lightning Source LLC
Chambersburg PA
CBHW030825310726
48980CB00006B/647/J

* 9 7 8 0 8 2 7 6 0 7 2 2 4 *